"Peredur?"

He froze, turned a[...] shapes had risen [...] dimness of the roo[...] wasn't the maid. Even if the tiring woman would never have addressed him by his name, he recognized Rhlanon's voice, her slender form, the cascading fall of her hair.

"I was making sure the fire still burned," he whispered, startled at the hoarseness of his voice. "Go back to sleep."

"What hour is it?"

"What hour?" Peredur shook his head at the strange question. "I know not. Does it matter?"

There was a little silence. "No, not really." Another silence. "It's just...there are no church bells here to mark the passing of the night."

"No, there are no bells," he responded, his pulse beginning to beat a little faster as the firelight danced at the base of her throat. "But it must be well past midnight."

He'd studied her face keenly enough as they'd sat before that other brazier on that other midnight, their wedding night. But he hadn't seen her in a shift then as he did now, nor beheld the smooth, bare skin of her arms. And now his imagination proceeded to paint a vivid picture of the naked body *below* the shift.

Author Note

Ynys-hir, the Royal Society for the Protection of Birds (RSPB) nature reserve in the Dyfi Valley, mid-Wales, has always drawn me, not just for its dramatic beauty but also because it houses the remains of a medieval motte and bailey castle. While researching the historical background for this, my third novel, I discovered the true significance of this castle and its strategic importance in medieval Wales.

Today, Ynys-hir—the long island—is a tranquil haven for birds and other wildlife, but in the twelfth century it was the foremost frontier post of the much-fought-over land of Ceredigion, standing as it does on the headland of the Dyfi Estuary and looking northward to Gwynedd. I am extremely grateful to RSPB Ynys-hir for their welcome and help, and to Comisiwn Brenhinol Henebion Cymru Royal Commission on the Ancient and Historical Monuments of Wales (CBHC/RCAHMW) for confirming that the castle of Abereinion (Domen Las) is indeed the one built by Lord Rhys, Prince of Deheubarth, in 1156.

LISSA MORGAN

The Warrior's Reluctant Wife

Recycling programs
for this product may
not exist in your area.

ISBN-13: 978-1-335-59568-3

The Warrior's Reluctant Wife

Copyright © 2023 by Lissa Morgan

For questions and comments about the quality of this book, please contact us at CustomerService@Harlequin.com.

Harlequin Enterprises ULC
22 Adelaide St. West, 41st Floor
Toronto, Ontario M5H 4E3, Canada
www.Harlequin.com

Printed in U.S.A.

Lissa Morgan hails from Wales but has traveled far and wide over the years, usually in search of the next new job, and always pursuing her love of the past along the way. A history graduate and former archivist, she now works in website design and academia. Lissa lives between the mountains and the sea in rugged North West Wales, surrounded by medieval castles that provide the perfect inspiration for her writing—the best job of all! Visit her at lissamorgan.com, Facebook.com/lissamorganhistoricalromance and Twitter.com/lissamorganauth.

Books by Lissa Morgan

The Welsh Lord's Convenient Bride
An Alliance with His Enemy Princess

The Warriors of Wales

The Warrior's Reluctant Wife

Visit the Author Profile page
at Harlequin.com.

I Deulu Ty Ffwrnais

Chapter One

Wales, January 1157

'Has the *bwgan* stolen your tongue?'

The words cut through the cold air like a knife and the chatter going on among those assembled ceased abruptly. Rhianon turned her head and looked at the man at her side who had spoken them.

Peredur ab Eilyr's grey eyes met hers, glistening like the frost on the trees around Llanbadarn Church. Even the January weather was casting an ill omen on this marriage, it seemed, with its leaden sky and the ground still white with rime even now at well past noontime.

And then came a movement of his mouth that might almost have been a smile, albeit one of irony. 'Or perhaps the frost has claimed it?'

Rhianon's mind whirled. Was he jesting? Surely not! Of all the tales that she'd heard of this man she was marrying today, none involved humour. Peredur Galon Gudd-Peredur of the Hidden Heart—called so by friends and enemies alike. Some said he had no heart at all…

'I…' Rhianon's voice stumbled as those eyes seared

her to the spot, reflecting the iron will for which their owner was legendary, despite his relative youth, for he was not yet seven and twenty.

Perspiration oozed down between her breasts, making her bridal gown cling uncomfortably to her body. Could the far-fetched stories she'd heard about the warrior with no heart really be true?

Behind her someone shouted. 'Get on with it, girl. Answer the man!'

Her father! Shaming her even now by voicing his contempt of her before the kin of both their houses. A flush burning her cheeks, Rhianon glanced over her shoulder to where her family stood, shuffling their frozen feet.

Her mother's gaze was downcast, her younger brother, Llywelyn, was frowning, her older brother, Rhodri, looking simply bored. Conversely, the face of her uncle Edwin was serene, his sightless eyes almost hidden by his monk's cowl.

Peredur's kinfolk too were looking perplexed as they shivered in their cloaks. And then someone else spoke, loud, clear and authoritative. The splendidly dressed man who outshone everyone around him on this bitter afternoon.

The Lord Rhys ap Gruffudd, Prince of Deheubarth, who had commanded this union between the two warring chieftains—her father, Cadwgan of Uwch Aeron, and Peredur's father, Eilyr of Penweddig—and so, not even the harshest winter weather could stop it.

'*Ust*, Cadwgan, your daughter is nervous, as all brides are.' The keen eyes, as black as his neatly cropped beard, locked onto hers. 'But best get the vows said and done, *forwyn*, before we all freeze to death!'

But his smile sent the encouragement that *should* have come from her family, but didn't. And all at once a semblance of dignity came out of nowhere, just as the sky darkened and the snow began to fall.

Rhianon turned back to the priest, quaking with cold in his long robes before the church door. She *was* nervous, yes, but she hadn't completely lost her tongue, even if some bogle *had* robbed her momentarily of the will to use it.

'I do take you as my wedded husband,' she said, the snowflakes that fell on her lips melting away as quickly as they had come.

As they knelt before the altar, the tiled floor as cold as the ground outside had been, Peredur was keenly aware of the woman at his side. Rhianon *ferch* Cadwgan seemed older than her twenty-two summers, not in her face or her form, but in her bearing. Tall and slender with a curling mane of wild black hair that fell to below her waist, she was also beautiful.

Her eyes were the colour of gentian and fringed with long black lashes, as silken as the wings of a moth. Her face was flawless, her skin without blemish, and her lips as soft as autumn raspberries.

Too soft for a man such as he and doubtless she knew it.

The blessing bestowed and the ceremony over, Peredur rose and, taking his bride's hands, drew her upwards. He received the kiss of peace from the priest and then bent to kiss Rhianon. Her chin lifted and her mouth surrendered obediently but her eyes were veiled, looking *through* him as opposed to at him.

Peredur knew that look well. He'd seen avoidance,

distrust, or fear, or myriad shades of all three, all his life. From the people of the village where he'd been born, and afterwards from Eilyr's people, who had never quite accepted him even though he was Eilyr's adopted son.

And worst of all, the resentment of the grandmother who had raised him after his mother had died birthing him.

His birth, his lineage, his very appearance, had set him apart always, made him different. As a boy, it had hurt him deeply. As a man he'd learned not to let himself feel that hurt. But now, it surfaced and cut as keenly as if he was six years old once more.

'Do you not wish for the kiss of peace, Rhianon?' he asked.

Her eyes cleared and, suddenly, his hurt withered away before the depth of beauty in them—and not just beauty, but dignity and pride and courage.

'Why would I not wish for peace, my lord?'

'Because you seemed so reluctant to say your vows that I was beginning to think you would refuse to wed me.'

Her reply held both a tremor and a thin edge of defiance. 'Refusing is a choice I do not have.'

No, she hadn't had a choice, had she? The Lord Rhys meant this marriage to bind their two families to him and so strengthen his rule over Ceredigion, the ancient lands of his royal dynasty that he'd wrestled out of the hands of the Prince of Gwynedd.

Unlike Rhianon, however, Peredur *had* had a choice. He'd chosen to marry, something he'd vowed never to do. The expectations of marriage, and the consequences that might result, were forbidden to him. *He'd* forbidden them because he'd vowed long before he'd even reached manhood that he'd never become the murdering man his Flemish father was.

And he'd chosen to marry *her*, partly because of a distant memory that should have been long forgotten—and partly to save her from his brother. Maelgwn was vicious, deviant, and not even his vow of chastity, not even his fear, could allow Rhianon to fall prey to his brother's whims.

For that would *certainly* condemn her to a life of suffering. Perhaps even the same suffering his blood father Letard had inflicted on his mother, something he had also vowed never to inflict on *any* woman.

'But if you *did* have a choice?' he pursued, curiosity pricking at him like the needles of hoarfrost that hung at the windows. The shutters were open and, as the daylight fell on her face, there it was again, that flash of defiant rebellion.

'Then I would not marry again,' she replied, bluntly, almost with pride. 'I have been wed and widowed once already and would sooner take the veil!'

The tension in the church was palpable now, every ear strained to listen to what was being said at the altar. Puzzled whispers started up and the priest leaned towards him.

'Lord Peredur…'

Peredur gave an impatient nod. Choices, or the lack of them, were irrelevant now. This wedding was arranged, a strategic union, just as her first marriage had been. And to seal it and give it the blessing it would no doubt need, he had to kiss her.

He bent his head and once more sensed her withdraw, even though she actually didn't move. Her eyes stared through him once again as she yielded her mouth—but not herself.

Her lips were as cool and as distant as her gaze. All the same, as their mouths met, something unexpected happened. Something pulled hard inside him and heat surged in his loins.

Peredur reined in the reaction immediately, shock thudding into him like an arrow. He'd long since mastered the carnal side of his nature, suppressed the base bodily urges that other men indulged and enjoyed. The unbridled lust that had condemned his mother to a cruel fate at the hands of his blood father and led to his own tainted, shameful birth.

How, then, could his body jolt and his blood stir at so light and fleeting a kiss? How, when he'd only seen this woman once before when she was a child of twelve summers? He'd never even spoken to her, let alone touched or kissed her, until today, at the door of the church.

But he *had* been jolted, his blood *had* quickened, and when the day was out, he would have to rein himself in tighter than ever. Because he'd have to do much more than simply kiss Rhianon *ferch* Cadwgan. He would be expected to bed her.

The hall of Llanbadarn Castle was as warm as the church had been cold. A fire blazed in the central hearth and flaming braziers lined the whitewashed walls. Heavy linens covered the windows and the rushes lay thick on the floor, fragranced with winter evergreen.

The meat that came up from the kitchen was piping hot too, and cups of wine and mead flowed thirstily down everyone's throat, thawing chilled bones and blood.

But Rhianon's body refused to thaw and her heart remained a frozen lump in her breast as she sat at the high table between her new husband and their patron, the Lord Rhys, at the wedding feast.

Beyond Peredur was his father, Eilyr ap Bleddyn, frail and white-haired. Next to him sat Peredur's brother, Maelgwn, slight and dark and comely, and as different to Peredur as night was from day.

Suddenly, her new husband spoke, his observation ending the silence that had reigned between them since leaving the church.

'You are remarkably like your mother in appearance, Rhianon.'

'Am I?' Rhianon looked to where her mother sat, not at the high table, but at the long table to their left, with Eilyr's wife and two daughters.

'You are indeed,' he said, spearing roast boar onto the point of his knife. 'But you also look as sad as she does this evening.'

Rhianon said nothing but the similarity he'd commented on sent a thrill of terror through her. Had Tangwystl been sad on *her* wedding day too, or full of hope and joy as brides were meant to be? If so, her husband had beaten all those things out of her long since.

And now, she was walking in her mother's footsteps towards the same fate, all over again! If Peredur's reputation was true—and it far outdid her father's prowess and her former husband's courage on the battlefield—how could her fate be otherwise?

Then Peredur leaned towards her, a wine jug in his hand, the sleeve of his tunic brushing hers. 'More wine?'

Rhianon met his eyes and shook her head. 'No... thank you.'

She studied him properly for the first time that day. Torchlight glanced off the strong planes of his face, followed the sculpted lines of cheekbone and jaw. His golden hair was like ripe wheat under sun and, by contrast, his clothing relentlessly dark. The few adornments—the clasp of his cloak and the thread that lined his collar, cuffs and the edges of his cloak—were silver, a bright but equally forbidding colour.

He was handsome, in a roughly hewn sort of way, like all the men of Flemish blood were reputed to be, not that she'd ever seen any. She'd seen *him* though, just once before, when he'd been a youth of sixteen. He'd been one of the war band that had gathered in the courtyard of her father's castle of Ystrad Meurig for yet another battle against the Normans.

From her window, she'd stared unseen, fascinated by his golden head amidst all the darker ones, the quiet way he sat his horse. And now she saw that the latent force she'd sensed in him then had matured into the indomitable warrior who had become her husband.

'Then perhaps you would prefer mead instead?' he offered.

Rhianon shook her head again, and, with a shrug, he filled just his own cup. As she watched the wine rise to the brim and all but overflow, misery filled her heart too. If she were exactly like her mother, would her second husband turn out to be exactly like her father, just as her *first* husband had done?

And if so, sitting here like a mouse in the presence of a lion would give him the wrong impression entirely. Delude him into thinking that, if she were like her mother in *every* way, not just in appearance, he could treat her how he liked.

'Do you not like the wedding gift I gave you, my lord?' she asked, bluntly.

His brows lifted and she coloured. Asserting her person was one thing but seeking acknowledgement of her gift, even his gratitude, sounded like desperation! 'I mean…do you think it fitting?' she amended.

He glanced down at the gauntlets she'd given him. Soft dun-coloured leather with thread of gold stitched at the cuffs, they lay next to his plate where he'd tossed them earlier, as of no consequence.

He muttered something that might have been a 'thank you,' but the remainder negated the courtesy completely. 'The gloves are very fine, but too fine for winter wear, perhaps.'

Rhianon blinked away an odd sense of disappointment. He hadn't given her a gift at all, fine or otherwise! And that omission only served to confirm her standing in his eyes—worthless but for the price of political alliance.

Then, almost as if she'd uttered her thoughts out loud, he spoke again. 'I have a gift for you too, naturally, but now is not the time to give it.'

Her cheeks grew hot. Yes, she knew that all too well. A man may have *his* gift at the wedding feast, but the bride receives *her* gift the morning after the bedding in return for her body. A fact her new husband confirmed a moment later.

'I will give it tomorrow…when we leave.'

On the morrow, they would depart for his castle to the north but, before then, tonight would end as her first wedding feast had, leaving her body bruised and her soul shattered.

Rhianon dragged her gaze up from the spurned

gauntlets and met his again, but it was impossible to discern any expression there. Like it was impossible to see the bottom of a river that was covered with a thick sheet of ice.

'What is it?' she asked, trying not to think of what this night held, and what would come with the dawn. 'The gift, I mean?'

He smiled—or was it a smile? He wore no beard, and his mouth was wide and generous, with an old scar faded to white that cleaved through the left jawbone. 'If I tell you, it will spoil the giving.'

And then, as she met his eyes again, the ice in them seemed suddenly to melt. She blinked but it was still there, that sudden thawing that sent a strange sort of warmth right through her.

She turned away, not trusting her eyes, not able to trust them. If her experience had taught her anything, it was that a husband will take all but rarely *give* anything. And if this marriage was to be different to her last one, she had to make it so, now, right at the start.

Although she had no appetite, Rhianon helped herself to another portion of the succulent goose that sat in a rich sauce on the platter, even though the first portion she'd forced down still churned like poison in her stomach.

'You look so different to your kinfolk, and everyone else here tonight, my lord.' She took up her eating knife and dug its point deeply into the fowl. 'Is that because you favour your Flemish father rather than your Welsh mother?'

Peredur winced inwardly. Everyone knew his history, of course, so she must know it too. And everyone knew also, as must she, the manner of his begetting—that he was the result of the despoiling of an innocent at the hands of a monster. Was that why she looked at him with undisguised contempt and gripped that knife as if it were a weapon?

'I may look unlike everyone else here tonight, my lady,' he replied. 'But my Welsh blood is more than equal to the Flemish.'

'Yet it is well known that the blood of the Flemings runs thick with lust for war and conquest.'

Her words curled around his entrails like a snake, crushing the breath from his lungs. 'And blood will out. Is that what you are saying?'

'*I* do not say it, but the poor, persecuted Welsh of Dyfed might say so.' She twirled a sliver of meat onto her knife and lifted it to her mouth. '*They* know better than anyone what the Flemings are like.'

Peredur inclined his head, said nothing, since she spoke the truth. But she might just as well have driven her eating knife deep inside him instead of into the goose, which she was devouring now as if she hadn't eaten for a week.

At that moment, the Lord Rhys, sitting to Rhianon's left, rose and went to use the latrine. There was the scraping of a chair and Maelgwn dropped down into the vacated seat, latching on to his wife like a leech.

'Well, my lovely new sister, an opportunity to talk to you at last.'

Rhianon started and then shifted to face his brother, touching her napkin to her mouth and laying her knife down beside her plate.

'Good eve, my lord.'

Peredur sat back, the irony almost amusing. Rhianon

didn't know it but she would need that knife now more than ever! Every woman without exception swooned in the presence of his dazzling sibling. Maelgwn was everything he was not—raven-haired with eyes of forest green, his body lithe and graceful, possessing a beautiful face and an irresistible charm. A false charm that women and occasionally men too discovered to their sorrow.

Would his new wife fall into the snare like all the rest?

'I had hoped to be the blessed one today, Lady Rhianon,' his brother was saying, laying his hand expressively over his heart. 'But instead I find myself utterly desolate.'

'How so, my lord?'

'*I* had asked for the honour of becoming your husband but my brother insisted that you be *his*.' Maelgwn smiled his brilliant, devious smile. 'Strange indeed since he has fought so shy of marriage up to now.'

Rhianon's head tilted, the yellow flowers in her bride's garland like spots of sunlight against the midnight black of her hair. 'Perhaps you have had a lucky escape, my lord. We might not have suited each other.'

Peredur felt a smile tug at his mouth, albeit a grim one. She might be far better suited to Maelgwn in looks than she was to him, but at least she would never find out just how accurate that observation was.

Seeing his smile, his brother's mask slipped into malice. 'Even so, I would have made you a better husband than my foundling brother here will make you, Lady Rhianon.'

'Oh? In what way, my lord?'

'Peredur worries from dawn to dusk, rides for hours on end, toils like a serf and fights like a demon of hell.'

Leaning back in his chair, Maelgwn poured more wine into Rhianon's cup and then drank of it, wetting his lips with viciousness. 'And doubtless you have heard that he has no heart? Mayhap it was left behind in Pebidiog where my father found him and took him in out of pity.'

Peredur's smile froze on his lips. Since their boyhoods, his brother had delighted in taunting him with the odd nature of his heart, misplaced as it was, and therefore misunderstood, a subject for scorn and superstition.

'But that was an act of kindness on your father's part, surely, not just pity?'

'Was it, Lady Rhianon?' The green eyes glittered. 'You can dress a wolf up in the fleece of a sheep, but it will still be a wolf. So it follows that you can robe a peasant like a lord—but he will still be a peasant.'

Peredur clenched his teeth as the blood began to pound at his temples, but he held his tongue. To rise to his brother's baiting, as he had done so often when they were growing up, would only end one way—in bloody noses and bruised knuckles.

Maelgwn, however, seemed determined to provoke a quarrel, no matter what. 'My virginal brother knows nothing of leisure or pleasure…or of lovemaking. A poor husband for *any* woman, Lady Rhianon, whereas I…'

Then, his brother went too far. Taking Rhianon's hand, he turned it and kissed the inside of her wrist, where the blue veins showed beneath the delicate skin. Not the courteous kiss of respect, nor even one of kinship, but the kiss of a would-be lover.

Rhianon gave a little grimace of pain and Peredur was on his feet in a flash, his self-control shattered. Behind him, he heard Eilyr rise from his seat, ready to intervene in his sons' quarrels as he'd done so often in the past.

Quarrels that he'd never once instigated and had tried his utmost to avoid, until it was clear there *was* no avoiding them. Maelgwn, three years younger than he, had hated him from the day he'd arrived, resenting both Eilyr's affection for him and the circumstance that he was no longer their father's sole heir, even though as his legitimate son he would still get the greater portion.

This, however, went far beyond a quarrel. It was a deliberate affront to Rhianon that Peredur had no intention of letting pass. 'Take your hands off her, Maelgwn!'

His brother sprang to his feet, relinquishing Rhianon's hand, just as the Lord Rhys reappeared, with fortuitous timing, and averted the dangerous moment. Maelgwn, all innocence now, bowed low, his apology coming as slick as grease off a knife.

'Your pardon, a*rglwydd*. I was merely greeting my new sister before my brother whisks her away to their bed sport.'

'Is it so late?' The Prince's shrewd eyes assessed the situation accurately and at once, since he knew—as did everyone present—of the animosity that existed between the sons of Eilyr. Taking up an empty goblet, he banged it down three times on the board. 'The hour has come to cheer the newlyweds aloft! Let everyone wish them a night of pleasure and an heir to be made before the morrow!'

Rhianon sat rigid in her chair and rubbed her wrist where the skin still smarted. She felt like a bone that had been fought over by two snarling dogs. But then, that's exactly what she was. A prize for the victor—although she hadn't realised there had even been a contest until a moment ago.

She let out her breath as Maelgwn scowled his way back to his chair, followed by the icy stare of his brother. A stare that turned, a slow moment later, to bear down upon her. Peredur held out his hand and her stomach clenched hard with trepidation. But, since she could do no other, she placed her palm in his.

The next instant, trepidation turned to surprise. For the calloused palm and strong fingers were so different to the soft hand of his brother—which had been anything *but* soft. Whereas Maelgwn's hand had gripped like the teeth of a viper, hard enough to break the bones, Peredur's somehow…did not.

Rhianon stared up into his eyes and, as his fingers wrapped gently around hers, a strange sensation of being safe, *protected*, caught her off guard. And, in its wake, an even stranger flood of attraction warmed her blood for the first time that day.

She didn't let that surprise, or that startling, *shocking* attraction, show on her face as her new husband drew her to her feet. Instead, she kept her features impassive, her whole being apart, as her mind whirled with confusion.

A mass of people had gathered around the top table, baying like hounds before a kill. Everyone would try to get a piece of her clothing, or the garland from her hair, or the garters from her knees, as tokens of good luck.

Luck and sport for them but sheer humiliation for her.

But there was no escaping the dreaded ordeal. Peredur bowed to the Lord Rhys and Rhianon dipped a curtsey too, her heart beginning to pound. She sought her mother's eyes, but Tangwystl's head was turned away.

Her father and elder brother didn't even bother to look at her. The only support came from her youngest brother, Llywelyn, his blue eyes so like hers, sombre and sympathetic.

And then the howling crowd surged forward. She braced herself for the onslaught, tipping her chin up defiantly and daring everyone to do their worst. She'd survived this moment, she'd even survived marriage, once before. She could do so again. She *would* do again.

And then, so unexpectedly that she gasped, Peredur lifted her up into his arms. The next instant, he was striding swiftly down the hall, his long legs outpacing all those that ran after them.

Faces blurred around her as he shoved and elbowed away the grasping hands that tore at her clothes. Nevertheless, a shoe disappeared and someone ripped the stitching of her sleeve. Rhianon winced as the flowers were wrenched from her hair and, above her head, she heard Peredur curse violently.

But soon they were on the stairs that led upwards and then over the threshold of their chamber. Peredur shouldered the door shut, putting her down so that he could ram the bolt home before anyone entered behind them.

There was some futile complaints and half-hearted thumping on the oak, but the revellers quickly returned to the hall and to their ale. It was the custom and all in good humour, but Rhianon found herself shaking with the intensity of the last few moments, like a startled bird fluttered at the bars of its cage.

And now, an even greater ordeal had yet to be faced— or rather circumvented. The bedding.

In the silence of the chamber, the noise from the hall below seemed muted and distant. The fire crackled in the brazier and the wind rattled the shutters over the windows. Rhianon fought to regain her breathing, and her dignity, straightening her ruffled clothing and smoothing out her tangled hair.

And then something struck her, something incredible, impossible. All the time Peredur had been carrying her, her head had lain on his chest, her ear pressed close to where his heart should lie. But she'd not heard nor felt a single heartbeat.

Chapter Two

Peredur swore under his breath. Despite the flight from the hall, Rhianon hadn't escaped completely unscathed. The flowers were gone from her hair and there was a rip in the sleeve of her gown at the shoulder, through which a glimpse of bare flesh showed. She'd lost a shoe too, for the stockinged toes of one foot peeped out from beneath her hem.

But, standing there in the centre of the room, her stance proud and erect, her beauty stole his breath away. Her wild black hair flowed down over her shoulders, making her pale face seem even paler, her eyes larger, bluer.

'Why did you do that?' she asked, her tone more challenging than curious, yet somehow defensive too.

And, as Peredur looked deeper into those eyes, he saw beyond the challenge, to something bewildered, wary... afraid. The same expressions he'd seen below when Maelgwn had gripped her wrist and caused her pain.

'Do what?' he asked, cursing himself as much as his brother for not seeing the incident coming, and for not intervening quicker than he had.

'Carry me from the hall.'

'Did you think I'd let them tear an expensive gown to shreds?' Though it was *she* who might have been torn to shreds by the roughness of the crowd, albeit unintentionally. And the way her fingers had tightened around his as they'd faced the crowd told him that she knew it—and dreaded it. So he'd picked her up and carried her, the urge to protect her far greater than the obligation to indulge wedding custom. 'They stole your garland, however,' he said.

She lifted a hand to where the wreath of flowers had been—hardy winter buds of golden gorse—and then she looked down at her feet.

'And they got my shoe too.' Her eyes met his again. 'Will I get it back in the morning?'

Peredur shook his head and fought to steady his breathing, not just because of the way he'd taken the stairs two at a time, but because of what more she might have endured had he not managed to deny that howling mob its sport. 'I doubt it.'

She laced her fingers together in front of her and he noticed the tremble in them. 'No,' she agreed, with a strange note of acceptance. 'I don't suppose I will.' The blue eyes stared at him for a moment. 'Thank you…for what you did. It was…considerate.'

Her composure might have fooled another man, but because he felt as nervous as she clearly was, Peredur saw through it. Despite her thanks, she looked not like a woman going to her bridal bed but more like a sacrifice going to the slab!

'It was nothing,' he said. Crossing to the table next to one wall, he poured out two goblets of wine. His throat was parched and sweat trickled down between his shoulder blades. The room was too warm, the fire too high, the aroma from the freshly strewn rushes on the floor too potent.

And, beyond that heavy curtain that divided the living from the sleeping area, their nuptial bed lay...waiting.

It could wait a little longer, as long as possible.

Peredur turned around. 'Come, we'll sit and talk before the fire for a little while.'

Her gaze widened. 'Talk...?'

He nodded and, putting the wine cups down on the table near the brazier, he pulled the two chairs in the room closer to its warmth. A shadow of doubt flickered over her face before she lowered herself into one of them.

'Very well,' she said, her hands folded in her lap and her wedding ring winking in the firelight. 'What do you want to talk about?'

Peredur sat down opposite her, his blood flowing warmer in a way that had nothing to do with the heat from the fire. Below them, the feast had become merrier, voices growing louder. A bow scraped across the strings of a *crwth* and singing rose to the rafters. Perhaps there would be poetry too, and dancing.

But here in this chamber there was just he and Rhianon. Most newlywed men would be eager to learn their bride's body first and only afterwards get to know her mind and soul. He, however, he was not like most men. How could he be given the accursed bloodline that had marked his boyhood? When, in his manhood, he'd witnessed women blanching and crossing themselves, lest the Fleming's son prove the same sort of man as his infamous father.

Unlike his lustful brother Maelgwn, with his smooth

tongue and ardent body, he had no experience of women. That had never mattered before. It had been a necessary abstinence, so long and so deeply ingrained that it had become who he was—until tonight…

Peredur cleared his throat. 'Tell me of your life,' he said at last, picking up his wine cup and sitting back in his chair. 'Up to now, I mean.'

Her head tilted, the gesture like a habit, as if she was listening for something all the time. The gentian eyes were as dark as twilight in the glow of the rush lights that flickered on the walls.

'My life has been like that of any woman born into a noble house.'

'That doesn't tell me much,' he said, when she fell silent again, sitting upright in her chair and seeming much further away than the mere yard that separated them.

'And, as such, I have been raised to be married as well and as profitably as possible,' she added. 'What else is there to tell?'

The reply was given without expression. If he hadn't been looking at her, Peredur might have taken it as glibly as it had come. But he *was* looking at her and he saw the emotions behind her eyes that spoke too eloquently of what had been censored on her lips.

'Yet, that was not what you wished for, was it?' he said, probing carefully as he lifted his cup to his lips. 'You said at the altar that you would have preferred to enter the religious life.'

'I am the only daughter. For me, there was…is…no such escape.' There was a flash in her eyes as she went on, far more candidly than he'd expected. 'Should you die in battle, like my first husband did, my father will give me to another, and so on, until I become a worn-out brood mare!'

Peredur almost choked as he swallowed the heady wine. At least that was *one* thing she didn't have to worry about. He might have taken a wife but he would never expect her to breed. For that, he'd need to bed her first…

'I could never envisage you as a brood mare, Rhianon.'

'It doesn't matter what you do or do not envisage. As long as I am young and able to bear children, that is my fate.'

'Yet, your first marriage produced no children.'

'No.' Her lashes lowered, hiding whatever inner thoughts might lie behind her words. 'My husband died within a fortnight of our wedding.'

'Seisyll,' he said. 'Yes, I knew him, slightly.'

She looked up at him again and a flush mounted her cheeks. 'Then you know he was a man who lived only for war, possessing great valour but very little else. I was his possession, nothing more, to do with as he liked. Few women, if any at all, are so lucky as to be wed to a man they love, or can grow to love, or at least to a kind and honourable husband. Such men do not exist.'

The speech was the longest she'd uttered all that day, and the vehemence in it was palpable. Were the words intentional, telling him in no uncertain terms what she thought of *him*, her *new* husband?

His fingers tightened around his cup as a shaft of pain lanced him. Whatever else he was, whatever else he tried to be, *wanted* to be, he was his Flemish father's son. There was no denying that. Anyone who had ever seen Letard looked at him, the warrior's bastard spawn, as if they couldn't believe their eyes, some with fear and others with hatred, but all with distrust and dislike.

Peredur forced another mouthful of wine down his throat. It tasted suddenly sour, though he knew it wasn't the wine that was tainted, but *he*.

'And you believe that I am such a man?' he said, with slow deliberation. 'Neither kind nor honourable, nor lovable, a man who also lives only for war, and who sees you too as nothing more than his possession?'

Rhianon had no idea how to answer that unexpected question. She'd witnessed the changing moods of men often in her own house, in her volatile and violent father, and her elder brother, Rhodri, too, who was cut from the same cloth as their sire.

Seisyll, her erstwhile husband, had been by turns brutal and indifferent, and it had been a merciful escape when he'd been killed and the torture of his lovemaking had no longer to be endured. Now she saw her new husband's mood change, like a sky turning from light to dark, but it wasn't quite the same.

'I do not know *what* you are, my lord. I only know what I have *heard* about you.'

His jaw tightened until it seemed hewed out of stone, the faded scar like a slip of the chisel. 'And what is it you have heard?'

Rhianon lifted her chin higher and met the steely grey gaze. Unlike her mother, she would not lie or hide or cower away. She'd learned, at the age of eight, never ever to do that, always to look strong, resistant, untouchable. As she must look, and must *be*, throughout all the days of this marriage, be those mercifully short or endlessly long.

'The same things your brother talked of earlier in the hall,' she said.

'And you believe everything you are told?'

The fire crackled and sparks flew upwards as a log shifted. In his eyes, Rhianon saw the flames reflected there, the cool challenge behind them. Was he testing her in some way? For surely, he wasn't really interested in what she thought and felt!

'No, I don't,' she replied. 'But he *did* say something that puzzled me.' Deftly, she turned the conversation around, although the truth was it *had* puzzled her. 'Why did you thwart him by choosing me to be your wife, as he claims? A woman you'd never even seen before?'

'But I *have* seen you before...once.'

Rhianon felt her mouth drop open. Could he have seen her, that day she'd watched from her window as he'd sat his horse? Young, silent, calm, while the lesser warriors—even the older and battle-hardened ones—had yelled and waved their swords in the air?

'*When* did you see me?'

'Ten years ago, when I came with my father to Ys-trad Meurig to join with Cadwgan's forces against the Normans.'

Her heart leapt into her throat. 'And you *saw* me, above, at my window?'

He shook his head. 'I saw you *below*, in the bailey, the day before we left. I was in the great hall, at one of the windows, while our fathers talked strategy at the table. You were berating one of your father's men for beating a horse.'

Rhianon nodded. 'I remember now. The horse was restless and the man lost his patience.' She put her wine cup down, looked at her hands a moment, and then back at him. 'But…why would you remember such a trivial incident that happened so long ago?'

His answer was almost as long in coming. 'Because I also cannot abide senseless cruelty to any living being, beast *or* man.'

The shifting log broke in two and disintegrated in ashes. Peredur rose and took another log from the pile to the side of the brazier. As he threw it onto the fire, sparks flew upwards. One flew outwards and landed on the skirt of her gown with a little hiss and an acrid smell of scorching.

Quickly, Rhianon bent forward to brush the glowing ember away. But before she could reach it, Peredur was squatting down in front of her, dousing the spark with the palm of his hand.

'Forgive me, that was careless of me.'

She blinked. Contrition? Care? Neither of those were qualities she'd expected from him or even thought… hoped…to look for. Neither of them matched his reputation of the cold warrior with no heart. And yet, if he had spoken truly, if he really *did* abhor cruelty to man or beast…then was that reputation false?

'It was an accident,' she said, her heart suddenly beating hard. Despite what she'd said a moment ago, she *had* accepted what she'd heard of Peredur without question, assuming that *all* men who lived by the sword were the same. But…could she be wrong? 'There was no harm done.'

'Nevertheless…'

As he spoke, Peredur tucked the bottom of her gown out of range of the fire, his fingers touching the foot that had lost its slipper. And even though she still wore her thick stocking, Rhianon felt her skin quiver in response.

The chamber seemed suddenly smaller, as if the walls had closed in upon where they sat. Her stomach began to roil with nerves as his gaze bored into hers and, instead of returning to his seat, he remained squatting on the floor in front of her.

'What you did that day stayed with me, Rhianon. Your compassion was memorable…admirable.'

Rhianon stared at him in astonishment, his words becoming stranger all the time. The flames from the brazier glinted on the golden hair, exposing one side of his face and darkening the other, until he seemed like two men, one in the light, one in the shadow.

'But you didn't marry me just because of that,' she said. 'You wed me merely to please the Lord Rhys.'

'No.' He shook his head and a bead of moisture slid slowly from his brow down his temple. 'Rhys would just have happily seen you married to Maelgwn.'

Rhianon held her breath as his hand lingered on her foot, as unsettling as his words. Did he mean to feel his way *all* over her body? Take her here and now, fully clothed, in this chair before the fire?

Or would he pick her up and carry her over to that bed? Peel her clothes from her body and slake his lust there, at his leisure, among the furs?

He was kneeling so close that she could see even clearer now the things she'd noticed down below at the table. The strong bones of his face, the eyes that no longer seemed ice-like but glittered like sparks of iron, the mouth that wasn't cruel at all, but sensual…beautiful.

Her heart started to beat hard and something unfamiliar began unfurling in her stomach, a strange sort of need she'd never experienced before, but which suddenly made her want the hand that rested on her foot to move to other places, to touch her and caress her in more intimate parts.

'I married you because I wouldn't leave even my worst enemy to suffer the vices of my brother.'

The noise from the hall faded away, the crackle of wood from the brazier fading with it. And then only the sound of humiliation filled her ears. He'd married her out of *pity*?

As he got to his feet at last, Rhianon jumped up too, indignity banishing that inexplicable yearning and spurring her to a tart retort. 'You needn't have been so noble,' she said, her voice shaking. 'One husband is very much like another, at the end of the day!'

A look of surprise travelled briefly over his face and then he retook his chair. And the eyes that had gleamed so warm a moment ago were suddenly like ice again.

'Perhaps. But evidently one wife is not at *all* like any other.' He lifted his wine cup to his mouth. 'And now, you should retire, my lady. I will sit here a while.'

Rhianon stared at him, her indignity, her humiliation, even that treacherous hunger for his touch, eclipsed by a sense of deflation, as if he'd outmanoeuvred her even before she'd put her strategy into motion.

She inclined her head and, with far less guile than she'd prepared, she placed her hand on her midriff and gave a little wince.

'I think that will be best… I feel a little sick.'

His brows drew together. 'Are you not well?'

'I'm not sure,' she said, silently asking forgiveness for a lie. 'My stomach is queasy. Perhaps the goose was too ripe…'

Rhianon forced herself to meet his stare, boldly, wondering if he saw right through her gown to the naked skin below. And worse, *through* her skin and right down to her deception and the reason for it.

'You did have quite an appetite,' he said, without inflection, although a brow rose with a discernible hint of scepticism.

She flushed. Was that remark meant to be humorous—or reproachful? It was utterly impossible to tell. 'Yes, I did,' she admitted, suddenly feeling exactly like that child of ten years ago, being admonished for doing wrong, even though it was right. 'But it was a very excellent goose!'

Rhianon threw her defence at him but it fell far short of target. Because even her father in his worst moments had never glared quite in the way Peredur was doing now. Dark and brooding, intense and so potent she could *feel* him. Yet so remote she had no idea at all of what he was thinking.

He stretched one long leg out towards the fire and rested his elbows on the arms of his chair. 'And so, since you are…discomforted, I will not disturb you tonight.'

The words, dry as they were, were also weighted with something Rhianon couldn't interpret. Just as his fingers had been weighted, for all the lightness of their touch, on her foot a moment ago.

She breathed in a sigh of relief and yet, somehow, the sense of deflation persisted. Had he guessed at her ploy and, if so, why was he allowing it?

'Thank you,' she said, lifting her chin with all the dignity she possessed, but her hot cheeks surely giving her away. 'Then I will bid you goodnight.'

His head dipped, perfunctorily, and he turned back to his wine. 'Goodnight.'

Feeling more and more as if *she* had been thwarted,

not him, Rhianon crossed the room, stepped through the curtain and closed it again behind her. Then, with thoughts that trembled as much as her fingers did, she undressed quickly and put on the clean nightshift her maid had laid out earlier.

Getting into the square box bed, the straw rustling beneath her, she pulled up the furs. The wood crackled loudly on the fire without and the sound of the *crwth* and the singing from below filled her head until it started to ache.

Then, her heart thumping and her fingers pleated tightly in the bed covering, Rhianon listened and waited. And, as the moments passed with agonising slowness, her stomach really did begin to feel queasy.

For even if Peredur had *said* he would not disturb her, had he really meant it?

Peredur lost count of how many hours passed, how many cups of wine he'd poured and drank. Too many and yet not nearly enough, for his mind, and less still his body, wasn't numbed at all. Instead, every thought, every feeling, every sense was keenly alive to the woman in the bed beyond the curtain.

Had she stripped herself of her wedding gown? Was she lying now beneath the furs, nothing but a night shift covering that glorious form? Was that wild black hair splayed out across the pillow? Those soft lips parted as she breathed…with anticipation or with apprehension?

Was she waiting for him to make her his wife and the mother of his children?

She needn't wait. Marriage was one thing but…

With a grimace, he poured another cup of wine and emptied it down his throat. The fire grew cold but he didn't bother feeding it more wood. Better his blood be allowed to grow cold too, the flow stop altogether, his loins freeze. Anything but this hot rushing urge to go to that bed and claim her as his wife.

Because if he bedded Rhianon, consummated this marriage as he ought, how could he face the possible consequences? If he got her with child, as he ought, and then she died, as his mother had died...

No, he couldn't take that risk. He didn't *need* to take it, since she didn't want him to. She didn't want *him*, and had told him as much in plain words.

That should have made this night easier—but it didn't. Instead the desire that had reared its head so unexpectedly made this marriage more difficult than he'd ever imagined when he decided to snatch Rhianon to safety from under his brother's nose.

What had she called him? Noble! No, he wasn't noble. He may have had her wellbeing in mind when he'd thwarted Maelgwn, but it had been much more than that.

For it hadn't only been Rhianon's compassion that had stayed with him over the years. She herself had remained there, at the edges of his memory, all the time. And now, to find her grown to a lovely womanhood, beautiful and desirable—and *his*—had suddenly thrown him headlong into a hell of his own making.

The next morning, Rhianon was woken out of a nightmare by a shout. She sat bolt upright, blinking the sleep from her eyes. The place in the bed beside her was vacant, cold and undisturbed. Drawing the covers back up over her, she listened, but the shout had come from outside, down in the bailey, not within the chamber.

Peredur hadn't appeared all night but she'd sensed his presence in the outer room, heard his occasional shifting in his chair, the splash of wine into his cup, sometimes a heavy breath that sounded more like a sigh. But, as the revelry below had ended and silence had descended, he hadn't come to her bed. And as the night had dragged by, it was clear he didn't intend to.

Rhianon slipped from under the furs and peeped through the curtain. The room beyond was empty, the chairs they'd sat in looking forlorn beside the cold brazier. Shivering, she washed quickly from the ewer and basin on the table and dressed herself. All the while, her mind raced after explanations.

Why hadn't he come? Had he actually believed her when she said she'd felt sick? And been more magnanimous about it than her first husband would ever have been?

Rhianon was fastening her girdle at her waist when a knock came at the door. Turning, she drew herself up to her full height and, finishing the knot, linked her fingers together in front of her, her pulse starting to race.

'Come in.'

However, it wasn't her husband, as she'd anticipated, but her mother who pushed the door open. Tangwystl looked as if she hadn't slept much either, with dark circles under her eyes and a brow that was furrowed deeper than usual.

'Good morn, daughter.'

Rhianon's heart swelled and then sank. She and her mother had been so close once, since she was the only daughter among sons. But that had changed, dramatically and irrevocably, the day she'd turned eight years old. The day she'd tried to save her mother from her father's fury but had ended up bearing the brunt of it herself.

Tangwystl hadn't been there then to protect her. Instead, she'd left her defenceless and at Cadwgan's mercy. And she wasn't really here now. She was hidden somewhere deep inside herself, somewhere she'd gone to seek safety and had never re-emerged from.

Somewhere that Rhianon had sworn to herself, then and there, on her eighth birthday, never to retreat to no matter what she had to bear.

'What's amiss below in the bailey?' she asked, taking her comb from the small sack of possessions she'd brought with her and sitting down in the chair she'd occupied the previous night. 'Why is there so much noise?'

Her mother came to stand behind her and, taking the comb from her hand, began to run it through her hair, like she used to do when she'd been a very young child.

'Ystrad Meurig is under attack.'

Her home! Rhianon stiffened as a shock ran through her, although the castle of her childhood had never been a *home*. 'Attack? From whom?'

'Roger de Clare, aided by the Welshmen of Buellt, or so I have heard.' The hands that combed her hair were shaking even though Tangwystl was long used to such news. 'Peredur, and your father and brother Rhodri, are riding at once with the Lord Rhys.'

The sounds made sense now. Men running and shouting, the rasp of steel and ring of horses' hooves, all the necessary preparations for battle. It was a sound she'd heard many times.

'So…' The thought was on her tongue even before it had taken shape in her head. 'I might be made a widow before I'm properly made a wife.'

The comb paused. 'Did Peredur not…?'

Rhianon shook her head. 'No.' And she left it at that. She had ceased sharing confidences with her mother a long time ago, along with her trust, when Tangwystl had stopped listening, stopped even noticing, what was happening to her children.

'Perhaps it is just as well.' The comb recommenced its untangling of her hair, more unruly than usual this morning after a restless night. 'If Peredur does not return, you will still be suitable for remarriage, since you are yet childless.'

The stark yet common-sense remark was also a callous one. Once, before her first marriage, it would have struck at Rhianon's heart, drawn forth tears, but not any more. She was hardened now by that experience with Seisyll, whose pleasure in causing her pain had only confirmed and entrenched the lessons she'd already learned in the house of Cadwgan.

'No,' she said. 'If I am widowed again, then I will take the veil.'

Tangwystl began to plait her hair, her fingers making haste. 'I'm sorry, Rhianon. If it were in my power to grant your wish, I would do so but…'

'But if my father decides I will marry for a third time, then marry I will.'

Rhianon finished the excuse for her, winding the tie to secure her plait. Then she rose and turned around to face the pitiful figure that had given birth to her.

'But *you* know, mother, better than anyone, that I will never make *any* man a good and willing wife.'

To her astonishment, her mother gave a gulp and pulled her into a quick and tight embrace. 'I wish sometimes you'd been born male, daughter. It would have been so much easier for you, for us both.'

Rhianon stiffened in shock. Her mother hadn't held her like that since…she couldn't remember. But, even as her arms went to return the embrace, with an instinctive impulse of gladness, and of unexpected need, it was gone as suddenly as it had come. And, even though she knew the gesture held no hope of reconciliation, sorrow for what had been lost filled her eyes.

'However, it is as it is, and you must bear it as best you can.' Tangwystl turned away, emotion subdued beneath efficiency once more, and looked around the room. 'Now, where's your cloak? We must hurry down and bid farewell to the men.'

Blinking, Rhianon followed her mother downstairs, still reeling from the display of affection, the anguish that had followed. Had *remor*se sparked that fleeting embrace? Sadness, even, that her fate was indeed as it was and could not be otherwise?

But, if nothing else, Tangwystl had taught her well in one respect. The only way to survive a marriage was to keep the real self out of it, even in the act of yielding to it.

In the courtyard, a thick white mist covered the ground, swallowing up the feet of men and horses. The day was bitterly cold, turning breath to clouds and making faces tingle. Her father was already mounted, as was Rhodri, while Llywelyn was holding their sire's stirrup, obviously not going with them. Not because he was too young to fight, but because—since he had no lust for war—their father considered him a coward. But Llywelyn wasn't a coward. He was gentle and pious, learned and cultured, a poet and a thinker, and for that he'd suffered worst of all at their father's hands.

Cadwgan didn't even glance at his wife, let alone bid her farewell. Rhianon hadn't seen him spare a thought for her mother once, not even when he was girding himself for a battle he might not return from. But today, that insulting neglect hit her harder even than his fist had so often done over the years.

Without knowing why, she turned her gaze to search for Peredur and found him at the gates. Mounted on a tall dapple-grey stallion, one hand was reaching for his shield, the other gathering up his reins.

Beneath his cloak, and over his short riding tunic, he wore a dark brown gambeson, the leather jerkin laced tight around the broad chest and narrow waist. Strong thighs clasped the saddle and calfskin boots reached to his knees, while leather gauntlets covered his forearms to the elbow.

A shiver passed through her that had nothing to do with the cold. She'd seen her father and brother dressed for war many times but they'd never looked the warrior that her husband did now, and had done, even ten years ago. Like then, he sat calm, silent and aloof from the chatter of excitement and the enthusiasm for killing that all the other men around him evinced.

Then, suddenly, he looked in her direction and those intense and forbidding eyes locked onto hers. He didn't come over to her. He didn't say anything. He didn't even raise a hand in farewell. But, as his gaze lingered, the ice in them seemed to turn to quicksilver, lancing her where she stood, potent enough to melt the rime that froze the earth beneath her feet.

Rhianon forgot that her face was stinging in the bitter wind, that her feet were numb, that she should have put gloves on, for she couldn't feel her fingers any more. Instead a thrill raced down her spine and something pulled hard, deep down in her belly. She snatched a breath, feeling the cold turn to hot in her nostrils, and her blood began to race fast through her veins.

And then, still without any acknowledgement other than that blistering, impenetrable stare, he turned away. At the side of the Lord Rhys, with her father on the other side, he rode out through the gatehouse into the snow. A shaft of thin sunlight broke through the clouds and glinted like gold on his hair for a brief instant and then the war band disappeared into the mist.

Chapter Three

Rhianon was alone in the church of Llanbadarn, three days later. She'd gone there every day to pray with her mother and her brother Llywelyn. The folk of Castell Llanbadarn too had gone to pray for the safe return of their men. This morning, however, none had accompanied her, for snow had begun to fall heavily again just after dawn.

But Rhianon went anyway, even though the church was a goodly walk from the castle. And, in the snow, a difficult one, down the hill and across the narrow wooden bridge over the Rheidol river.

Now, kneeling on the tiled floor at the stone altar where she'd been married, the eyes of the painted saints on the walls watching her, Rhianon prayed. Not for Peredur's return or lack of it. That was already in God's hands. Rather she prayed for the strength to bear this marriage if her husband *did* return from battle.

'Rhianon…' A deep voice came from behind her and she turned to see her uncle coming down the aisle, his footsteps firm and sure, even though he was blind. 'I did not expect you today in this weather.'

Edwin ab Ieuaf knelt down beside her, his head bowed and his face hidden by his cowl. He wasn't a monk—though he wore the habit of one—but a *duwiolfrydog*, a contemplative who'd given his life to God. He occupied a small cell attached to this church that had taken him in after his brother Cadwgan had maimed and blinded him twenty years earlier and so ended his worldly life.

'My mother and Llywelyn decided not to come today,' Rhianon said, 'but I felt the need.'

His head lifted and turned towards her and she shuddered at the place where his eyes had been. The empty sockets and sunken lids bore witness to the brutality that marked her family. At least Cadwgan had left him his life, unlike his two other brothers, who he'd killed to gain the supremacy.

'The need for God's mercy and understanding?'

Rhianon nodded and a wave of sadness swept over her at how different her mother's life might have turned out. For Edwin had been Tangwystl's betrothed until his brother had deprived him of his sight, his manhood and the woman he'd loved.

'When my husband returns we will leave for his castle to the north,' she said. I don't know if there is a church there.'

Edwin smiled and she saw how comely he must have been when young, his face still pleasant, despite the marks of violence.

'No, there is no church there, but the folk of that district sorely need spiritual guidance,' he said. 'Perhaps your husband will build one?'

Rhianon bit back the impulse to speak of her wedding night. What could she ask, after all, of this man who knew nothing of marriage? He might have known of love once but marriage wasn't love—something that *she* knew all too well.

'I doubt that he has much faith in God,' she said. 'From what I have heard, he is a warrior, first and foremost.'

'Do not believe all you hear about Peredur, Rhianon, especially if it comes from the mouth of his brother. I do not need eyes to see which is the better of the two.'

As he spoke, the sound of hooves came crunching through the snow and Rhianon's breath caught. No one would be riding in this weather so it could only be the men returning from Ystrad Meurig.

Her uncle crossed himself and then stretched out his hands to help her rise. 'Here is Peredur now.'

She peered at him, her nerves pulling tight at the prospect of meeting her husband again, and her heart recommencing that strange fluttering that had afflicted it the day he'd ridden away.

'How do you know it is he?' she asked.

'I recognise the gait of his horse.'

'But how can you tell Peredur's horse among so many?'

'My hearing has become very keen over the years, to make up for my sight,' he replied, with a smile. 'His stallion has a fault in its right foreleg that causes it to go short on that side.'

Rhianon's mouth dropped open and his smile broadened, as if he saw her surprise as easily as he had her thoughts. 'Now, let us go out and welcome your husband home.'

Outside, the priest and his laymen were offering the returning men warm ale from the *bragdy*—the brewing house—next to the church. Only a dozen or so of

Eilyr ap Bleddyn's men had gone to Uwch Aeron and it seemed they had all come back whole and unscathed.

Including Peredur who, in lieu of his aged father, had led them, seconded by his brother Maelgwn, whom she saw had also returned unharmed. There were two of her father's men also, but no sign of Cadwgan or her brother Rhodri.

Which could only mean they had either remained at Ystrad Meurig or else had been injured or killed in the battle.

In the shadow of the church door, Rhianon drew her cloak tighter as the prospect of that—and the implications it would have for Llywelyn—sent a shudder of dread down her spine.

Peredur had dismounted and was drinking deeply of the warm ale, his hood thrown back from his head. His hair was wet with snow, though no snow was falling now. Handing the cup back with a nod of thanks, he turned and saw her. There was a discernible hesitation and then he made his way to where she stood.

Lifting her chin, and her heart beating hard, Rhianon walked forward to greet him. She noticed, with a start, that the dapple-grey stallion did indeed go short in front, not lame exactly, but its stride noticeably uneven.

'Welcome back, my lord,' she said, as Peredur came to a halt before her. If Edwin was right about the horse, perhaps he was right about its rider too? 'I did not expect you to return so soon.'

'What are you doing *here*, Rhianon?'

Rhianon bridled at the abruptness of his reply. So much for her uncle's inner sight! 'I came to pray.'

'You *walked* all the way here from the castle, *alone*?' he asked, his brows lifting.

'Yes,' she said, returning his frosty stare with one of her own. 'I *wanted* to be alone and… I *like* to walk!' she added tartly.

A flicker of astonishment crossed his face—or was it disbelief? 'Over half a league or more and in the snow?'

'Especially in the snow!' Rhianon bit back another inexplicable urge to gainsay him. The strange exchange wasn't one she'd been expecting at all. But then, after their nuptials night, she hadn't known *what* to expect when next they met, least of all the churning in her stomach that sent a blush into her face.

'Then I see you are fully recovered from the effects of the goose you ate at our wedding feast?'

She felt her cheeks burn hotter still but she inclined her head politely. 'Yes… I am, thank you.' Smoothly, she turned the conversation in a less embarrassing, more appropriate, direction, and tried to pretend the unwelcome yet undeniable stirring of attraction didn't exist. 'I am pleased to see you returned whole and well, all your men too.'

His face changed. 'We are not *all* well and whole,' he said, after a short pause. 'Your father is unharmed but your brother Rhodri is dead. Cadwgan has remained at Ystrad Meurig to do vigil for his son.'

Peredur saw shock transfigure his wife's countenance for an instant, and then it was gone, leaving her expression blank, her face ashen, all the colour that had been there before draining away. Had it only been three days since he'd seen her last, kissed her, albeit fleetingly, before the altar? It seemed much longer.

'H-how did Rhodri die?'

The question came shakily and she swallowed several times, as if suppressing an outpouring of grief. Her fingers clasped themselves tightly together in front of her until the knuckles shone white, and Peredur cursed Rhodri ap Cadwgan's folly.

'Recklessly and without need.' He stroked a gloved hand down Tarth's neck and stamped his frozen feet. 'De Clare's men had been warned of our approach, and with the Lord Rhys's forces joining us from the south, they retreated without giving battle. Cadwgan gave chase and your brother was killed in the pursuit, along with several other of his men.'

She nodded. 'My father is not one to let an enemy go free, no matter what it might cost him—or cost others. Though he will mourn his son.'

There was no sorrow in her voice, but rather a note of sad regret. It puzzled him. He knew of her brother's warlike reputation, of course, his lust for battle. It was a case of like father like son, both of them rash, violent and cruel—as his own blood father had been.

'And doubtless, so will you,' he said.

'Yes…in my own way.' Her lashes fluttered closed for a brief instant and then she crossed her breast quickly. 'Thank heaven Llywelyn was left behind.'

There was a shiver in her voice, despite the thick woollen gown and cloak of sage green that she wore. Her hood was damp and, beneath, her hair was covered with a white linen coif, as befitted a married woman.

She met his eyes again, the gentian blue startling against the cold whiteness of her face. 'I will need to be with my mother when she hears this news. Rhodri was her son…despite everything.'

Peredur nodded, relieved not to have to break the sad tidings himself, though he would not have shrunk from doing so either. But it was a duty he'd done far too often this last year of fighting alongside the Lord Rhys to free Ceredigion from the rule of Gwynedd, with too many widows made on *both* sides.

'Then you will ride back with me.'

She shook her head, colour rushing once more into her cheeks. 'I would prefer to walk than double your horse's load, since he is lame.'

Peredur grimaced inwardly. It would be far easier for him if she *did* walk, given that the intervening days had done nothing to cool the desire he'd felt on their wedding night. If anything, despite the cold, it had kindled all over again, as hot as ever, when he'd seen her standing in the porch of the church.

But there was no question of her walking, of course, so remounting Tarth, he stretched out his hand. 'You will be quicker and safer riding, and my horse isn't lame. He was born awkwardly and it left a fault in his leg.'

Her eyes widened and she glanced over at her uncle, who was looking straight at them. Peredur followed her gaze. He'd known Edwin since boyhood, when Eilyr had brought him to this church to be baptized with the name he now bore. Edwin couldn't see anything, of course, but he'd always had the feeling the holy man saw everything he needed to see.

'Besides which, if you walk, I must walk with you,' he went on, looking back again at his wife. 'And I would rather get my men home sooner, since they are tired and hungry, as well as frozen to the bone.'

Still she wavered, her mouth beginning to set stubbornly. But as the wind whipped up and sent snow spiralling around the churchyard, she gave a curt nod. 'Very well, then I will ride.'

Putting his foot out for her to step upon, Peredur took her hand and drew her up into the saddle. Settling herself, she clutched her cloak together with one hand and wrapped the fingers of her other hand in Tarth's mane.

Gathering his reins, Peredur placed an arm around her waist. Immediately her spine stiffened against his chest and she attempted to move a little further forward. But as there was nowhere to go other than to sit on Tarth's neck, she had no option but to sit in his lap.

The snow began to fall again but his blood went from cold to hot in an instant. It was too late to rue that he hadn't put her up *behind* the saddle, on Tarth's rump. But his horse's coat was wet with snow and she was cold and damp enough already. So, gritting his teeth, Peredur thanked the priest again for the ale then, motioning to his men, touched his heels to Tarth's flanks.

They rode in silence down the slope to the bottom of the valley floor and crossed the bridge over the river. The water was frozen, the wooden bridge slippery, but they crossed in safety. And then, as they climbed the hill on the other side, Rhianon spoke and her head, which had been averted up until then, half turned.

'Does your horse's injured leg not hurt him?'

Peredur kept his gaze on the road ahead as her scent drifted to his nose—winter rose and wild heather—and began to play havoc with his senses. 'No, his leg is ill-formed, not injured.'

Beneath her hood, her brows rose and her eyes found his. 'Ill-formed?'

'He was birthed badly, a breach.' Peredur felt his palms grow moist inside his gauntlets and sweat trickled down his back as her gaze searched his, bluer than ever against the snow all around. 'I pulled him from the womb as cleanly as I could…but his dam died.'

'In my father's house, lame animals are of little worth.' Her voice was flat, without expression, merely stating a well-known fact. 'The foal would have been slaughtered and used as food for the hounds.'

'Tarth might have been too had I not asked for him,' he said, losing the battle with the desire that had begun to stir uncomfortably in his loins. 'But Eilyr allowed me to keep him.'

'But if his dam had died…?'

'He was put with another mare that had recently foaled.' Peredur swallowed as the horror of that breach birth came vividly back to him, eclipsing desire abruptly as it drove visions into his soul of his mother's suffering and death—things that he could never actually have seen. 'Luckily, she accepted him. Not all will, some will reject an orphan at once.'

'And you mended him?'

'For the first few months, I kept his leg strapped in a splint until the bone had strengthened,' he said, blinking away the terrible images. 'It didn't grow completely straight and was left a little shorter than the other.'

'It must have been a lot of trouble, to raise him that way.'

Rhianon's gaze, wide and vivid, searched his curiously. Her breath came warm and tantalising at his throat, and her hood brushed his chin. She wasn't sitting quite so stiffly now and her weight leaned lightly into him. 'That was a kind thing to do, especially…'

He gave a grim smile as her voice trailed off and uncertainty clouded her eyes. He might at least save her the trouble of finishing her sentence. 'Especially for a man with no heart?'

No sooner had the words left his lips than his brother's laughter rang out behind them.

'Why don't you ask him outright, Rhianon?' Maelgwn had ears like a bat and was as quick to strike as an adder. 'My brother's horse isn't the only unnatural creature among us.'

Peredur said nothing. Retaliation would only add fuel to his brother's fire, as it had almost done at the wedding feast. But, as Maelgwn's taunting filled his ears and echoed around the silent hills, he felt his face grow hot.

'Peredur cares more for horses than for women. But doubtless you found out on your wedding night, my poor sister, that you have married a mongrel and not a man!'

Rhianon went rigid in his arms and her gloved fingers tightened in Tarth's mane. She turned her head to the front again and the little moment of closeness, so unexpected yet so pleasant, was severed. A moment of common ground, discovered and shared for the first time, that he'd found himself enjoying, and now it was over…missing.

In the bailey of Castell Llanbadarn, Peredur dropped down from the saddle then lifted Rhianon down. As she landed lightly on her feet, she slipped, and to steady herself, planted a hand on his left breast. At once, her mouth fell open in a gasp.

The activity going on all around, as stable lads ran to take horses and tired men stripped off their armour, faded into silence. Even the snow stopped falling as they stood and stared at each other, without words but with a question that screamed out loud.

And then Rhianon snatched her hand away and curled

it into her midriff. Peredur waited, his hands still on her waist, bracing himself for her to ask why it was she could feel no heartbeat there.

She could never have felt his heartbeat, of course, through the thick gambeson he wore, even if she had known that all she needed to do was move her hand from one side to the other…

Her eyes were searching his face avidly, as if she really *did* want to ask him outright, as Maelgwn had urged her to do. But the question never came. Instead a voice called her name and then her mother was hurrying towards them, the younger brother, Llywelyn, at her side.

Rhianon stepped back, out of his hold, and drew her cloak about her. 'I will tell her about Rhodri. It will be easier to hear from me than from…anyone else.'

Or from him! Peredur didn't need to hear that in words to know it was in her thoughts. And as she left him and ran to meet her mother, he led Tarth towards the stables, his stride suddenly as uneven as that of his horse.

Would he have told her, had she asked, why he was called Peredur Galon Gudd? Would he have told her that his brother was right? It wasn't just Tarth who was badly birthed and ill-formed, but that *he* was too.

'God keep you, Rhianon…and Cristin also.'

The next morning, in the courtyard, her brother Llywelyn kissed her goodbye. Rhianon nodded, misery clutching at her heart, tighter even than she clutched her brother's hands. She and her maid would indeed need God's protection where they were going. And so would Llywelyn.

'God keep you too,' she replied, her voice choked. She

might not see her brother again for a long time, if ever. 'You are the only son now that Rhodri is dead, and our father will expect much of you.'

Too much, she thought, but left it unsaid since it needed no saying. As Cadwgan's heir, there could be no question of Llywelyn entering the religious life now, as he'd wished.

He nodded, his face grim. 'I know.'

His eyes moved briefly to Cristin, standing just behind, and when they returned to hers, the blue depths were more troubled than ever. His mouth tightened, as if to say more, and then he seemed to change his mind.

'If you ever need me, sister, you only have to send word and I will come.'

With a quick squeeze of his long, slender fingers on hers, Llywelyn kissed her mouth once more. Then he turned away and joined their mother, already mounted, her eyes turned towards the gate.

There had been no such painful farewell from Tangwystl, still mute with mourning for her dead son. But Rhianon hadn't looked for any. Their relationship was dead too, all the mourning for it done long since, at least on her part. Whether Tangwystl mourned it, missed it, she didn't know. And now it was far too late to ask.

The party rode through the gates, accompanied by the two men-at-arms her father had sent back from Ystrad Meurig. At the last moment, Llywelyn turned and looked back, just once, and then they were gone. But at least her family knew what they were returning to, and were doubtless already prepared for it.

Like her mother, like Llywelyn, she had suffered the violence, the brutality, the fear, in silence and dogged resistance. It had made her stronger, not weaker, but now, however, she felt far from strong. For she and her new husband would soon ride out as well, northwards, to the castle of Abereinion, into the unknown, for which she wasn't prepared at all.

As if the thought had conjured him up, Peredur appeared at her side. Rhianon hadn't seen him since they'd parted in the courtyard yesterday. She'd taken supper and slept with her grieving, tearful mother, her own eyes dry, although inwardly she'd wept too for Rhodri's short, violent and wasted life.

No one had been sent to fetch her or to enquire after her absence, and now, as she turned to face Peredur, she wondered if he'd even missed her from either his chamber *or* his bed.

'Are you ready to depart, Rhianon?'

He was dressed in dark colours as usual and looked the same as he had on their wedding day—tall, hard, remote and forbidding, the icy warrior of reputation. Yet today…there was something else, something that didn't sit at all well on those broad shoulders, for it struck her suddenly that he seemed bashful…unsure of himself.

He held the reins of a horse, not the one she'd arrived on but a chestnut mare she'd not seen before. 'This is for you,' he said, in clipped tones.

Rhianon recalled the conversation they'd had about gifts on their wedding night. Was this the one she should have had the morning after in exchange for her body?

'This isn't my horse,' she said, unable to stem the hope in her voice. 'I rode here on a roan, with my mother.'

'Mêl is the gift I had no chance to give you before.'

'Mêl…'

She repeated the lovely name that so suited the pretty

mare, and suddenly had to blink back silly tears. It seemed hope wouldn't be dashed after all.

'Is she called so because her coat is the colour of honey?' The swell of gratitude caught her unawares since it was a sentiment unfamiliar to her. Gifts given in her father's house were rare and came from custom, not from thought or kindness.

'And for her temper also, which is also sweet as honey, though she can be skittish when startled.'

Rhianon stroked the mare's soft muzzle and Mêl snuffled into her gloved palm, bringing a lump into her throat and smile to her lips. 'Thank you, she's very lovely…but do you mean she is really mine?'

'I have just said so.'

Rhianon held those frosty eyes, so at odds with the giving of a gift, as his curt response banished gratitude and left her feeling only sheepish. 'I've never had a horse of my own before,' she explained, pulling her hood up to hide her embarrassment. 'My father breeds horses for war, not for pleasure riding for womenfolk.'

She saw his mouth tighten but he said nothing. Was he thinking of that day, ten years ago, when he'd seen her stand up for the feelings of a horse? Was that the reason behind this wonderful gift he'd given her?

'Then it is time you did. As my wife, it is fitting that you have your own horse.'

No, it seemed it wasn't thinking any such sentiment! Rhianon lifted her chin higher as the satisfaction of being proved right only made the snow that started to fall come even colder to her face. 'Yes, of course, I understand that, Peredur.'

It was the first time she'd used his name and, for a brief instant, he glared at her as if she'd insulted him with it. 'We must leave now,' he said, looping the reins over the mare's head. 'Abereinion isn't far but we should make the most of the daylight.'

Rhianon nodded but her mouth went dry with dread now that the time had come. Her fleeting moment of pleasure over Mêl vanished as Peredur stooped and linked his hands for her foot.

Yesterday, when she'd laid her palm on his chest to steady herself, she'd felt no heartbeat through his thick gambeson. Today, if she reached out surreptitiously as he helped her mount, she still wouldn't find one, since he wore the same garment.

She should just ask him, of course, boldly and out-right, as his brother had advised her to do. But today she wasn't feeling bold at all. So instead she stepped mutely into his waiting hands and was lifted into the saddle as if she weighed nothing.

Peredur turned abruptly and strode to where his grey stallion was waiting. Swinging himself up onto its back, he gathered the reins and touched his heels to its flanks. There were no cruel spurs on his boots like other men wore and no harsh word either, she noticed, but a softly encouraging click of his tongue that was answered with a twitch of the horse's ears.

What had he called the stallion? Tarth? That meant mist—an element that was grey and unfathomable, im-possible to see into or through, enveloping, disorientat-ing and mysterious. As Peredur himself was.

Peredur Galon Gudd—Peredur of the Hidden Heart.

Rhianon gathered up her reins too, her thoughts whirling faster than the snowflakes in the wind. He was a man like any other. He was made of flesh and blood, he lived and breathed and walked as others did. No man could exist without a heart…so he *must* have one!

They rode out through the gates into a winter that seemed to have no end to it. The lifetime that lay ahead of her seemed endless too, like that leaden sky that lay ominously on the horizon.

Would she discover, in the long years to come, whether that name rang true or whether it did not? And, even if Peredur did have a heart, would it prove to be as cold and as pitiless as the harshest of winters?

Chapter Four

As they rode northwards, the weather worsened. Their horses sank to hock and knee in the deep banks of snow that piled up along the route. The journey to Castell Abereinion was less than five leagues, half a day's ride at most, but it seemed double that, as daylight began to fade and the gloom stretched like talons from within the trees that lined the road.

Peredur cursed. If the Lord Rhys hadn't insisted he take possession of Abereinion immediately, he would have delayed this journey and waited, like any sensible man would do, for more clement weather.

Pulling his cloak tighter around his damp shoulders, he looked back to see that all his men were still with him. They were, indistinct shapes huddled in their cloaks too, their heads bent before the driving snow, their mounts blowing and labouring, as were the four packhorses at the rear.

Apart from his own *teulu* of twelve men—his personal war band—two carpenters, a stonemason, a blacksmith and a cook rode in his train. He would also take command of the five men already garrisoned at Abereinion, his task to enlarge and reinforce the castle. Turn it from a deserted outpost to a formidable fortress that would make any enemy think twice before assaulting it.

But twenty-two soldiers was a pitifully small force to hold the frontier against Gwynedd and Powys should the rulers of either kingdom attack.

Rhianon's voice broke the eerie quiet that always accompanied dense snow. 'H-how much further is it?'

Peredur glanced sideways at his wife. She'd hardly spoken since they left Llanbadarn, let alone complained, and neither had her maid, who rode sullenly in the entourage behind.

'Not too far,' he said. 'We are nearer the coast now and the land will soon flatten out.'

She turned her head to look at him and an ache opened up in his gut. Her face, almost hidden beneath her hood, was drained, her skin so pale it seemed translucent.

'The castle lies on the coast?'

Peredur nodded and fixed his eyes ahead of him again, away from her beauty. 'On the southern side of the estuary of the Dyfi.'

But the ache persisted. If he was honest with himself, the same ache had been eating away at him since the night of the wedding, when they'd sat before the brazier. When they'd talked and he'd touched her foot and desire had flamed up inside him, far higher than any fire.

'Though I doubt you'll see the sea today,' he added. 'Unless we get there before dark.'

Two of his men were riding in front, forging a path through the deep snowdrifts. Now one of them drew rein and turned in his saddle. 'The miller's house, my lord.'

The mill loomed into sight. The waterwheel was idle, icicles dripping like silver daggers from its teeth. Even the waterfall that fed the wheel hung eerily still, its torrent frozen into a solid column of white water.

The miller, who he knew to be called Hywel Felin Ddŵr, and his wife were gathered in the lee of the house. There was a whole brood of children around them, wrapped up in swathes of wool until only their eyes were visible. But no greeting came from any of them, only dull and resentful stares.

Then, a small russet brown dog ran out at them, barking sharply. Rhianon's mare startled and shied, barging into Tarth, her stirrup clashing with his in a loud ring of iron. One of his men drew his sword swiftly, another rasp of iron echoing the first, and, leaning low, swung it at the dog.

The nimble creature dodged it with ease and barked even louder. One of the women in the group—the mother of the brood or perhaps an elder daughter—gave a scream and hauled the smallest of the children back behind her skirts.

'Uffarn dân!' Pushing his hood down, Peredur put a hand on Mêl's rein to steady the mare. 'Call your dog off, man!'

The miller jerked his head and a child darted forward and wrestled the animal into its arms. Both child and dog were small and unkempt, and both were grinning from ear to ear—if dogs could grin.

And then, as one entity, the whole family turned away and disappeared into the mill house, the door closing behind them with a thud that shook the snow off the lintel.

Peredur almost flung himself out of the saddle, ready

to stride across and pound on that dismissive door, and take the miller to task for his show of insolence. But Rhianon and her maid were frozen to the bone, and so were his men. So was he, come to that.

He breathed out, his breath a cloud of frustration in the cold air, and then turned his stallion around. Hywel Felin Ddŵr would have to wait.

'Come, we'll press on,' he said to Rhianon.

There was no reply. She'd not made a sound, he realised, when the mare had almost unseated her. Extreme cold could lead to inertia and the dulling of senses, he knew, having endured it many times over on winter campaigns. Perhaps he should have left her behind at Llanbadarn, her maid too, and sent for them when the snow melted.

Drawing his hood up again, Peredur gave a mental shake of his head. Even his father's watchful eyes didn't see everything and his brother was more than adept at sneaking by them. Rhianon wouldn't have been safe for a moment under the same roof as Maelgwn.

They continued on the last part of the journey, mercifully short now. Fording the Einion river, shallow from lack of rain, their horses' hooves broke through the layer of ice on its surface, like hammers on glass. The northern bank of the river along which they rode had been cleared of trees and the going was far easier now that the land was flatter.

As they neared their destination, Rhianon gave a little gasp and, drawing rein, Peredur turned to look at her. Her face was filled with both wonder and dread, as if she'd suddenly found herself in a magical but awful place.

'Oh… I never expected this.'

He followed her gaze to where the mountains of Gwynedd rose loftily before them, like spectres out of the gathering dusk. On this side, at the edge of the land, the sea sat pale and unmoving. It was if some ancient *dewin* had cast a spell and frozen the world, not just in winter, but in a time that was centuries old.

In many ways, the place *was* magical, at least at first sight, with its bleak and unforgiving beauty, the sense of a wilderness without end. But she would soon discover that spending a lifetime here would be anything but magical.

'Castell Abereinion,' he said, without need, since it couldn't be anywhere else. Perhaps it was just the light, but the tower, set on a mound at the point of the head land, looked more like a lone and immoveable sentinel at the edge of existence.

'Our home,' he added, as if to make it seem more appealing than it was. A sense of shame fell over him, heavier even than the snow had done on their journey north. She deserved better.

'The castle was built in haste by the Lord Rhys a year ago to forestall a rumoured attack from Gwynedd,' he explained, his words sounding more and more like an excuse. 'That threat was averted and this outpost has been more or less abandoned ever since.'

'Abandoned? You mean it is not garrisoned?'

'There is a custodian in charge, with a small band of men, who will have maintained the place somewhat.' Peredur met her gaze and found it dismayed. '*We* are to be the garrison.'

'Is there no village nearby? No settlement?'

He shook his head. 'Only the mill we just passed

by, where corn is ground and wool weaved, and there are some outlying farms. But no, there is no village.'

Had she expected more? Well, she would be disappointed. There would be nothing more, only the hardship and isolation of a frontier post and a husband who was not worthy of her.

Rhianon's voice came again, pensively, as if she'd been chewing over all he'd told her and found it not just distasteful but indigestible too. 'I see…then we will be quite alone here.'

Peredur looked away and towards the mountains that heralded the southern border of Gwynedd. Alone? With enemies to the north, and to the east too, both with greedy eyes set on Ceredigion, they wouldn't be alone at all. But she was right all the same.

'Yes,' he replied, as the wind suddenly lifted from the wide stretch of water that surrounded the headland and swept down to where the estuary opened out to the sea, and on to oblivion. 'Quite alone.'

There was a long silence, filled only with the primitive and unearthly sounds of the landscape around them. Loudest and most eerie of all were the haunting cries that rose from the desolate shore, sending a sudden tingle down his spine.

Rhianon turned towards him. 'Are they birds I can hear?'

Peredur peered through the twilight towards the shoreline. He couldn't see them, however, but he knew what they were. 'Those are the *morloi*.'

'*Morloi?*'

'Sea calves. This estuary is the Dyfi but the local people call it Glan Morloi—the Shore of Sea Calves. You'll be able to see them, tomorrow, in daylight.'

Why was he expounding on the creatures that would become their neighbours when he should be getting them all inside and warm?

'Night falls later here than it does inland since we are on the western coast,' Peredur added, touching his heels to Tarth's flanks and moving his party onward. 'But even so, we should hurry indoors before it becomes dark.'

And once indoors, he would have to show Rhianon to their chamber. And, after supper was over, she would surely expect him to take her to their bed, consummate their marriage, as he should have done already almost a week since. Tonight there would be yet another struggle to resist her and master himself.

But as they rode into the castle, a trickle of unease slid down his spine. The gates were wide open, not a light showed anywhere, there was no call from the watch—in either greeting or challenge—and no one came to meet them.

Halting in the middle of the unkempt bailey, Peredur stared about him, the hair lifting at the back of his neck. The three-storey keep and outbuildings were almost as weathered as the gates were. And most foreboding of all, there was no sign of the five men that were supposed be garrisoned here.

After a moment of stunned silence, he called out. But there was no answer, just his voice echoing around the walls and disappearing beneath the wailing of the *morloi*.

'Wh-where is everybody?'

Rhianon's question came through chattering teeth. Her lips were almost blue, her eyes dull, her too-pale skin an indication that her blood flow had slowed down, failing to warm her body at all.

'I don't know,' Peredur replied, dismounting swiftly and gritting his own teeth against chattering. Handing Tarth to one of his men, he beckoned to his *penteulu*—the captain of his guard.

'I mislike this, Meirchion. Organise a thorough search. There must be *somebody* here!' He looked up at the sky, darker now, oppressive. 'We'll need food too but it's too late to hunt anything tonight.'

He pulled some silver from the purse at his belt. 'If there is nothing eatable to be had in the kitchens, send someone to the mill to ask for meat enough for tonight, and pay the miller well for it.' He paused, recalling the insolence of earlier. 'If he won't give it, then take it.'

As his captain hurried away, Peredur lifted Rhianon down from the saddle. Her body was stiff in his arms and she landed heavily on her feet, causing her to clutch at his forearms to steady herself.

Her eyes flew to his and, like a reflection in deep water, Peredur saw in them that moment of yesterday, when she'd put her palm over his breast. Then snatched it away again, as if the contact had singed the skin from her hand.

Today, however, she didn't snatch it away immediately. Instead, she stood and stared up at him and, for a moment, the cold and the desolation ceased to matter as those eyes seemed to pull him in and drag him down into their lovely depths.

Then, even if she didn't snatch herself away exactly, she removed herself from his hold with deliberate intent and pulled her sodden cloak tightly around her.

'Beth ddiawl!' Swinging around, he pushed his hood

down and dragged his fingers through his hair. Because even the beguiling beauty of those eyes hadn't blinded him to the pinched whiteness of her face, the shiver of her lips, the frost that spiked the long silken lashes. 'What in God's name has happened here!'

As if in answer, one of the men that had been sent to search the keep returned, his face bemused. 'There is no one inside the tower, my lord, neither in the hall nor aloft.'

Peredur swore again, under his breath this time, and then turned to Rhianon. 'You and your woman will be warmer in the hall, even if it is empty.'

She nodded and, linking her arm through her maid's, followed in his wake to the keep, the fading daylight picking out their way. The doorway, though open, was dark as night, the flight of wooden steps that led up to it covered in white rime.

He placed a foot onto the first and felt it slide immediately. Calming his temper with an effort, Peredur extended his hand to Rhianon. 'Lest you slip,' he said, when she frowned. 'The steps are treacherous.'

After a slight hesitation, she placed her palm in his. It was like ice, even through her thick glove, her fingers so brittle it seemed they might break should he hold them too tightly. As quickly as was safe, Peredur guided her upwards. Then, leaving her at the top, he returned and extended the same service to her maid.

Inside the hall, it was almost too dark to see. The one long table down the centre was strewn with dirty trenchers and overturned cups, and stools lay upside down on the bare earthen floor. The hearth was cold and the rush lights on the walls long burned low and extinguished. Somewhere in the rafters, a rat squealed.

Peredur turned to Rhianon, to find her face pale and drawn, her eyes dim with fatigue, and the maid looked just as weary. 'We'll go aloft and find a chamber,' he said, remorse biting deeper than any cold. 'And hopefully one with a brazier to light.'

By the saints in heaven! What sort of place had he brought her to, brought them *all* to?

Rhianon followed Peredur up the wooden stairway, Cristin at her heels. She could hardly see the steps in front of her but thankfully they were not as slippery as the ones outside had been.

And, as if by divine justice, a cruel but timely retribution for the deceit of her wedding night, her stomach was gripped with the stabbing pains that came every month, and her head ached until it hurt even to keep her eyes open.

At the top, there were two chambers, one small with a pallet on the floor and nothing else, and the larger one—the lord's room—containing a bed and some pieces of furniture. Someone had obviously slept here and left in a hurry, judging by the untidy bedding and few dirty utensils that lay about.

In the larger room, Rhianon wrapped her arms around her midriff as, muttering under his breath, Peredur went over to the iron brazier that stood on a stone slab in the centre. Pulling off his gauntlets, he took out his knife and a piece of flint and tried to kindle a fire on the twigs that were piled inside it. It wouldn't take, however, and she felt his frustration grow as all his attempts failed.

'Is the wood too damp?' she asked.

He sent her a swift look of incredulity and Rhianon

bit her tongue. But the oppression of this place, the dreadful emptiness, a weariness she'd never dreamed was possible to feel, the excruciating pains that wracked her abdomen and his rapidly fraying temper were shredding her nerves to ribbons.

And far worse was the darkness that was creeping in through the open windows, the drawing in of the night when she and her husband would retire to that unkempt bed. Unless she contrived it otherwise...

Finally, Peredur threw down his implements and, planting his hands on his hips, glared at the brazier with such venom that it was a wonder the wood didn't spark to life, in sheer fear.

But when he spoke, there was no anger in his voice, nor even frustration now, but a sense of futility, almost defeat. 'This is useless.'

Despite her misgivings, and her aching belly, a wave of sympathy rose up inside her. He was just as cold and wet and tired as she was, and as dismayed too to find such an inhospitable welcome, the place deserted, the garrison mysteriously absent.

Shaking his head now, he chewed his lip and frowned until his brows met. With a sigh, he gripped the edges of the brazier as if he'd like to choke the life out of it. Then his eyes found hers.

'Yes, as you said, the wood *is* too damp, Rhianon.' A wry grimace twisted his mouth. 'But I don't know what else to try.'

Rhianon felt a blow smite her heart, sharper even than the pains in her womb. Her father, were he in Peredur's place, would be resorting to his wine now, yelling and cursing and kicking his blameless servants for failing to get a fire going. Not valiantly, if hopelessly, trying to do the task himself as her husband was doing.

'There is a trick to light a damp fire, my lord,' she ventured, taking a step forward. 'Perhaps it is worth a try?'

She pulled her braid out from beneath her cloak. It was wet where the snow had fallen on her shoulders but the ends of her hair, tucked well down inside her clothing, were dry. 'Cut a good handful of my hair.'

His brows lifted. 'Your hair?'

Rhianon nodded. 'It might be sufficient to start a flame but we'll need some dry material too…perhaps some hay from the pallet next door?'

With a word, she sent Cristin to fetch some, hoping the hay wouldn't prove as uncooperative as the wood. Peredur was looking at her intently, doubt etched deeply on his face, and suddenly, her idea seemed anything but practical. If it didn't work, would he yell and curse and take it out on *her*, as Cadwgan would?

The night of their marriage feast came back to her, the crushing grip of Maelgwn's hand, the contrasting gentleness of Peredur's, the protective way he'd carried her from the hall, away from the grasping hands that tried to steal a wedding token.

Would a man who showed that consideration for her by turn shout at her and strike her out of sheer temper? But then, how could she know for certain that he *would not*?

Lifting her chin, she forced those possible consequences from her mind as necessity took precedence. 'We must do *something* else we'll all freeze to death this coming night!'

Before she could take her offer back—for she wasn't

sure at all now that this *would* actually work—Rhianon went over to the table next to the wall and placed the end of her braid on its surface. Then she took a deep breath. 'Cut it.'

After a moment of pause, Peredur nodded and joined her at the table. His knife flashed and sliced four or five inches off the end of her braid. As he went to take up the chunk of hair, however, his hand stilled. Then his fingers stroked gently over the severed locks.

Rhianon's heart started to drum as his eyes lifted and blazed into hers. A muscle clenched in his lean cheek but, in the rapidly darkening room, it was impossible to read what lay behind those eyes. Was it regret, even apology, for robbing her of the hair she'd offered freely?

Or was it something else entirely? The same thing she'd seen, sensed, on their wedding night, as his hand had touched her foot and his eyes had burned then too, if only for a moment?

'It doesn't matter,' she said, her voice quaking a little and not just with cold, or from the clawing pains in her belly. 'A few inches of hair is a small price to pay for a fire. No one would even notice it has been cut and it will soon grow again.'

His hand hovered a moment longer and then he gave a short nod. Snatching up the hewed-off locks, he strode back over to the brazier. Laying some wisps of the hay—thankfully dry—over the damp wood, he placed the hair down atop it. The knife flashed again as he struck his flint once more.

It still took several attempts, and Rhianon, going to stand at his side, began to pray silently but fervently. It didn't seem it would work after all. As the long moments dragged out, and the noise of stone on steel started to grate, and Cristin gave a little sob of despair, her heart began to sink too.

And then, at last, a spark caught. The lock of hair sizzled and the straw and the twigs below began to glow. With fingers that visibly shivered, Peredur fed the struggling fire with more hay and the flames leapt higher. And then the fire took hold and the larger pieces of wood below the brash began to hiss and smoke.

It was then, with the first feeble beginnings of heat, that they turned and smiled at each other. Really smiled, his transforming his face and turning the harshness of his features to utter beauty.

'Where did you learn such a trick?' he asked.

'From my brother Llywelyn,' Rhianon replied, her cheeks heating for reasons that had nothing to do with the fire that was crackling merrily now, as if it had just been toying with them all the time. 'He's very resourceful.'

Cristin was lighting the rush lights from the brazier, bringing light as well as warmth into the room. But, between she and Peredur, a different sort of warmth had gathered. One that warmed her frozen toes and fingers and banished her belly ache as if it were nothing.

Had Peredur leaned closer suddenly? Or was it *she* who'd leaned closer to him? For there were mere inches between them now, their clothes steaming together in the heat, the cold from his body touching hers through them.

'And evidently so are you, Rhianon.' His face too was close to hers, his breath misting and mingling with the smoke from the fire. 'Resourceful, I mean.'

And like that other night before that other brazier, Rhianon saw his eyes turn from ice to fire, then drop and linger on her mouth. The scorch of it seemed to ignite her blood and she found her lips parting, felt herself wanting to lean in closer still, compelled by something she knew not what, to feel the touch of *his* lips.

Instead, she jerked away, just as Peredur did the same. Pocketing his flint and sheathing his knife, he strode swiftly to the doorway.

There, almost as an afterthought, he turned and cast a keen glance over her sodden figure, his gaze ice-like once more.

'I'll send a man up with your belongings. You should get out of those wet clothes at once, your maid too.'

Rhianon moistened her lips then cleared her throat, urgent reality overcoming whatever had just occurred between them. Her words came fluently, even before she'd composed them in her head. 'This evening…'

His brows lifted. 'Yes?'

'I will require…privacy.' Her voice faltered as the room, no longer dark, illuminated the mortification on her face. 'My courses have begun…the *misglwyf*…and therefore… I trust you will take the other chamber?'

There was a beat of silence when even her maid's embarrassment was tangible at the emphasis of spelling it out, so that there should be no misunderstanding. And there wasn't. Peredur coughed and then, inclining his head, he stepped quickly over the threshold.

'I understand.' His hand paused on the door latch. 'Then I will see you at supper, my lady.'

He closed the door behind him. Rhianon listened to his footsteps descend the stairs, heard the door to the hall shut behind him with a bang. Drawing a deep breath, she gazed around the sparse chamber, at the damp wooden walls, the ill-fitting shutters and bare floorboards.

She let her breath out again in a sigh of relief. As inhospitable as it was, this chamber was her place of sanctuary for the next five moons, at least. But even as the comforting thought came, it vanished and the stabbing ache in her belly intensified all over again.

Rhianon sat down on the bed, her head aching too now, and the dampness of the bedding seeping through her clothes into her bones. Privacy for five nights, yes... but what of all the other nights that would come after?

Chapter Five

Much later, Peredur stood on the battlements and stared outwards. There was a full moon high in the starlit sky and the snowy landscape was as bright as day. The water in the estuary, by contrast, was a black as pitch except where the moonlight reflected in a rippling swathe of silver.

Pulling his cloak tighter around him, he listened for sounds that weren't there. Not even the *morloi* were calling, since they were sleeping. It was quiet. Everything…everyone…was asleep but he.

How long had he been standing up here? It had been three hours, perhaps four, since they'd eaten a late and cheerless supper in the hall, the meat grudgingly supplied by the miller despite being paid well for it.

Rhianon and her maid had retired upstairs and he'd resumed the task of making this place something like habitable. Now every man had a full belly, a warm body and a bed. Every horse too had been fed and watered and now slumbered in its stall.

An owl shrieked close by and the flap of ghostly white wings over the battlements started him. And it was only when his frozen limbs failed to react that Peredur admitted the folly of this vigil. None was necessary since not even the most reckless enemy would venture out in deep snowfall on a clear moonlit night.

He descended the ladder, feeling for the rungs with numb toes, his fingers like ice inside his gauntlets. The two men on duty at the gates barely lifted their heads in acknowledgement as he passed by, doubtless as chilled as he was.

'Reduce the guard rota from three hours to two,' he instructed them, indicating the candle with its time-keeping rings that sat on a shelf within the recess. 'It's too harsh for any man to stay out longer.'

Peredur climbed the steps to the keep, not slippery now due to the straw he'd ordered to be laid down, plenty of which had been discovered in the outbuildings. As well as straw, there'd been cut wood, peat turfs and dried rushes, while the kitchen had revealed a barrel of ale and another of salt.

There was still no sign of the errant garrison, however…

Frowning, but unable to even speculate at the disappearance of a seasoned custodian and four men-at-arms, he entered the hall. There was a roaring fire now in the central hearth and exhausted men slept soundly around it, none waking at his footfall.

Peredur climbed the stairs that led to the upper levels, passing quietly by the second floor where other men slept. Then, reaching the top floor, he hesitated, halfway between the two rooms. He looked towards the door of the smaller chamber, where his pallet of hay and a blanket awaited.

Then he looked long at the other door. What if the

brazier he'd lit earlier had burned low, or gone out altogether? Finally, he reached for the latch. It hadn't been oiled in God knew how long and gave a click as loud as a hammer on iron. Peredur stilled but there was no sound at all from within. So, carefully, he eased the door open and stepped over the threshold.

The room was unlit, apart from the fire, and the sturdy wooden shutters he'd ordered nailed over the windows barred the moonlight. As his eyes adjusted, he made out two shapes beneath the furs in the bed. Rhianon and her maid, deep in sleep and huddled close together for warmth.

The brazier was still burning but it could do with feeding all the same. Dragging his eyes away from the bed, Peredur crossed the floor, his footsteps making no sound. Taking up a few peat turfs, he laid them carefully on the fire and was turning to leave when the rustle of bedding broke the silence.

'Peredur?'

He froze, turned and caught his breath. One of the shapes had risen up in the bed and, despite the dimness of the room, he knew it wasn't the maid. Even if the tiring woman would never have addressed him by his name, he recognised Rhianon's voice, her slender form, the cascading fall of her hair.

'I was making sure the fire still burned,' he whispered, startled at the hoarseness of his voice. 'Go back to sleep.'

'What hour is it?'

'What hour?' Peredur shook his head at the strange question. 'I know not. Does it matter?'

There was a little silence. 'No, not really.' Another

silence. 'It's just…there are no church bells here to mark the passing of the night.'

Through the dark, the flames picked out the curve of her cheek, the bridge of her nose, her wide brow. Her face seemed paler, her eyes bigger, her lips fuller.

'No, there are no bells,' he responded, his pulse beginning to beat a little faster as the firelight danced at the base of her throat. 'But it must be well past midnight.'

He'd studied her face keenly enough, as they'd sat before that other brazier, on that other midnight, their wedding night. But he hadn't seen her in a shift then, as he did now, nor beheld the smooth, bare skin of her arms. And now his imagination proceeded to paint a vivid picture of the naked body *below* the shift.

'Then why are *you* still up and about?'

Why? Peredur gave a grim smile. With his back to the brazier and his face in shadow, she wouldn't see the fantasy that was colouring his thoughts, nor the carnal desire that came in its wake. 'I couldn't sleep.'

That was the truth, at least. If she hadn't been suffering her monthly *misglwyf*, if she hadn't requested privacy, if she hadn't banished him to the room next door…

He'd been spared temptation this night, and the few to come, but what then? One night soon he would have to make Rhianon his wife. He would be expected to consummate the marriage to make it valid in the eyes of the Church. He would be expected to provide for heirs to come after him. And to do that he would have to let that fantasy in his head become reality.

But if he did, he would never know a moment's peace from then on.

'What do you think happened to the garrison?' she

asked, still sitting up in bed, her face clearer now as his eyes adjusted to the light.

Peredur shook his head. 'Perhaps they mistook their orders,' he said, not really believing it was true, any more than he believed that forbidden fantasy in his head could ever become true. 'And instead of remaining under my command have returned south to the Lord Rhys.'

'And left the place unguarded?'

He shrugged, sharing her scepticism. 'Tomorrow, I will send men to ask at the outlying farms for information, since someone hereabouts *must* know what happened to them.' His suspicions were that they were either dead of disease or from violence. But, if so, where were the bodies?

'Go back to sleep, Rhianon,' he said, not voicing his suspicions, since it wouldn't serve to worry her. And the longer he remained, the more lurid his fantasy would become, until it might blind him altogether and make him want to *make* it reality. 'I'm sorry I woke you up but the fire will stay in until morning now, so I'll not disturb you again.'

Turning, he closed the door behind him and entered the small chamber. The brazier here had long gone out and only the moon beyond the un-shuttered window lit the room. He flung himself down on the hard pallet and sighed. It felt more like a hair shirt than a bed but he welcomed the scourge of hay through his clothes and the chill that began to bathe his skin.

As difficult as it would be, better to adhere to abstinence, endure frustration, loneliness even, than to give in to desire. Better by far to ignore fantasy and neglect his wife than to add to the weight of responsibility, and accountability, he'd carried since boyhood and always would.

A burden placed there by the grief-stricken grandmother who had raised him and who had hated him for being born alive while his mother—her daughter—had died.

After Peredur had closed the door behind him, Rhianon lay down again and pulled the furs up to her chin. She stared up at the ceiling, watching the flicker of flames cast eerie designs there. None of them made sense and neither did her husband.

With the click of the latch, her heart had leapt into her throat at the thought that her courses weren't enough of an excuse. That he'd come anyway, that he'd dismiss her maid, and then take his husband's due, *misglwyf* or not.

Yet he'd come only to feed the fire! Why had he done that? Out of duty? From consideration, even care? Or simply plain common sense since it had been so much trouble to kindle a fire in the first place, best not let it go out again?

And why was he still awake and on his feet instead of sleeping under the blessed comfort of furs in a warm room?

Rhianon sighed and gave up on the unfathomable puzzle that was the man she'd married. She closed her eyes but, as if the turmoil of her thoughts was palpable, Cristin stirred at her side.

'*M-meistres*…are you awake?'

'Yes.'

To her astonishment, her maid began to cry. 'Oh, I

don't think I can bear it here! This place is terrible… all this snow…'

'Cristin, what's amiss? Did you have a bad dream?'

The girl's voice was quivering with fear. 'It's those w-wailing sounds from the sea. They aren't a dream, no, nor a nightmare either, they exist! D-demons that lurk beneath the water, waiting to lure us all in, one by one, until there is no one left.'

Rhianon's astonishment turned to fear at the images the girl had drawn. 'Don't be silly, *forwyn*! There are no demons in the sea.' Though she didn't know that for sure, did she? 'Perhaps far out, there exist things we don't understand. But not so close to land, and those sounds are only the creatures that live here.'

'The devil's creatures!' Her maid shook her head vehemently. 'His familiars sent here to drive us mad, like that poor garrison before us!'

Rhianon drew Cristin into her arms, shocked. She'd never heard her maid— usually so silent and composed—speak like this before. But, coming from peasant stock as the girl did, perhaps it was simply superstition that fuelled her fearful imaginings.

'All places are strange at first, even a little frightening,' she said, as calmly as she could, though her imagination began to run amok too. 'The snow will thaw soon and those sea calves will swim back out into the ocean come spring. There is no need to fear them.'

'But what if they *don't* go? What if we're all *dead* by spring? What if…what if they take our souls with them, to the bottom of the sea?'

'Cristin, hush!'

'We'll never rest in consecrated ground but suffer eternal torment for sins not confessed nor absolved!'

Cristin was sobbing piteously now, her fingers clutching at her shift. 'Oh, *meistres*, I want to go home! There isn't even a church here where we can confess, nor or a priest to save us from certain damnation if we stay!'

As if to echo her maid's words, a long eerie call broke the night. Not the *morloi* now, but the haunting howl of a wolf, somewhere in the forested hills beyond the river. January was *mis y blaidd*…the month of the wolf! The thought sent a shaft of horror to Rhianon's heart.

'Be easy, *forwyn*.' She stroked her maid's hair, like a mother would do a frightened child, as *her* mother had done, a long time ago. 'You are overtired after our journey, that is all, and your thoughts are playing tricks on you. It will not seem so frightening on the morrow, you'll see.'

But, as Cristin's tears subsided at last and she drifted into a fitful sleep, Rhianon held tightly on to the girl all the same. Not just to give comfort if she should wake again but to take comfort for herself in return.

Unlike Cristin, she might be able to separate superstition from knowledge, but she was also disturbed by this unwelcoming place. She too was unsettled by the haunting calls of the *morloi* and the wolves, by the desolate white landscape that hemmed them in, by the lack of spiritual guidance…

Unlike her maid, however, she could not voice such fears, or even allow them. She was a wife and had to simply endure them in silence.

'I wish to send Cristin back home to her parents.'

It was three days later that Rhianon made the request of Peredur. By then, she truly did worry for the girl's sanity. Neither of them had slept a wink during the previous two nights and, by day, her maid was too distracted by the *morloi* to carry out her duties anyway, no matter how gently she chided and helped her.

Peredur, just mounting the steps as she was going out of the hall to find him, paused. His head was bare, his hair windswept, and his boots covered with mud. He'd been hunting with some of the men and, behind him in the bailey, two red deer and a wild boar hung across the backs of horses, together with the carcasses of several hares and fowl.

'Cristin?'

'My maid.' Three steps above, Rhianon looked down upon him, not up as she usually did. That didn't give her any sense of advantage however, nor make this man— her husband—any more approachable, although today, fresh from the exertion of the hunt, he was undeniably attractive.

Since the day of their arrival at Castell Abereinion, Peredur continued to occupy the small chamber, as she'd requested of him. By day, except during meals, he was either busy setting the castle to rights or riding in the outlying lands seeing to defences and getting to know his bond tenants, few as they were.

'Why do you wish to send her away?'

His words now came as they usually did—short and to the point. After the day he'd cut her hair, and that strange moment beside the brazier, and later when he'd come to feed the fire, all his words were short and to the point, if he uttered any at all.

'Cristin is unhappy here,' Rhianon explained, his taciturn manner and remoteness unnerving her as always. 'The *morloi* frighten her and she is not used to this…isolation. She's never been away from home, so

far from her family, before. She is too young and un-
prepared for it.'

'Yet, you are not much older, and, doubtless, neither
have *you* been used to isolation. Do *you* wish to leave
too, Rhianon?'

His blunt question came more like an accusation.
Had she given him cause to think so? How could she
have, when they hardly ever crossed paths less still
crossed words? A marital situation that *should* have
relieved her but only left her confused!

'I have no choice but to stay. I am your wife. Cristin
has no such…' Rhianon searched her mind for the expression she needed. 'Such obligation.'

She saw his face flush. But why should either of
them be embarrassed, since it was so? It was bitterly
ironic that a choice between this house and the house
of her father was no choice at all, even if she *had* been
able to choose!

'However, I can choose for Cristin,' she went on,
'and I would like to return her to her parents in Uwch
Aeron, which is what *she* would choose were she able.'

His grey eyes were locked on hers, glinting like frost,
just as they had on their wedding day. 'Who will tend
to your needs if she goes?'

Rhianon had thought that through already, at least
the domestic and servile needs she assumed he was re-
ferring to. The other needs—unexpected and unwelcome but distinctly womanly—that had begun to shape
her dreams these last few nights, those she tried to ignore.

Needs that now brought a flush to her face too and
forced her to have to clear her throat before she could
speak.

'I noticed, the day we arrived, that the miller has a daughter close to my own age,' she said, linking her fingers together and willing her skin to cool, refusing to allow those troublesome dreams to invade the clear light of day. 'Could *she* not become my maidservant?'

His head tilted, his golden hair catching the sun as it fell over his brow. He was wearing his customary dark colours and they looked even more forbidding than usual today, except…

As he lifted a hand and rubbed his chin, Rhianon saw he was wearing the dun-coloured gauntlets she'd given him. Why that should touch her was a mystery, and yet it did, swift and startlingly.

'I'm not sure she would be suitable.' Peredur's response came after a moment of consideration. 'I don't trust the miller and I'm certain that he, living so close, must know what happened to the garrison.'

The day they'd arrived, when the dog ran out barking, crossed Rhianon's mind. The miller and his family huddled against the wall of their house, their faces resentful and not at all trustworthy, the utter lack of greeting to their new lord.

'If the people here are as you suspect, Hywel's daughter coming as my maid might help win them over?' she suggested, recalling too her husband's tolerance of the insult, one that another man—like her father, like her first husband—would have retaliated against at once, and with violence. Yet Peredur had not.

Had that been because he'd deemed it more important to reach the castle before nightfall? Because they'd all been frozen to the bone and a fire and a bed had taken priority? Or had it been because Peredur was not

like Cadwgan or Seisyll at all, despite what his reputation said?

'I doubt that very much,' he said, taking a step up,
as if to move on and pass into the hall. 'Not if what I've
seen so far of my tenants is anything to go by. None
have given me any cooperation in discovering what
happened to the men of the garrison.'

Rhianon drew a deep breath, both at his sudden prox-
imity and because she sensed the topic was now closed.
With the continued mystery of the missing men, and
the truculence of his bond tenants, Peredur had more
pressing matters to deal with. But…should she insist
all the same?

She'd long learned not to ask for anything, less still
plead, since in Cadwgan's house, and also in Seisyll's,
she would be refused anyway. But she was mistress
here now, and a wife, and if she were to succeed in both
roles—survive both—she would have to draw her line
firmly. 'Nevertheless…' She inched sideways a little,
deliberately barring his way. 'I would like Cristin to go
as soon as possible, so I would like to speak to Hywel
Felin Ddŵr today.'

His mouth tightened. 'For all we know, the daughter
might be as intractable as the father.'

'Perhaps.' Rhianon lifted her chin higher until she
was almost looking down her nose at him. 'Even so, I
would like to give the girl the benefit of the doubt. As
lady here, do I not have the right to choose my own maid
and to decide whether she is suitable or not?'

Squinting against the morning sun, Peredur stared
up at Rhianon. She did indeed look every inch the lady,
and not just because of her fine clothes. She wore a dark

red cloak over a kirtle the colour of autumn leaves, colours that struck him as forcibly as her mood today. Her gloves were of brown leather and a girdle was looped at her waist, from which dangled her pouch and the keys to the castle stores.

A white linen coif covered her head and her hair hung in a shining plait over one shoulder. Five inches shorter now, of course, since he'd cut it.

She also looked more beautiful than ever, the bold colours of her clothing a striking contrast with the raven-black hair, complimenting the pale countenance and the dazzling blue eyes.

Peredur shook himself free of the beguiling thoughts in his mind that pulled his body tight, and he brought himself back to the matter in hand. Her request wasn't unreasonable. In fact, if her present maid was so frightened and unhappy here, perhaps it *was* wise that she go, and soon. If this oppressive place had driven a hardy garrison of soldiers to flight—if that was indeed what had happened to them—what hope did a frightened maiden have of surviving it?

'Very well,' he said, making his mind up, swiftly as he always did. I will send for Hywel in day or two and I…*we* will discuss the matter with him.'

'Will you not send for him at once?' An imperative note entered her tone. 'I mean, now, today?'

'No, it's not advisable.' Peredur shook his head. 'The snow is still thick and the road too perilous for riding.'

'But the mill is quite near. I could ride there, or even walk.'

'Walk?'

She nodded then added, with obvious reluctance,

'Or, if you think it unsafe for me to go alone…you may walk with me.'

It was almost ludicrous! Walk *with* her when he needed to walk *away* from her? As far away as possible from the desire that, instead of decreasing over the last days had only piled up on top of him, thicker and far more perilous than any snow.

'No,' he repeated, more firmly now. 'That would not be any safer than riding.'

Her eyes clouded and she tilted her head to one side, exposing the creamy column of her throat. If he moved up another step, he could place his lips there, just where her pulse beat below the soft skin. Perhaps even touch his lips to hers…

Lips that, the next instant, set rebelliously. 'And that is the end of the matter?'

'Yes, Rhianon, it is.' But Peredur sensed it wasn't the end of the matter at all as far as she was concerned. 'What difference will a delay of a day or two make?'

'It might make a great deal of difference to Cristin!'

Then he *did* take another step upwards until his gaze was level with hers, reasoning with her as patiently as his carnal thoughts permitted. 'Cristin could not leave yet, in any case,' he said. 'The way south to Uwch Aeron would be impassable.'

'But we came that way, did we not, and the snow was worse then.'

'Er mwyn Duw!' Too late, Peredur bit back on a curse as his patience finally frayed, weakened like an outwitted foe by the unseen enemy—desire. 'What would have me *do*, Rhianon? Wave my sword and make the snow disappear, like a magic wand!'

Her eyes flew wide and, moving back a little, she

drew herself taller. 'Of course not! I want you… I *expect* you to listen to me.'

Peredur dragged in a deep breath as what had started as a discussion flared into unexpected, inexplicable argument. 'Have I not been doing exactly that?' he countered, inhaling, against his will, the scent of heather and winter rose, and some other essence that was purely she.

'Your insistence is baffling,' he went on. 'I understand your concern about your maid, of course, but she is not in any danger. It needs only to wait a little longer.'

She folded her arms across her midriff, the movement lifting her breasts and exposing her slender waist, the gentle slope of her hips beneath her cloak. 'I see,' was all she said.

But suddenly, it was as if she stood at the far side of the courtyard, not right there, two steps above and a mere arm's length away.

'When it is safe to do so, and your new maid is in your service—providing she proves suitable—I will send two men to escort Cristin home. Will that satisfy you, Rhianon?'

She nodded but her gaze had become veiled, her stance remote, as if she wasn't satisfied at all, nor even as if she believed him.

'And may *I* be the one to decide if she is suitable or not?' she asked, haughtily.

He inclined his head. 'Of course.'

There was a taut silence and then her breath came in a sigh, as if she'd held it in too long. 'Very well,' she said. 'Then I suppose I *must* be satisfied, since it is your will.'

Peredur sighed too. This wasn't about his will or even hers. Did she really expect him to let her ride out in such treacherous conditions to talk with a man who might be even more treacherous?

Pulling off a glove, he ran his fingers through his hair. Then he glanced down at the gauntlet he'd removed, clenched in his other hand. The gauntlets she'd given him on their wedding day. Soft and skilfully made, they fitted well, yet he'd barely acknowledged the gift, let alone thanked her for it.

As if she'd read his mind—or seen the remorse on his face—she spoke again, her words as pointed as a spearhead.

'I see you are wearing my gift, even though they are not at all adequate for winter!'

It was a challenge that she didn't even attempt to disguise, or perhaps—having lost the argument over her maid—she needed to claw back some ground. Peredur let her have it.

'They are warmer than they appeared at first sight,' he admitted, feeling lower than the worms. It didn't matter that his ingratitude had been born out of embarrassment and his sense of being not worthy of them, for they were the most exquisite gift he'd ever been given. It was still ingratitude in her eyes. 'And come spring, they are not too thick for wearing in kinder weather either.'

And before that kind spring, there were still long months of harsh winter to get through. Long months when, once the castle was made fully habitable, once all its defences were strengthened, once the tenants were firmly under his rule, there would be no more avoidance.

No excuse to stay abroad all day and lie awake all night in that accursed chamber, feeling the rough hay of the pallet scratch his skin and gnaw like rats at his nerves, knowing all the time that Rhianon lay just beyond the wall.

No way to prevent his blood quickening with desire even at an argument!

'And now, unless there is more you wish to speak of, I have business to attend to,' he said, grateful that none of that relentless torment sounded in his voice.

She shook her head and, without another word, moved past him and down the steps, as if no dispute had erupted between them at all. Bemused, Peredur watched her make her way towards the stable to see her mare, as she did every day.

The gift *he'd* given *her*. One inspired by a distant but unforgotten memory, and which Rhianon *had* thanked him for, with embarrassment, too, but also with a gratitude that had touched him deeply. Too deeply.

Moving into the shadow of the doorway, Peredur leaned back against the wall and swore softly. Perhaps he should never have married her, but left her for Maelgwn. Never have brought her to this God-forsaken place, to waste her beauty, her spirit, in a lifetime of loneliness.

He could bear that loneliness. He'd always *chosen* to be alone, instead of turning to a woman for companionship, for comfort, for lovemaking to ease loneliness, as other men did.

But he could not be like other men any more than he could have left Rhianon at the mercy of his brother. How could he risk bringing her harm, albeit unintentionally, in the way Maelgwn and men of his ilk would do without a thought, let alone a shred of remorse on their conscience? Letard had never spared either thought or remorse for his mother, dead in childbirth, after he'd indulged his lust on her without restraint. Letard hadn't cared either that he'd left his bastard son to bear that burden instead, the guilt that he would carry all his life, right to the grave—and perhaps beyond it.

Why then, didn't that knowledge make it any easier to pretend, to Rhianon, and to himself, that he didn't desire her at all? And why, now, as that pretence failed him utterly, did he feel lonelier than he'd ever felt in his life?

Chapter Six

'Lady Rhianon, welcome!'

Rhianon ducked her head to enter under the low lintel of the miller's house. His wife, Elen, greeting her with a beaming smile, gestured to her to sit down on a low stool next to the fire, and then pressed a cup of ale into her hands.

'This is an honour, my lady!'

Was it? After Peredur had ridden out early that morning, Rhianon had made up her mind to visit the mill, snow and all, to speak to the miller's wife. And to do so alone and not in the shadow of her husband, regardless of his refusal of yesterday...or rather, because of it.

Perhaps it *was* risky to come alone but old habits, long learned, died hard. She, and her brother Llywelyn, had chosen the hard way, many years before. While Rhodri bowed to and emulated Cadwgan, losing all compassion in the process, they'd evoked their father's wrath instead by resisting and challenging him at every turn. It had enabled them to survive, made them strong, kept their souls intact and their spirits unbroken. But now, sitting next to the wide hearth, on which a pot of something very sweet bubbled, Rhianon began to rue she'd come. Because, despite the hearty greeting, the smile, the ale, she felt her presence was not welcome at all.

'It was high time I paid a visit,' she said, looking about her and taking a moment to compose herself. It was a poor house and, although spotlessly clean, it seemed far too small for a family of eight. It suddenly became even smaller as the children of the house came, like so many mice out of so many holes, to crowd around her.

They arranged themselves on the earthen floor at her feet, their mouths open and their eyes round and avid. Rhianon's heart heaved as she felt herself swallowed up, not just in frank curiosity but in an abundance of joy and belonging. Even the dog—the same one that had run out barking the day they'd arrived, and wriggling now in the arms of one of the younger boys—was clearly part of the family!

Clearing her throat, she looked up at the miller's wife. Elen Felin Ddŵr was standing with her hands planted on hips that were broad with childbearing. She wore a rough homespun kirtle, with a stained apron over, her hair shoved into a casually fixed coif.

'But I have a reason for coming, too,' she began. 'I would like to ask you if your eldest daughter will serve as my handmaiden, since my present one is returning to her family in Uwch Aeron.'

'Esyllt has more than enough work to do here.'

Rhianon blinked at the blunt answer, totally devoid of the ingratiating tone that had greeted her—or had it been a *mocking* tone? A trickle of discomfort slid down her spine. 'Then perhaps she could come and help me only part of the day, and return to her duties here when she is finished?'

Elen's shrewd eyes narrowed. Her mouth was very red, as if she'd just eaten a basketful of berries. Then she turned to her daughter. 'Do you think you can do both, Esyllt?'

The healthy-looking, brown-haired girl standing behind her mother nodded, her eyes agog. 'Yes, I can, mam. I would like very much to be maid to the lady.'

Rhianon breathed a little easier. That was half the battle won, at least. She considered a moment, pretending she did this sort of bargaining every day of the week.

She didn't of course, though from the age of ten, she'd helped run her father's house, aiding her mother who, as the years went by and Cadwgan's abuse got worse and more frequent, coped less and less well. Who would be helping Tangwystl now she wasn't there?

'Then can you come to the castle soon after the hour of Terce?' she asked, pushing that futile worry away and, with it, a sadness for things long lost—a mother-and-daughter relationship that was nothing like the closeness that clearly existed between these two women.

'Terce?' The miller's wife laughed, head thrown back, and this time the mockery was unmistakable. 'And how will we know when it is *Terce*, lady, with no church bells to tell us?'

Her daughter laughed too and even the younger children were giggling, everyone enjoying the jest except her. Blushing, Rhianon lifted her cup to her mouth. She didn't know when Terce was either, nor any other of the hours of devotion.

Then the girl, Esyllt, spoke again. 'I can come when my morning chores here are done and return here in time to do my afternoon chores. Would that suit you, my lady?'

Rhianon had no idea precisely what times the girl meant but she nodded all the same, since she had no alternative suggestion. 'Then let us say from when the sun is halfway to its zenith in the morning and halfway from it in the afternoon.'

'And the payment, my lady?'

It was the mother who spoke but this time Rhianon had her answer ready. That much she knew of experience and she wouldn't let the woman mock her a second time.

'As our bond tenants, there is no monetary payment, naturally, but Esyllt will take her midday meal with us and may bring back whatever meat and ale is left over at table. And you will all receive gifts at Christmas and Eastertide, as is customary.'

Was that sufficient? It would have been not just sufficient but generous in the extreme in her father's house, who treated his servants even worse than he did his kin.

Elen Felin Ddŵr nodded. 'Then we are agreed.'

Rhianon laid her cup aside. She couldn't have paid Esyllt anyway, since she had no means to do so. Suddenly that dependence—which in reality was no less than that she'd had before she'd wed—turned the few sips of ale she'd swallowed sour in her stomach.

Putting out a hand, hiding her discomfort, she patted the dog. It licked her with relish, its tail wagging furiously. 'What's his name?' she asked of the boy who held it.

'Fawrgi, my lady.'

Fawrgi? The name meant Big Dog! Rhianon couldn't help but smile, despite her longing to be gone from this irrepressible and irreverent household. 'That is a strange name for such a tiny creature!'

'When he was pupped, we thought he would grow

as large as his sire but he favoured his mother instead.'
Another child spoke. 'Tada wanted to drown Fawrgi
because he was the runt of the litter and thought not
likely to live, but we wouldn't let him.'

Rhianon's smile vanished and a lump lodged in
her throat. In Cadwgan's house, his children would
never have dared be so bold, and the pup would have
been drowned the moment it came from the womb.
Quickly she rose to her feet, the comparison dragging
her down like a swamp, choking her until she could
hardly breathe.

'Then I will send word when Esyllt is to start,' she
said, turning for the door, away from the unbearable
happiness that filled the house to the rafters. 'But it will
certainly be within the week.'

Before she reached it, however, the door swung open
and the huge bulk of the miller filled her vision, dark
against the light behind him. He was scowling and the
deep and jagged scar that ran from brow to jaw made
his face look more threatening still.

Rhianon's feet faltered and she felt panic rise into her
throat. Suddenly, it wasn't the miller that stood there,
but the image of her father, standing as he had so often,
making her cower before him. The instant of utter stillness, the dreadful sense of danger starting to choke
her, the rush of terror that she refused to let him see…

'I am just about to take my leave since my business with your wife is complete.' Lifting her chin, she
stepped purposely forwards and looked him straight
in the eye. 'Thank you for the ale…and the welcome.'

But the miller didn't move and, short of pushing him
out of the way, she could do nothing but stare up at him
and hold her nerve, hide her fear from him as she'd done

from Cadwgan. For an endless moment, Hywel Felin Ddŵr stared down at her, seemingly with no intention at all of letting her pass.

And then, just as the panic threatened to overwhelm her, he stepped out into the daylight of the yard, and bowed from his thick waist. 'Be sure to call again, my lady, but perhaps when the weather is more clement.'

He gestured to the boy standing behind him, who she'd not seen until then since he'd been hidden behind his father. Aged about sixteen, he was the image of the miller, but lacking the scar.

'Escort Lady Rhianon back to the castle.'

'I don't require an escort,' Rhianon said, quickly, her feet itching to run as fast as they could to where Mêl stood, tethered to the gate. 'I know the way well enough.'

But the miller shook his head. 'Hywel Fychan will go with you. It is treacherous underfoot.' His brown eyes narrowed. 'I'm surprised that your husband let you venture out on your own in the first place, since you are a stranger in these lands.'

Rhianon flushed. It was almost a reprimand! Yet who was he to reprimand her? Stranger or not, she was his lord's wife and lady of these lands now. But she forced a smile and omitted to mention that her husband didn't know she'd ventured out at all!

'Very well, then your son shall see me home...and thank you for the courtesy.'

She rode back the way she'd come, Mêl slipping now and again as the snow balled in her hooves, the boy striding sullenly alongside. And the nearer home she went, the less Castell Abereinion felt anything *like* a home, for all its high walls and fortifications.

The humble house she'd just left, despite its simple structure and mean furnishings, was a home. It contained a family. One that toiled and played, laughed and bickered, a family that loved each other. A family that reminded her, with an anguish that she hadn't dreamed she'd feel when she'd set out earlier, of things that had never been hers and never could.

Peredur mounted Tarth and turned the horse towards home. He'd learned nothing about the fate of garrison from the ancient drover at Llaethdy, the stony reception confirming what he already suspected. He'd met with the same response at every place he'd stopped at that morning, and it seemed that winning over these people, gaining their trust and their loyalty for the Lord Rhys, would be a mountainous task, if not an impossible one.

As he drew level with the mill, his last calling place, he saw tracks in the snow, different to those Tarth had made going southward that morning. These were the hoof prints of a much smaller horse, coming from the direction of the castle and going away again the same way, the second time accompanied by footprints.

Peredur's blood chilled and his hands tightened on the reins. There could only be one explanation for those prints. Rhianon had ignored his warning of yesterday and had come after all to ask for the miller's daughter.

At that moment, Hywel Felin Ddŵr strode around the corner of the house. The man stopped dead at sight of him, though the same dog as before ran out barking.

Peredur ignored it and addressed the miller with no pause for greeting. 'Has my wife been here?'

Hywel's eyes narrowed and he shrugged. 'Been and gone…my lord.'

The reverence was given grudgingly, as a deliberate afterthought, but he ignored that insolence too. 'Gone? How long?'

'A short while ago. My son escorted her back to the castle, since she rode down alone.'

The knot of tense alarm that had tightened between Peredur's shoulder blades loosened and relief flooded his limbs. 'Then I thank you for that courtesy.'

The miller spat, the phlegm making a little hole in the snow at his feet. 'I have no need of your thanks.'

Peredur stared down at him, taking the opportunity to study for the first time this most unruly of his tenants, who was also their headman. Hywel Felin Ddŵr was as tough a man as he'd ever encountered. The deep scar that cleaved through the left cheek was unmistakably a sword wound, indicating he'd once been a soldier and seen at least one battle.

'Even so,' he said, mildly. 'You have them.'

The dog was now sniffing around Tarth's heels, making the stallion stamp and sidle. Its master didn't call the animal off but remained standing, feet planted wide and hands fisted belligerently.

And then Tarth kicked out and sent the little cur flying with a yelp. The miller's wife peeped her head out through the mill house door, and a gaggle of children appeared from behind her. One of them, a scruffy boy of about twelve, called the dog to him.

Hywel Felin Ddŵr spat again and then grinned, mockingly. 'It must be that golden hair of yours, my lord, that puzzled my dog so. He's never seen the like, having never beheld a Fleming before.'

The waterwheel suddenly started to turn, the noise of the cascading flood breaking through the tension like a blade. Peredur kicked his feet free of the stirrups and, swinging his leg over Tarth's neck, dropped down from the saddle. Taking two long strides until he stood eye to eye with Hywel, he stared straight into the other man's face.

'Then perhaps he'd like a closer look?' he said. 'And his owner too?'

Another long stalemate stretched out. Peredur's blood coursed faster even than the water over the wheel now, the torrent filling his ears as a cold resolve sharpened all his senses at a single point. If he and the miller had to come to blows, it might as well be here and now.

But Hywel shrugged and, shaking his head, he took a step back. 'I've seen all I need to see, my lord.'

Peredur exhaled silently. The miller was heavier than he, just as tall, but less nimble. It would have been an interesting and hard-won contest between them. Perhaps they would still have it, one day sooner or later.

However, while he had the man's attention, if not his respect, he issued a parting shot as he reached for Tarth's reins. 'I wonder, since he has such sharp eyes, if your dog happened to see what happened to the five men that garrisoned the castle?'

The unmistakable inflection of challenge drew the air bow-tight again. Hywel's grin faded and the sudden twitch of his cheek that made the scar jump grotesquely indicated his arrow had hit its mark.

'If he did, then he cannot speak of it, can he, my lord? Perhaps the *morloi* took them!'

Somehow, Peredur held his temper, though the sarcasm told him all he needed to know. Proof that the garrison had neither deserted nor returned south to their overlord, but had suffered a much more sinister fate.

But he wouldn't get the whole truth out of the miller, not today at least. And the most imperative thing now was to get back to the castle and see for himself that Rhianon had indeed returned home safely.

'Very well,' he said, his tone calm, but deadly serious. 'Though I'll wager that whatever happened to those men, the *morloi* had nothing to do with it. So I will ask you again, one day soon, Hywel Felin Ddŵr, and perhaps by then you'll have come up with a better answer!'

Mounting, Peredur touched his heels to Tarth's flanks and, with a cursory nod, rode for the castle. Once across the ford, he pushed the stallion into a gallop. His common sense told him the miller wouldn't have dared harm Rhianon, and the fact he'd sent his son to escort her homeward safely bore that out.

Yet…if Hywel had had anything to do with the disappearance of the garrison, then who knew…?

By the time he trotted in through the gates of Abereinion, Tarth's sweating coat was sending up mist into the air. Peredur was sweating too as he flung himself from the saddle, though not with exertion but with foreboding.

Foreboding that dissipated somewhat as he saw Rhianon come out of the keep and walk purposely in his direction, her eyes blazing like blue fire. Halting before him, she flung her head up and addressed him curtly, without preamble.

'I went to the mill earlier today, while you were out, to ask if Esyllt will come as my maid.'

Peredur felt his jaw drop and his whole body jerked in surprise. He stared at her for a moment and then handed Tarth to the man that came running. 'Walk him a while,' he ordered, 'until he has cooled down.' Then, taking another moment to steady himself, to try and cool *his* blood too, he nodded.

'I know. I called at the mill on my way back from Llaethdy.'

Her gaze flew wide. 'Oh. Did you? Then I suppose there is no need for explanations.'

There was indeed a need for explanations! It made no sense at all, and her lack of prudence, her decision to ignore his advice that the ground was treacherous, that Hywel was not to be trusted, was beyond comprehension.

'So…why did you go today?' Peredur asked. 'Why did you not wait a little longer, as I advised yesterday?'

'As I said… I didn't want to wait. I wanted the matter settled sooner, so that Cristin can go.'

'I understood that, Rhianon, and I thought you had understood me'

He held her gaze, which was boldly returned, though she made no further explanation. And her silence only baffled, and exasperated, him all the more. She'd escaped harm *this* time but he had to ensure there wouldn't be another time.

'What you did was rash as well as inexplicable,' he said. 'The road is dangerous and your mare could have slipped or fallen, you could have been thrown.'

Peredur stepped closer, making sure she listened, and understood the import of what he was saying. And then, as his blood began to rush hot and fast all over again at her nearness, wished he'd stayed where he was. 'And if an accident *had* happened, there is no physician here, nor anyone to properly treat man or beast.'

Colour washed into her face. 'Yes, I suppose that's as may be, but….' She chewed her lip a moment and then turned on her heel, as if to walk away. 'But as you see, no accident occurred.'

'Perhaps not this time.' Peredur put out a hand, touched her arm, and stopped her in her tracks. Beneath her sleeve, her skin was warm, soft, beguiling and, of their own accord, his fingers curled more snugly. 'But accidents aside, until I ascertain where the miller's loyalties lie, I don't want you going there alone.'

She turned back towards him and her brows arched. 'Then you can be at ease,' she said, shrugging his hand off. 'I have no intention of visiting the mill again in any case.'

There was strange undertone to the petulant words and, as she made once more to leave, he stopped her again, this time with a question instead of a touch.

'Why? What occurred?'

'Nothing…occurred.' She held his eyes frankly enough but there was a hesitation before she went on. 'I merely think that perhaps you are right about the miller…and that I shouldn't have gone alone after all.'

With that admission, the tension in the air seemed to pull to breaking point. A tension that it was up to him to diffuse, since he'd been the one to cause it in the first place, even if out of worry for her safety rather than any intention of rekindling the argument of yesterday.

'So…how did you find Hywel Felin Ddŵr?' he asked.

'Intimidating.'

Peredur nodded. 'I guessed as much. Did he say anything untoward or disrespectful? Did he insult you, or threaten you in some way?'

There was a wavering of her eyes, another discernible pause before she answered. 'No.'

Her stance was erect and proud, as always. But once

again, just like on the steps yesterday, he got the impression that her feet might fly at any moment. And yet, folly aside, it had taken courage too to venture to the mill on her own, which made her actions even more perplexing.

'And did you engage the girl?' he asked, biting his tongue from the urge to warn her again. No harm had come to her, thank God, and pressing the point might do more bad than good, now it was all over.

'Yes, I engaged her.'

The wind picked up, howling eerily around the courtyard. It whipped Rhianon's plait around her shoulders, blew her kirtle close to her body, so that her shape was visible. The small breasts, the neat waist, the gently flaring hips, the long legs...

Peredur dragged his eyes up from her body to her face. Her lips were slightly parted, white and even teeth just showing. 'Then, if the miller is disloyal,' he said, his mind exploring the possibility while his senses explored something else entirely, 'having a member of his family in the castle could prove advantageous.'

Her brows knit together. 'In what way advantageous?'

He moved a little closer and her scent drifted once more into his nose...winter rose with a hint of summer heather. 'The girl might be induced to talk or she might let something slip.'

Rhianon was staring at him intently now. 'Do you expect *me* to try and get information from her?'

Peredur gave a nod, though the thought hadn't occurred to him until that moment. 'You would be best placed to do that, innocently, in conversation, of course.'

There was a little silence and her tongue came out

to moisten her lips, her eyes going past him to fix on some point beyond, where they lingered.

'Yes, I suppose I could try…'

Then she drew herself visibly taller, her gaze meeting his again, bold, and at the same time, strangely defensive.

'Then I take it…you are no longer angry?'

The question caught Peredur unawares, so startling that even the impulse to move closer and kiss those moist and enticing lips faltered a little. 'No longer…? I wasn't angry to begin with, Rhianon. Did you expect me to be?'

Rhianon's eyes didn't waver at all. 'Yes,' she said, with the frankness that was becoming so familiar to him. 'I did. So…are you?'

He shook his head. 'No.'

But, *myn uffarn*! Yes, he *was* angry. Angry at himself for keeping her here talking when he should be letting her go. Angry for standing here when he should be walking away from temptation as fast as his legs could carry him.

Angry that he wanted to reach out and draw her near, not push her far away. Angry with himself for desiring her, for marrying her when he could never possess her, *must* never possess her lest that desire caused her harm.

Peredur shook his head again. 'No, I'm not angry, Rhianon, but…'

He left it unfinished. He could admit to the alarm he'd felt when he'd discovered she'd gone to the mill, but never to his desire. Even if he *could* have given in to it, she didn't desire him at all, something she'd made abundantly clear from the beginning.

'But…?'

She prompted him, stepping a little closer, so that if

he'd wanted to, he *could* have reached out and drawn her to him, whether she wanted him to or not. Held her safely in his arms and let himself taste that mouth at last, as he so badly wanted to do. Held her and keep her safe from danger, even danger that hadn't really existed—at least not outside the castle walls.

Within them, it might indeed prove dangerous for her should he take her in his arms. Should he kiss her, carry her aloft, disrobe her, give his desire its head and possess her...

'But I want you to promise me you'll not venture out alone again, to the mill,' he said instead, 'or anywhere else for that matter.'

She gave him a long and thoughtful look. 'I have already stated I have no thoughts of visiting there again.'

Then, with a dismissive nod of her head, she turned and walked quickly away. Peredur, watching her go, got the distinct feeling she'd promised him nothing at all. Just like at the altar, when she'd vowed to be his wife, but had not meant anything then either, any more than he had. Those vows had been empty for both of them and for that he only had himself to blame.

Rhianon climbed the stairway to her chamber. Her feet were steady in their course, her breathing shallow and oddly calm, and her eyes fixed on each step as she mounted it. Inwardly, however, she was trembling like a leaf. Not with fear, or terror, or even shock, but with...disbelief.

As a child, and as she'd grown to womanhood, whether she'd done something wrong, or done nothing at all, the pattern was always the same. She'd challenge her father and then make herself confront him.

Force herself to stand there, unafraid, as she told him of whatever it was she'd done, proudly, defiantly, and had dared him to do his worst.

And then it would come. The shock of his hand across her face, the lash of his belt on her body and, on one occasion, the snapping of her bones.

And the more he punished her, the more she did it. To prove to herself, even more than to him, that he could never break her as he'd broken her mother, no matter how he bruised her skin and shattered her body.

Rhianon had expected all that when she strode out to meet Peredur just now, her head high and her heart quaking. She was so certain that, even if he hadn't actually gone so far as to strike her, his anger and a tongue-lashing would more than justify her expectations, reinforce her convictions, prove her right.

But she'd been wrong. There had been no admonishing at all, less still any physical retaliation. Instead, he'd looked at her with genuine perplexity in his eyes, and something else that was too deep to see, less still to interpret. Yet she'd recognised it, not with her eyes or her mind, but with an instinctive part of herself, an intimate part that had felt it and known it for what it was. Desire. And when his eyes had dropped to her mouth, lingered long, *she* had felt desire too.

And that, somehow, had left her reeling far more violently than her father's fist ever had.

Chapter Seven

A week later, the snow was gone. The sky was clear blue and the sun shone, though the wind that blew from the estuary was still bitter. Rhianon's monthly courses had stopped and, free of the gnawing stomach pains, now worry nibbled away at her instead.

Cristin had gone too, and Esyllt, the miller's daughter, had taken her place. Rhianon liked the girl immediately, despite the long green cat-like eyes that hinted at cunning. Esyllt was always smiling, always willing, with a carefree attitude to life that mystified Rhianon.

But then, unlike her, Esyllt had clearly grown up in a loving, happy household, not one where every word and every footstep had to be meticulously thought out beforehand lest they prove to be the wrong ones.

'Then, after Hywel Fychan, my father's eldest son and namesake, there is Idwal, who is thirteen, then my two younger sisters, Anest and Lleucu, who are eleven and eight, and finally Ithel, who is six.'

Carrying out her morning duties, her maid paused for breath and Rhianon got a word in at last. And even though she tried to hide it, a note of envy edged her words that thankfully her maid didn't notice.

'Six children in all, then, three of each sex?' she asked, even though she knew exactly how many children Elen Felin Ddŵr had birthed, for she'd counted them, each and every one of them, at the mill house a week ago.

Esyllt nodded. 'There were three other babes besides, but they died in the womb. That's when my mother decided six was enough. Now she uses the red wimberry to ensure there is not a seventh!'

'Red wimberry?'

'A fruit that stays the *misglwyf* so a woman cannot conceive of a babe.'

Rhianon's jaw dropped. 'And your father *knows* your mother prevents her monthly flux?'

Her maid giggled. 'He thought six was quite enough too. He says he can tumble my mother into bed now whenever he likes without worry, and so can *she* tumble him!'

'Esyllt!'

'Your pardon, *meistres*…but you did ask.'

There was no contrition in her new maid's tone as she folded yesterday's kirtle and put it in a coffer. In fact, she began to hum quietly under her breath, as if such remarks were the order of the day. Perhaps they *were* in the miller's household, where nobody had to hold their tongue, keep their place, watch their step.

But as for this magic fruit Esyllt's mother took…? Rhianon searched her mind for words that didn't sound like she wanted to know more, because she *shouldn't* want to at all. 'Doesn't God's holy church permit marriage in order to bring forth children?' she argued. 'And condemns those who try to prevent that?'

Her maid shrugged and the coffer lid closed with a bang that made the rush lights flicker. Esyllt did everything well but never did anything quietly!

'If God didn't mean us to use fruits for *all* their virtues, why did He put them on the earth? The wimberry grows on the high ground here without the need for cultivation so it must be divine, must it not, *meistres*?'

'Yes… I suppose it must…'

'Anyway,' Esyllt went on. 'There is no priest here to tell us what to do and what not to do, not that anyone would listen.' She took up a comb in one hand and some braiding in the other. 'Shall I do your hair now?'

Rhianon sat in a chair, her mind reeling as the comb went to work, untangling the knots of sleep, her maid chatting without pause.

'You should have heard Fawrgi barking in the night, *meistres*, loud enough to wake the dead! Horsemen passing by, my father said it was, heading north. Strange to travel in the dark, though, do you not think?'

Rhianon nodded but hardly listened as very different thoughts, ones that she shouldn't be *thinking* at all, began to unravel, even as her hair did. If Esyllt's mother took this fruit to stay her courses and prevent conception, couldn't other women do likewise? And if, as Esyllt said, there was no sin or harm in it, couldn't *she* take it too?

Otherwise, if she conceived of a babe, of many babes, how could she know what their fate would be? The fate of the miller's children, blessed with love and joy, or the violent and fearful existence she and her siblings had known in the house of Cadwgan?

And would it be better not to have to find that out one day when it was too late to prevent it? When perhaps, she might prove as powerless to protect her children as Tangwystl had been, and be forced to stand by and watch helplessly, and hate herself for that helplessness?

'Do *you* take the wimberry too, Esyllt?' Rhianon asked, possibilities taking shape in her head. Peredur still slept in the chamber next door but there was no harm in exploring the measures she might have to resort to should that situation change.

'Why on earth would *I* take it, *meistres*?' The comb didn't even pause. 'I'm not wedded yet and still a virgin.'

'And do you wish to be wed?'

'Of course I do!' Her maid laughed and tugged, none too gently, at a resistant knot. 'And I intend to have lots of children. All men need heirs, do they not, lords and peasants alike.'

The words scraped over Rhianon's skin far more roughly than the comb was going through her hair. Of course Peredur would need heirs too, one day. And the fact he still wasn't sharing a bed with her wasn't a state that would be likely to continue much longer.

A man knew a woman's courses didn't last indefinitely, though Peredur had not asked her as yet. But there had been moments when she'd glimpsed questions in his eyes. When their hands accidentally touched at a table. When she'd lifted her head sometimes and caught his piercing gaze. When she walked past him somewhere about the castle and felt those eyes follow in her wake.

As they'd followed the day she'd gone out to confess her visit to the mill—dark, puzzled, with a sort of hunger, but not angry.

Her maid's voice broke into her musing. 'Shall we go up onto the battlements this morning, *meistres*?'

'What for?'

'To look at the *morloi*, of course! Have you seen them yet?'

Rhianon shook her head, not at all sure that she *wanted* to see them, having heard them constantly since the day they'd arrived, at least during daylight. At the same time, now that Esyllt had said it, she found she *was* curious, after all, to know what they looked like.

And perhaps some fresh air would clear her head, sweep away the realisation that, every time Peredur had touched her, looked at her with that unfathomable look, those unspoken questions, the effect had been even more unsettling than the mysterious *morloi*, because she'd felt the same hunger too.

'Yes, let us go up then,' she agreed.

The sunshine was bright as they came out onto the parapet though the wind was keen. Up here, the tang of salt in the air was sharper, more pungent, but it wasn't that which suddenly brought a blur of tears to Rhianon's eyes.

For the landscape itself was truly wondrous. Hidden from view beneath its blanket of white all week, the beauty of it now it was revealed was breathtaking.

The mountains were still snow-capped, the trees still bare, and a thick sea mist blanketed the ground. But on the higher slopes, the grass was surprisingly green, as if a multitude of emeralds had been growing all the time beneath the snow.

Blinking against all that beauty and her ears filling with the deafening cries of the *morloi*, Rhianon didn't see Peredur at first. Then, as a footfall sounded behind her, she turned and there he was, the sun catching his wheat-gold hair and an expression of surprise and almost welcome alighting on his face.

'Rhianon…good morning.'

His presence took her unawares, his face and form even more breathtaking than the landscape. 'Wh-what are *you* doing up here?' she stuttered.

His brows rose, as well they might, since her question was a foolish one. When he wasn't about some business in the castle or beyond, Peredur was often up here, his eyes seeking the approaching enemies he seemed to expect any day. But the roads in all directions had been impassable for the last week and so far no one—friend *or* foe—had been spied travelling them.

'Looking.'

The simple word held a touch of irony and Rhianon felt her cheeks burn. Feeling wrong-footed now as well as foolish, she moved to the parapet to look outwards, conscious of a sudden and violent *inward* trembling.

'And have you seen anything?' she asked, leaning on her elbows on the wall as her heart quickened in her breast, aware that the sting on her face wasn't put there by the sharp wind.

'Nothing at all.'

She glanced sideways at him. 'And how long have you been up here…looking.'

'Since daybreak.' Peredur leaned his elbows on the parapet wall, right next to hers. 'The sun on the water is a glorious sight on a morning like this.'

Rhianon turned her gaze outwards to where the waters of the estuary shone through the mist like a silver ribbon. 'Yes,' she agreed, her voice suddenly sounding not at all like hers, as the warmth of his arm began to seep through her sleeve and the nearness of him brought a flush of heat to her face. 'It *is* glorious.'

The landscape was indeed lovely but, as they leaned close together, she was far more aware of the man at her side than the view. Especially since Esyllt had wandered off to talk to one of the guards further along the parapet, no doubt thinking it proper to leave her alone with Peredur.

'How do you find your new maid?'

The question was voiced with no inflection at all but Rhianon was immediately swept backwards to when she'd stood on the steps and argued with him against the folly of venturing out to the mill alone. And the lack of reproach, less still reprisal, later when she'd told him, with quaking heart, that she'd gone anyway.

Was he thinking of that day too, wondering at her insistence, her wilfulness? Was he at a loss to understand, as she was, the feelings that lay beneath the argument, why she'd needed to do the opposite to what he'd advised? Now her reasons seemed tangled and confusing, like the roots of a tree deep below ground.

'Irreverent, loud…but satisfactory,' she replied.

He gave a little nod and his mouth curved in something that might have been the beginnings of a smile, at least on anyone else's mouth. 'Good.'

Awkwardness dropped between them like a stone from the sky. It was too late to explain, to admit to her stubborn folly, let alone reveal the reasons for it. Instead, Rhianon studied her hands, then looked up at the sky, towards the mountains to the north, and then lastly, reluctantly, back to him.

Peredur's face was in profile, his features pensive, and his gaze steady on the shore, not wandering about as if lost as hers was, desperately seeking something to latch on to. And then he spoke, softly, and it was clear that—even if he'd been thinking on their argument of a week ago—he had no intention of revisiting it.

'Last year, when I was here with the Lord Rhys, when he surveyed this site for the building of a castle, it was summertime. It looked very different then and the water was warm enough to bathe in.'

Rhianon blinked. 'You *bathed* in the sea?'

He turned his head and met her gaze. 'Every morning.'

All at once, her senses seemed to come alive. Instead of sea salt, other aromas came to her nostrils—the wool of his cloak, the leather of the gambeson he wore beneath, and deeper still, the musky male scent of his skin, all of them heightened by the startling vision of him wading naked into the sea!

Clearing her throat, Rhianon looked outwards once more, but the scents and the shocking vision remained, in glaring detail now since she was looking right at the sea!

She'd seen her former husband naked, on the four nights he'd bedded her, but she'd never expected to wonder what a man looked like naked ever again. Not that Seisyll had been ugly—he had been simply brutal, unheeding of the fact he'd hurt her and frightened her, bent only on slaking his lust.

'Does the snow never melt on those mountain tops?' she asked, the memory of those nights serving to dim the unexpected and unsettling vision, like a blindfold falling over her eyes.

'Eventually, when the warmer weather comes. It's

still too cold in the uplands but at least the castle is warm and habitable now.'

Yes, Peredur had been efficient and thorough over the last week, making this place comfortable for both man and beast. Defensible and habitable, it wasn't a home however, not like the miller's house. Just as they were married but were not really husband and wife.

Did he intend to put *that* in order too now he'd finished seeing to their domestic and defensive needs? Now that she was no longer indisposed, would he bed her, hurt her as he spent his lust on her, as Seisyll had done?

The mist was fast retreating as the sun rose higher, dispelled by the gradual warming of its rays. The fear and violence of her father's house, the callous indifference of her first husband, seemed very far away this lovely morning. But she was not such a fool to think that both those states might not manifest themselves here.

'Do you see them?'

Peredur's arm lifted and he pointed to the opposite shore where, from the thinning mist, creatures were emerging that looked like enormous slugs, all over the beach, some small, others much larger.

Rhianon couldn't help but gasp. 'Are they the *mor-loi*?'

He nodded. 'Mothers and calves for the most part, but there are some bulls among them too. They breed again soon after the pups are born. The females carry their young almost a year, then come back here to birth and breed again.'

The grotesque mottled grey shapes seemed to possess no limbs, only paddle-like protrusions from their flanks. Some were lying dormant, either on their sides or on their bellies, while others were propelling themselves awkwardly down to the water's edge.

'How clumsy they seem without legs,' she remarked.

'They can move swiftly enough when alarmed, or enraged, and bulls have been known to attack,' Peredur said. 'But they swim gracefully indeed through water.'

Graceful or clumsy, the *morloi* truly were the most mysterious creatures Rhianon had ever seen. The heads that bobbed on the water seemed even funnier than the bodies on the beach, as if they'd become detached and floated away all on their own.

'But why do they call so mournfully like that, all day long?' she asked.

Peredur must have moved—or had she? Because the arm that had returned to rest next to hers on the parapet wall was now pressed lightly against hers.

'It's the pups that call…for their mothers.'

His eyes were fixed, like hers, on the opposite shore but a powerful connection seemed to flow between them, passing through her sleeve and lifting the hairs at the nape of her neck.

'Surely their mothers don't abandon them?' Perspiration trickled down between her breasts as that connection travelled further, penetrated deeper. 'Leave them to fend for themselves?'

'No, either the pups have wandered off, curious to explore and play, and can't find their way back. Or their dams are fishing in the sea and have left their young alone for the moment.'

His head turned and, as their eyes met once more, he almost smiled. Rhianon's breath stalled. He wasn't just comely, as she'd concluded on their wedding day, he was handsome, startlingly so.

'Pups?' She dragged her gaze up from his mouth. 'Then they are not demons after all!'

'Demons?'

Again, there was that elusive twitch that might have been mistaken for a smile. 'No, they're not demons.'

Rhianon thought back to that night she'd held her frightened maid in her arms, the night Peredur had come to feed the fire. 'Cristin believed them to be creatures of the devil,' she said. 'But perhaps if she'd seen them, as I do now, she wouldn't have let her imagination run away with her.'

'Did *you* think them demonic too?'

She shook her head. 'No, though hearing them calling so strangely, I almost began to believe they were. But there is no need to fear them, is there, even if they are half fish and half beast, neither one nor the other.'

Peredur didn't even flinch as the words struck him like a blow, square in the midriff. Rhianon might just as well have been describing him! She hadn't been but… is that how she thought of him? Half Welsh and half Flemish, neither one nor the other, as strange a creature as the *morloi* were? But unlike them, heartless as well? Why would she *not* think of him so? Everyone else did, after all—with the exception of the small band of men he commanded, who'd come to know him, and his father, Eilyr, who loved him.

He stared at the shoreline again. Over the tang of the sea came the subtle, yet so heady scents of the woman at his side. They clogged his nose, his throat, filled his lungs and swamped his senses.

'The *morloi* will be gone within a month or so anyway,' he said, his breath suddenly hard to draw. 'So you won't be troubled by them until they return next winter.'

She sent him a glance then, her gaze dark, as if she suddenly realised how many winters she would have to spend here, with him. 'They don't trouble me now,' she replied. 'Not now I know what they are.'

But she didn't know what *he* was! Not just a mix of two peoples but the worst of one and the best of the other. At least from what he'd been told, every day it seemed, for the first six years of his life, by the grandmother who had raised him—and hated him every day of those years.

Your father is a devil and your mother the angel he despoiled. But it was you, the devil's spawn, that killed her!

Peredur jerked upright, pushing Mallt's voice out of his head. He hadn't heard those words for twenty years and yet they were chiselled into his mind, as surely as if she'd carved them there.

Why did they resurface here, now, stronger even than the desire that had been curling in his loins from the moment Rhianon had walked out through the turret doorway and stolen the breath from his lungs?

'It's too cold to stay up here any longer, Rhianon,' he said. He wasn't a child now—he was a man. Why then, couldn't he *forget* those damning words? Was it because they were true that they were so entrenched in his soul, eternal and indelible? 'Best you and your maid go down.'

Her eyes searched his for a moment, as blue as the sea would be in summertime. Yet there was a cloud there now that hadn't been there a moment before.

'Yes, it has grown cold up here after all,' she said, with a little tilt of her head. 'I think I *will* go down.'

Yet, instead of moving away, she remained where she was. Her black hair hung, as always, in a plait over one shoulder, shining like jet in the sunlight. Beneath her red cloak clasped at her throat with a gold brooch, her body was slender, her waist so small he could have reached out and encircled it with his two hands.

But if he did that, he might be tempted to draw her closer, dip his head and breathe deeper still of her tantalising scent. Let it play havoc with his senses and stir his imagination to fantasies all over again.

The end of her plait didn't quite reach below her waist now, after he'd cut it. The ends were slightly ragged because his fingers had been frozen stiff and he'd used his knife clumsily.

But his fingers weren't stiff today. They were warm and pliant and eager and suddenly they were reaching out, taking up the end her plait, bringing it up to his face. Then he was breathing in those beguiling aromas that were uniquely hers—the winter rose, the hint of wild heather—all of them filling not just his nose, but his whole being.

'Wh-what are you doing?'

Rhianon's voice came as a whisper. What *was* he doing? Feeling her hair against his face, breathing her essence into his lungs, foolish indulgences that would lead him to want to feel *all* of her, breathe *all* of her, possess *her* completely.

'I cut it badly the other day,' he said, as if that explained it, which it didn't at all. 'I'm sorry.'

Her eyes widened. 'There is no need to apologise. It was necessary.'

Was it necessary to keep hold of that braid still? To want to undo the bonds that held it, to let that wild mane loose and thread his fingers through it? And from there, dip his head and take her mouth with his?

No, none of those things *were* necessary but all the same he needed to do them more than he needed to live. And, for that reason alone, Peredur let the plait drop from his fingers and, stepping back, he turned to look out over the parapet again.

She hesitated a moment and then, with a little frown, murmured a farewell and moved away. He remained staring outwards but the splendour had dimmed. The snowy mountains weren't so white now, and nor was the gleam of the water so silver as it had been a moment ago, when he'd looked at it with Rhianon.

Behind him, he heard her call to her maid and begin to walk towards the door in the turret that led downwards. Then her footsteps halted and her voice drifted back to him, laced with surprise.

'Who can that be I wonder?'

At once, Peredur's senses snapped back into their proper place. Spinning around, he strode to the side of the parapet that looked out over the land to the south. Sure enough, along the road they'd travelled on a week earlier, two men rode. Rhianon, coming to join him, gave a gasp, recognising them long before he did.

'It is Edwin, my uncle.' She squinted. 'And one of the laymen from Llanbadarn Church.'

By the time they went down into the bailey, the visitors had been admitted and were already dismounting. Peredur strode forward, calling two of his men to see to their horses.

And then, as Edwin ab Ieuaf's blind eyes unerringly

found his, he saw a rare expression of consternation there. His greeting froze on his lips as foreboding fell. Something was wrong.

'Lord Peredur… Lady Rhianon, *henffych*!'

His wife took her uncle's outstretched hands and squeezed them warmly. 'Welcome to Abereinion, uncle.'

'It grieves me to be the one to bring you these tidings, Peredur, but your father has met with an accident.'

The sun overhead suddenly turned cold and Peredur's foreboding weighed heavier. 'What sort of accident?'

'Two days after you departed from Llanbadarn, he fell from his horse, breaking a leg. With the snow, no one could come before and bring you the news.'

'Is there danger of infection, a worsening of his health, does he need me?'

Edwin shook his head. 'No, the break was clean, and has been well set. Lord Eilyr is in no danger, though I know he will welcome a visit from you.'

Peredur released a breath and uncurled the fingers that had clenched tightly at his sides. 'But…what was he doing on horseback at all in this weather, especially at his age?'

'The shepherds of Cwm Rheidol had complained that their sheep were being taken by wolves. Your father rode out with some men to hunt the predators down.'

'Was Maelgwn with him when this accident happened?'

'No. Your brother had declined to join the hunt.'

'Declined to join…!' Peredur shook his head in disbelief. 'For what reason?'

'None that I know of.' The man shrugged his bony shoulders, but there was nothing nonchalant about the movement. 'You will have to ask him that yourself.'

'I would do as much had my brother come here to tell me this news himself!'

'I thought—I hoped—that he *had* come, my lord. Last evening, your brother and two men-at-arms set out from Llanbadarn. I found it strange that he should travel by night, and stranger still that he told no one where he was bound.'

Peredur frowned. 'But Maelgwn has not been here or anywhere near, as far as I know.'

Rhianon, who had been silent all the while, suddenly spoke, her tone tentative. 'Peredur…perhaps I should have told you before…but I didn't think…'

He turned to her to find her brow creased in a frown too, and the eyes that met his were anxious. 'Then tell me now,' he said, softly.

'This morning… Esyllt mentioned that riders passed by the mill, late last night. The dog heard them and woke the household.'

Peredur drew a deep breath then let it out slowly. 'That doesn't bode well at all. But it wouldn't have mattered if you'd told me before now, Rhianon,' he assured her quickly, touching her arm. 'Maelgwn still has a good start wherever he is bound.'

He turned back to Edwin. And although he knew it already, given the direction his brother had taken, he asked it anyway. 'Where do *you* think he has gone?'

'I have no certain proof, my lord, but the word is that Owain Gwynedd is at present in Meirionnydd for the collection of renders. I suspect—as must you—that your brother rides for the Prince's court at Pennal.'

Chapter Eight

Rhianon sat next to Peredur at table that night long after supper was over. The boards had been cleared, the fire banked up, the men given permission to bed down for the night. They lay now, wrapped in their cloaks, around the hall or in the room above.

Edwin had also excused himself, soon after the meal was ended, and he and his layman had retired to the chamber made ready for them on the top floor—the one Peredur usually occupied.

Her husband hadn't told her to go to bed too and, not wanting to leave him without company, Rhianon had stayed. But he seemed so lost in his own thoughts that finally, as the silence became oppressive, and his preoccupation began to engulf her, she rose to leave.

'Stay.'

She froze. The word hadn't been a command or even a request. It had been almost a plea. She looked at him. His broad shoulders were hunched as he leaned forward on his elbows, as if his body were fatigued, yet he seemed resolved to shun sleep.

'You wish me to remain?' she asked, just to be sure.

He nodded, not looking up at her but down into his cup, the warm ale it contained surely long gone cold. 'Yes, I wish you to remain.'

Rhianon lowered herself back into her seat and then there was silence again. The fire in the central hearth cast leaping shadows on the bare walls. A grey pall of wood smoke hung in the rafters and the rush lights flickered in the draughts that crept in through every nook and crevice.

She waited, her hands folded in her lap, her thoughts in disarray. Did he want her company, her conversation, her counsel even, as ineffectual as that might be? But how could she know *which* to offer him if he didn't ask?

Finally, tentatively, she reached out and touched his arm where it rested on the table. 'You must be concerned about your father, Peredur. Why don't you go and see him on the morrow?'

He turned his head slowly towards her, his eyes troubled. 'Yes, I'll go and see how he fares as soon as I can, but not tomorrow. I must find out first what Maelgwn is about, since he has no reason I'm aware of to travel north, especially by night.'

'How will you do that?'

'By sending Meirchion ap Dafydd to follow discreetly in his tracks. If Maelgwn is headed for Pennal, then it can only mean mischief.'

'What sort of mischief?'

'Knowing my brother, the treacherous sort.' His mouth set grimly. 'Owain Gwynedd might have yielded Ceredigion to the Lord Rhys a year ago but that doesn't mean he won't try to regain it.'

'Then you believe that Maelgwn is involved in some plot with the Prince of Gwynedd?'

'I know that my brother will use my father's accident to his own advantage, in whatever way he can. Rhys is far to the south now, at Dinefwr, and only *we* guard his northern frontier.' He paused. 'And I fear for Eilyr. He is old, no longer strong, and Maelgwn has little love for anybody but himself.'

'Is that why you hate your bother so much?'

He gave a shrug but the lift of his shoulders was heavy. 'I don't hate Maelgwn, though I cannot find any affection for him either. It is *he* who hates *me*.'

'But why?'

'Maelgwn has grown up…awry. He is cruel and riddled with envy of anyone who has more than he, even though he lacks nothing. But as to why he hates me…'

He drew a breath and his fingers closed tighter around his cup. 'I tried to be his friend but, from the beginning, he resented my presence in our father's household and the affection Eilyr has always shown me.'

Rhianon searched his face, found the hollows of his cheeks deeper, the line of his jaw tense. And, suddenly, she saw something very clearly. Something his words hadn't really conveyed, or rather only hinted at.

'You have much affection for your father too, don't you?'

'Yes, I do, as *any* son should.'

The boards over the windows rattled as the wind wrapped around the outer walls. 'Is that because Eilyr took you for his own, when you were a boy?' she asked, sensing an opening in that other wall, the one that stood between her and her husband.

He nodded. 'But he did much more than that. He gave me a home and a family.'

'And before…you'd had neither?'

He looked away again and a muscle clenched in his jaw. 'I was an orphan, yes, if that is what you are asking. My mother died when I was born.'

'Yet you still had a father?'

His lips twisted. 'Of a sort!'

Rhianon realised her fingers were still touching his sleeve but she left them there. 'Tell me about Letard,' she urged, softly.

There was a hesitation. Around the hall, the snores of the sleeping men mingled with the hissing of the rush lights and the crackle of the fire. Then he drew in a breath and began to speak, though it seemed it was to himself, as much as to her.

'I was six years old when Anarawd ap Gruffudd, brother to the Lord Rhys, burned the village of Pebidiog, where I was born. The Flemings had driven most of the Welsh out of the district, but some remained, those who had nowhere else to go.'

'And your mother was among those who stayed?'

He nodded. 'She was of peasant stock, young, unmarried, and she and her mother, Mallt, were forced to serve the new lord—Letard.'

The torchlight played eerily over his stark features. Everyone said he looked exactly like his Flemish father and, with his face all angles and shadows, his hair glinting like gold, it was easy to believe.

'And when Anarawd came….?' Rhianon prompted.

'The Flemings fought like devils, naturally. Letard fought fiercest of all and then Anarawd engaged him… and slew him.'

The wind howled louder and Rhianon shivered at the vivid picture his words had conjured up, for all their practical description. 'And, when the fighting was over, you were spared because you were only a child?'

A ghost of a smile passed over his mouth. 'Oh, Anarawd wanted to kill me too. I was Letard's bastard son, after all, but Eilyr persuaded him to spare me.'

Rhianon's blood ran cold at what he must have witnessed that day. Was that why he was so remote now, as a man? Why he'd become the warrior of icy repute? After all, she herself had learned in childhood to keep aloof and apart, hide the fear and the pain deep inside.

'You said your mother died in childbirth…who raised you after?

'Her mother…my grandmother. Letard paid her well for the job!'

Rhianon bit back a gasp of shock at the brutal statement. 'But surely she didn't do it for that reason alone, only for money?'

Peredur shrugged, turned his head away. 'Why not, given the manner of my begetting?'

She searched his profile. Somewhere, somehow, she'd touched on a nerve, a raw and painful nerve. 'I don't understand,' she said, although she was beginning to, albeit dimly. 'Tell me.'

'Letard had forced my mother to be his mistress. Forced her into his bed then discarded her once he'd despoiled then tired of her. I was the result of that abomination.'

Involuntarily, Rhianon's fingers tightened on his arm as a blow smote her heart. 'Yet Letard acknowledged you, saw to your upbringing, gave you a name—'

Even before the words had left her lips, his gaze snapped round to meet hers.

'Until I was six years old, when Eilyr had me baptized, I *had* no name. I was called only the Fleming's bastard!'

His face had gone white and his words chilled her to the bone with their terrible conviction.

'The man was a monster, Rhianon. He acknowledged *nobody*, be they Welsh or Flemish, man or woman, old or young. He killed, raped, pillaged and ruled without pity. If Anarawd hadn't slain him, then *I* would have done so, one day.'

Rhianon snatched her hand away and stared at him aghast, her heart shrinking from the hate that glittered in his eyes. 'That is a wicked thing to say!'

His head tilted, an eyebrow arched. 'Is it? But I would have thought that *you*, possessing a father little better than mine, could understand that, Rhianon?'

She shook her head. 'I will never understand why those who should be the closest and kindest of all are usually the ones who do us most harm.'

His eyes raked hers, deep and grey and seeing too much. 'As your father did *you* harm?'

Rhianon balled her hands in her lap and looked away, down the hall towards the fire. But, even so, she felt those eyes burn into her cheek, far hotter than those leaping, dancing flames.

'Is that why you retreat into yourself whenever an altercation arises between us? Because your father has made you fear *all* men?'

She looked back at him, evading the last part and latching on to the first. 'I don't know what you mean. When has there been any altercation between us?'

'Frequently, even if hidden beneath the surface. Except on the day you asked me to send Cristin home.

And the day after, when you went to the mill and then came and told me so.'

'I was afraid you would refuse.'

'Or were you just *afraid*, Rhianon?'

Rhianon placed her palms down on the table, intending to push herself to her feet and leave him, but his hand closed over hers.

'And if so, why then did you persist in going to the mill, when I'd advised against it?'

She stilled, snatched a breath, held it. Anger she could have faced, violence she could have dealt with, even silence could be borne. But this quiet and insidious questioning was unexpected, disturbing, and she had no idea how to respond to it.

But worse was to come. His fingers closed tighter over hers and his words, gently spoken as they were, were keen enough to strip the flesh from her bones.

'And then, when you told me of your visit, boasting of it almost, I had the distinct impression that what you *really* wanted to do was run from me.'

Oh, how she wished she *could* run, not from violence, or from cruelty, or from fear, but from something even more terrifying. 'I… It's late,' Rhianon stammered. Withdrawing her hand from beneath his, she drew her cloak around her, hiding behind it as if it were a shield.

He sat back in his chair and was silent a moment. Then his voice came again, quiet yet penetrating, like a knife slid between the cracks of armour forged over long years of practice.

'And here you are, running once more.'

'No. I am merely tired.' Rhianon forced her words to be bold, to parry his bravely, even if in reality she *was* running. Seeking a hiding place to quickly seal those cracks tight again.

'You are reading too much into what was, after all, what men and women do once married,' she went on. 'They have, as you say…altercations.'

Peredur didn't contradict her yet again. He didn't have to. Altercations were one thing but he knew what sort of man her father was. The fate of Cadwgan's brothers was a vile testament to his cruel nature, with poor blind Edwin the only one he'd left alive. There was no need at all to ask if his womenfolk suffered similar brutality too,

'I was there, you know,' he said, instead.

Her gaze flew to his. 'Wh-where?'

'At our wedding. I saw how your mother sat mute and invisible, not looking at Cadwgan or speaking to him, nor he to her. As he didn't look at or speak to *you*—except to shout at you to say your vows outside the church door.'

She said nothing but her eyes told him everything. 'And the morning we rode for Ystrad Meurig, there was no farewell between Cadwgan and Tangwystl, despite the fact that he might not come back from the battle… as Rhodri didn't.'

Peredur saw her lashes flicker, her nostrils flare as she took a sharp intake of breath. 'Is that why you didn't mourn your brother, Rhianon, because you feared him as much as you do Cadwgan?'

She looked at him strangely for a moment and then her mouth curled. 'You think I *fear* Cadwgan?' A bitter laugh broke from her. 'You are wrong. I did once, when I was very young, but that changed when I reached my eighth summer. Then I saw him, saw everything, clearly for the first time.'

This time, it was *he* who drew a sharp breath. 'What happened?'

She shook her head. 'Simply that I learned to despise him, as I would any other man who takes pleasure in hurting the weak and the defenceless. And so I, and my brother Llywelyn, had to become neither. We had to defend each other, though it was he who protected me as we got older, he who bore the brunt…'

Her gaze dropped away and there was a rush in her voice, as if she didn't want to linger on that eighth summer and whatever it had held, or the years after.

'As for my other brother… I didn't *fear* Rhodri but I couldn't despise him either. He…changed as we grew up into someone I hardly recognised, yet the truth is he was as much a victim as any of us.'

Peredur couldn't speak for a moment, though he longed to ask, to take her back to the moment when it seemed it hadn't only been Rhodri who'd changed, but *she* had too.

But she was already getting to her feet, as if she really did want to flee from him as fast as she possibly could. And all at once he saw it, although the evidence had been there all along if he'd thought to look for it.

Victim. Is that how she viewed her role in this marriage? As something she had to suffer in silence or otherwise? An ordeal that she had to withstand, confront or run from, as circumstances dictated?

Dduw trugarog! Did she really fear that *he* was such a man as Cadwgan?

It seemed she read his thoughts—or perhaps his face betrayed him—for she drew herself tall and then said stiffly, 'I may be asleep by the time you come up-stairs…'

In the torchlight, her features leapt out at him vividly. Her face delicately carved, her high cheekbones and fragile line of jaw, the soft throat as pale as cream. Her body was as slender as a marsh reed, and seemed just as breakable. It might bend and sway before a prevailing wind, but it could so easily be snapped in two.

It was impossible to understand how any man could hurt her, intentionally or otherwise. How anyone could cause her pain, make her suffer, inwardly as well as outwardly. But men like Cadwgan and Letard knew only ugliness and cruelty, and nothing at all of compassion, as they set out to deliberately destroy everything beautiful.

A rush of feeling engulfed him—not lust, but something just as powerful, even more so. An overwhelming impulse to protect that fragile being that stood before him, cloaked in a strength of will, disguised in stubborn opposition, and shielded by an indomitable spirit…but vulnerable all the same.

Peredur rose to his feet and, now he knew where to find it, he saw the veil of defence come down, settling like an invisible and impenetrable mantle over the one she already wore.

'Then I will try not to wake you,' he said.

The flash of relief in her eyes before her lashes lowered only confirmed his suspicions. 'Thank you.'

He almost smiled. She didn't even make an effort to dissemble! Taking her hand, he lifted it to his mouth and kissed it, a chaste kiss goodnight. 'Sleep well, Rhianon.'

She inclined her head, her mouth pursing a moment,

and then she turned and walked quickly, though softly so as not to wake the sleeping men, down the hall.

When she'd gone from sight, Peredur retook his seat and leaned forward on his elbows, staring at the doorway she'd passed through. Her essence still lingered, on the air, in his senses, as elusive as she herself was.

He lifted his cup to his mouth and took a long swallow of ale. When his cup was empty, he took up the pitcher and refilled it. Then, drawing his cloak about him, he settled back in his chair and closed his eyes.

There was no question of him going aloft and sharing that chamber with her tonight, not after what she'd just told him. Or rather, after what she'd *not* told him, not in plain words. But he'd discovered it all the same.

And, as terrible as it was, it was also a merciful release—for him. How *could* he lie next to her, now, in their bed? Not just on this night but every night, and struggle, as he must, to master his desire, knowing she was not just unwilling but afraid too?

The next morning, Rhianon woke late. Peredur hadn't come to their chamber last night, after she'd left him in the hall, after that chaste kiss on her hand had stolen her breath, and made walking away so difficult to do when what she'd wanted to do was run.

Escape the knowledge that she'd almost spoken of something she'd never spoken of to anyone, not even to Llewelyn, whom she loved. The day, the incident, the revelation that had shattered and then reassembled her whole existence.

However, the things *he'd* said about his childhood had pierced her heart like a lance. No child should have to witness what he'd seen, lose what he'd lost, or be raised unloved by someone who should have protected him but hadn't.

It was cruelly ironic that they had that much in common at least. Both of them were the offspring of fathers that they'd grown up to hate and with good cause.

Getting out of bed, Rhianon washed in the cold water from the ewer then dressed herself. Then she sat a moment and looked around her. The chamber had been transformed from the empty shell it had been when they'd first arrived.

Now, sweet-smelling rushes covered the floors and shutters hung at the windows to keep out the draughts. Gaps in the wooden walls had been filled in and even a tapestry covered one wall, bringing both warmth and colour into to the room.

And a thick linen curtain, the same blue as her eyes, had been put up to separate the living and sleeping quarters.

Peredur had seen to that, of course, as he'd seen to everything else—with efficiency and consideration. Was *that* why she'd been induced to speak so candidly to him last night? Because, having witnessed his care and consideration on countless occasions since their arrival here, she'd trusted him enough to do so? Or was it because *he'd* spoken so candidly to *her*?

And, in doing so, had bolstered the growing instincts that told her Peredur was not the man his reputation claimed he was. But could she trust her instincts?

Esyllt, as usual, was late so plaiting her hair herself, Rhianon fixed a coif on her head. Then, pausing to quickly swallow a cup of ale, she went downstairs and straight outside into the winter sunshine.

Peredur was nowhere to be seen. She breathed a sigh

of relief. To meet him now, this morning, after the conversation of the night before would be difficult. To try to hide her relief, and her confusion, that he had hadn't come to their bed would be impossible.

Everyone seemed busier than usual, reinforcing ramparts, sharpening swords, burnishing shields, hasty preparations in the wake of Edwin's news of yesterday. At the storage barn, Hywel Felin Ddŵr and his eldest son were unloading sacks of grain from his cart, supplies that Peredur had ordered.

Nobody took any notice of her, though some bowed perfunctorily as they hurried by, bent on their tasks, their faces grim and shining with sweat. Finally, she stopped one of the carpenters as he was crossing the bailey, a length of wood balanced on his broad shoulder.

'Do you know where my husband is?'

The man eyed her from beneath bushy brows. 'Lord Peredur rode out an hour since, my lady.'

'Where has he gone?'

'Northwards with Meirchion, to the Dyfi crossing.'

In other words, tracking his brother's route. Would he cross the river into Gwynedd, or leave the pursuit to his *penteulu*, as he'd planned, and return to Abereinion? Or, another possibility, and one that sent a sudden shiver through her, would he find Maelgwn *this* side of the river and confront him?

'And have you seen my uncle Edwin this morning?' she asked. 'He hasn't returned to Llanbadarn yet, surely?'

'No, my lady.' The man shook his head and shifted the plank to his other shoulder. 'He and his layman have walked down to Ffynnon Non.'

'Ffynnon Non? What is that?'

'A holy well, they say, close to the ford.'

Rhianon thanked the man and, on impulse, turned for the gates. Since there was no church here, she'd sorely missed spiritual guidance. But, if there were a holy well, perhaps that would provide her with what she needed, today more than ever.

She didn't ride Mêl but went on foot, since with the thaw the way was easy to walk. At the ford, the ice had gone too, revealing a line of stepping stones across the river.

Unexpected delight rushed through her for no good reason other than the fact they'd been hidden all this time beneath the ice. But as she crossed over them with care, since they were slippery, it was as if those stones paved the way out of the stifling and confusing confines of the castle to somewhere she could see and think more clearly.

A little way beyond, in the direction of the mill, Rhianon found her uncle, standing head bowed underneath a canopy of trees. His layman, Iago, was sitting on a fallen tree trunk a few yards distant, his eyes closed and his lips moving in prayer.

Unbelievably, for it was not yet the end of January, the buds of spring flowers—green hellebore, winter aconite, anemone and even snowdrop—sprouted up through the dewy grass.

On her approach, Edwin's blind eyes found her unfailingly, as they found everyone. 'Good morn, Rhianon.'

'Good morn, uncle,' Rhianon returned, going to stand beside him and looking down into the well. It was no more than a square hole in the ground with some small boulders forming a low wall around it. 'Is it true this is a holy well?'

Her uncle nodded. 'Dedicated to Non, the mother of Saint David, who passed this way once, long ago.'

The Lady Non had died many centuries past but a sort of peace still inhabited this place, as pervasive as the breeze that whispered through the trees. A robin sang heartily from a branch overhead and, from here, the calls of the *morloi* couldn't be heard.

'Peredur is not with you?'

'No,' Rhianon replied, looking back up at her uncle. The sightless eyes no longer sent shudders of horror through her. 'He has gone north in Maelgwn's wake, as far as the Dyfi crossing.'

Then she broached, with no preamble or shyness, the topic of the man she'd married. The topic she'd really come here to talk of.

'You said, that day in the church at Llanbadarn, uncle, that I shouldn't believe everything I have heard about my husband.'

'That is what I advised you.' Edwin's brow creased. 'Has he given you *cause* to believe?'

Stooping, Rhianon plucked a snowdrop from the ground and searched her mind. 'Not exactly,' she said, lifting the bud to her nose and breathing deep, though it gave out no fragrance. 'The opposite, if anything. And, last night, when we were alone at table, he told me what happened at Pebidiog.'

Her uncle nodded pensively. 'I know of that from Eilyr, of course, but Peredur has never spoken of it— to anyone. It is well that he trusts you enough to do so.'

Trust? Perhaps. But that didn't mean she could trust in return, no matter what her instincts were telling her. 'Yet, they say he has no heart,' she went on, arguing against those instincts, as stubbornly as she'd argued with Peredur on the steps that day. 'Of course, I know that cannot be true but…he *puzzles* me. He is…distant and, sometimes, I can't help but wonder…'

As she hesitated to give voice to her confusion, since even her confusion confused her, her uncle read her mind.

'You wonder if Peredur is made of the same stuff as my brother Cadwgan?'

Rhianon chewed her lip. Did she still wonder that, truly? A week ago, she'd convinced herself it must be so. But the fact was Peredur had never given her reason to believe it, not once. And her uncle's next, and unexpected, comment came like a cold shower out of the cloudless sky above.

'Or are you trying to *prove* to yourself that he must be, despite what your eyes and your heart tell you?'

She stared at her uncle. Was he right? Was she testing Peredur in the same way she'd tested her father? Was she determined to find the proof, *any* proof, that her fears were well founded and that her husband was exactly the man his reputation claimed he was? Heartless?

'I don't know what I'm doing,' Rhianon said, the sting of being exposed staining her cheeks, glad her uncle couldn't see it. 'But… I am finding it hard to… trust.'

Edwin nodded. 'That is understandable.'

His tone was empathic more than sympathetic and, suddenly, Rhianon felt ashamed of burdening her uncle, who'd also suffered at the hands of Cadwgan. She touched his arm where it lay folded over the other inside the sleeves of his habit.

'I'm sorry for what my father did to you, Edwin.'

'You have no need to apologise for something your father did, Rhianon. It was twenty years ago.'

'But don't you hate him still?'

Her uncle shook his head. 'I've even forgiven him—though nothing is forgotten. After all, my fate brought me to my faith.' He tilted his head, his cowl slipping back a little, revealing his noble brow. 'But it is *your* fate that concerns me, Rhianon. What is it that stops you from trusting?'

Rhianon twisted the little bud between her fingers, the sap staining her skin. 'On our wedding night, he told me he only married me to thwart his brother, Maelgwn. Is that true?'

Edwin smiled. 'If you want the truth, daughter, you need to ask *him* for it, not me. Then look carefully beneath the words, listen to what they really mean.'

'But what else *could* they mean? And, from how he behaves... I doubt he wants a wife at all!'

Beyond the trees, but hidden by them, sounds carried from the mill house nearby. The yapping of the dog, children playing at some game or other, teasing and laughing, the admonishing tongue of Elen Felin Ddŵr as a child played too roughly perhaps.

Sounds of domesticity—simple, ordinary, content—all of a sudden, heart-rending. Up at the castle, the only sounds would be soldiers talking, jesting, cursing occasionally as they went about their tasks. There would never be a family there, in that barren outpost that was her home, not after she took the wimberry...

Edwin was studying her face, his own thoughtful. Did he see her shame, her thoughts, her fears...the intent that lay in her heart? Oh, if only she could voice it, confide in him, and seek his guidance. But perhaps she could, here in this holy place, with only Saint Non to judge her.

Rhianon gripped the snowdrop tightly between her thumb and forefinger, as if anchoring herself. 'Uncle, I need to speak of something....' She cleared her throat and forced the shameful confession to come out through unwilling lips. 'Peredur has not...that is, we have not... and I...'

At that moment, as if the words had conjured him up, hoof beats sounded and Peredur came towards them through the trees, leading his stallion. He looped the reins over a low-hanging branch and, as his gaze found hers, Rhianon willed the ground to open up and swallow her.

Had he heard?

'Good morn, Peredur.' Her uncle's greeting came without hesitation while her own faltered on her lips. 'Welcome to Ffynnon Non.'

Chapter Nine

Peredur hadn't heard everything but he'd heard, and seen, enough. His name, the halting words cut off so abruptly, then the wash of scarlet into Rhianon's cheeks. Had she spoken to Edwin of what he'd said at table last night? Things he'd never revealed to anyone, since the day he'd left Pebidiog with Eilyr.

Or had she spoken of what *should* have happened afterwards but hadn't? That, instead of going to her bed, he'd slept in his chair at the table.

'Good morn.' He returned the greeting, crossing the new grass to where they stood. Rhianon drew herself straighter, lifted her chin higher, as she always did whenever he approached her. Now it was so obvious it hit him like a blow.

'What are you doing here, Rhianon?'

Her eyes dropped to the little white flower she'd crushed between her fingers. 'I came to talk to Edwin.'

Her uncle nodded. 'I was about to suggest to Rhianon that a church might be built in this sacred place, my lord.'

The man's face was without guile and doubt rippled

through Peredur's mind. Had he misheard after all? Or misconstrued the words? Perhaps. But the knowledge that he'd interrupted something, the feeling of being unwelcome, was real, not in his imagination.

He knew that feeling of old because he'd felt it so many times before, when he'd been the worthless orphan of twenty years ago. Every time he'd entered the hovel he'd shared with his grandmother, he'd known himself to be unwanted, resented…hated. And not just by Mallt—the whole village too despised him for being the son of Letard, the man who ruled so brutally over them. It didn't matter that *he* felt himself one of the oppressed too—they shunned him anyway.

'There was a church here once, four centuries ago,' Edwin was saying. 'It burned down and was never rebuilt. Perhaps now it is time it was? The holy well will draw pilgrims, and with a new church, the community will grow.'

Peredur stared down at the well. It barely held any water, only the remnants of melted snow gone to mud, choked and strangled with weeds.

'A church will require a priest,' he said, as long-suppressed memories rose up inside him, filling his throat and strangling him too. Memories that had followed him from Pebidiog and haunted him down the years as the *cwn annwn* hounded lost souls to hell. 'It might not be easy to get one to stay, or even to get one at all.'

'I thought I would remain and fill that office, until a suitable priest is found.'

Peredur frowned, shook his head, dislodging those relentless memories, the damning and accusing voice of his grandmother that always came with them. 'You are not ordained.'

'No, but I can fill a void all the same if needs exists, as it does here.'

A void—another word for empty. Both apt words for the hollow that had opened up inside him, as if some giant claw had reached through his ribs and scooped his entrails clean out.

'I will think on it,' he said. 'For the present, I have other concerns to consider.'

Rhianon touched his arm, tentatively, yet with purpose. 'If we begin building at once,' she said, 'it can be completed in time for the Easter feast.'

Peredur turned towards her, the light touch making his pulse pound, even through the sleeve of his tunic. She wore a jaune yellow kirtle and green cloak, bold spring colours that complemented the raven hair and vivid blue eyes, enhancing her inner radiance.

'As I said,' he repeated, that radiance dazzling him. 'I shall give it some thought.'

'Then, in meantime, and with your permission,' Edwin said, 'Iago and I will continue to occupy the small chamber until a cell is built for me alongside the church.'

Peredur dragged his gaze away from his wife and looked instead at her uncle, the feeling of being excluded from something surfacing once more. 'You mean to remain indefinitely?'

'My work at Llanbadarn is done, and there is clearly a task for me to do here.'

That much was true. There *was* a spiritual lack here and his bond tenants sorely needed a man of God to guide them. He'd fully intended to see to that, and to build a church too, once the defences and comfort of the castle were completed.

But if Edwin stayed, Peredur would have to give up the small chamber and either sleep with his men—which was out of the question, even though he'd done so last night—or with his wife. And if it were simply a matter of *sleeping*, that wouldn't pose a problem. But it was far more complicated than that.

There could be no more excuses, no more avoidance, no more delay, tactics that had proved futile anyway. Every time he'd sat next to Rhianon at table, met her eyes across the courtyard, caught her scent on the breeze as she passed by, his desire had grown, not diminished.

'Of course, the chamber is yours for as long as you wish.' Peredur inclined his head in agreement, since he could hardly refuse the man. 'And Iago too is welcome to stay.'

Rhianon's face lit up. 'Oh, I'm so glad you are staying, Edwin. It's not just the common folk here that need a church, but we at the castle are also in dire need.'

She looked around her, a forefinger resting pensively at her chin. Then her gaze, bluer than the sky, found his again and she smiled with excitement, like a child who'd been given a priceless and longed-for gift.

'If you wrote to the priest at Llanbadarn, Peredur, and told him of our plans, he might come and hold a mass for Easter. If we haven't secured our own priest by then, of course.'

The sunlight that filtered down through the trees dappled the folds of her clothes, making her eyes sparkle. Around her feet, early spring flowers sprouted from the dewy ground, as if the warmth of her smile had opened their petals, even though winter had not yet passed into spring.

'I see you have both made your minds up already,' Peredur said, turning away from the impulse to linger longer here, with the dewdrops and the flowers, with the sunlight and with *her*.

But even so, the prospect of the coming night began to stir his senses, like a beguiling elixir. His blood quickened with anticipation and his voice sounded thick in his ears.

'Do you wish to return now to Abereinion with me, Rhianon?'

Rhianon hesitated, her answer freezing on her lips as realisation dawned. Edwin staying indefinitely in the small chamber, much as it delighted her, also meant that Peredur would have to sleep in the lord's room.

Her uncle was standing with his head cocked to one side, a smile on his lips as he listened to the robin singing in the branches overhead. There was nothing to suggest he'd decided to stay for reasons other than those he had stated, and yet... Had he heard her thoughts, known what she was about to confess, even before she'd spoken?

Panic rose up into her mouth. Should she get hold of the wimberry now, today, before nightfall? She could go to the mill this very moment, on the pretence of chivvying her errant maid, and ask Esyllt to slip her some of the magic fruit.

She might have to yield her body—she had no choice *but* to yield now—but to risk the possibility, the probability, that she might conceive a babe...

'Are you coming, Rhianon?'

Peredur asked her again, his voice strangely weighted, his gaze suddenly turbulent. His fingers were flexing where they held Tarth's reins, as if he was impatient to be gone.

As she stared at him in indecision, a flash of blue caught her eye. And there, on the road beyond, her maid was hurrying up towards the castle, depriving her of the only possible excuse to go to the mill.

Esyllt *must* have seen them there, at the well, and to escape a likely reprimand for her lateness to her duties had hurried on by, hoping she wouldn't be glimpsed. *Y gadnawes!*

So…the wimberry would have to wait for another day. What reason could she give now, after all? Even if she *had* a plausible excuse, Peredur had asked her to promise not to go to the mill alone and—even though she'd not promised in so many words—he might go with her and spoil her plan entirely.

'Yes,' Rhianon said, making her decision since it was already made for her. 'I'll come back with you.'

'Good.' He sent her a short nod. 'But we will have to walk. Tarth picked up a stone in his hoof. I've removed it but the sole is tender, so I would rather not put any weight on his back.'

They bade Edwin and Iago farewell and walked homeward. Esyllt must have raced before them like the wind, for she was gone out of sight completely. Rhianon's mind raced even faster, but Peredur—instead of being in a hurry—now seemed content to let the stallion go as leisurely as it liked.

At the ford, he strode straight into the river, leading Tarth, and Rhianon placed a foot on the first of the stepping stones, intending to cross them as she'd done before. But before her foot had reached the second stone, he took her hand, causing her to nearly fall off it in surprise.

Peredur wore no gauntlets today, since the day was fine, though the dun-coloured pair she'd given him was tucked into his belt. She wore no gloves either, having forgotten to bring any.

'I can manage by myself,' she said, trying to extract her hand as his fingers curled warmly around hers.

'The stones are uneven and might still be slippery,' he said. 'There was a frost in the night.'

Had there been? She'd been snuggled up under the furs in her bed—in their bed. Had he been cold down below in the hall or had the fire kept him warm? Had he looked out of the window, unable to sleep, and seen the frost wither with the dawn?

'They weren't slippery when I crossed a little while ago,' Rhianon lied, even though the stone beneath her feet did indeed seem far more perilous now than before. 'I crossed without mishap.'

'Nevertheless I would prefer to see you safely over them.'

Her heart began to thump but not because of any danger of slipping off the stones. Nor was it the same exhilaration she'd felt crossing over them the first time.

Now it was the strength of his hand, the warmth of his skin, the gleam of his eyes as the river reflected in them that made her blood gush so fast that her head felt dizzy.

'Oh…very well,' she said, her voice as unsteady as her feet and her heart starting to flutter in her breast. 'Better safe than otherwise, I suppose.'

Gathering her skirts up with her free hand, Rhianon took a step to the next stone, and then the next. And all the time, she felt she was crossing something else, not just running water. And even though she knew she wouldn't slip, that Peredur would not let her, she didn't feel safe at all.

Then, halfway through, Tarth stopped and thrust his nose down into the water, proceeding to drink with a loud sucking noise. It was so sudden that Peredur's arm was jerked back, and she was brought to an abrupt halt too, a foot poised between one stone and the next.

Rhianon gasped and swayed for a moment, really off balance now. Instinctively, she tightened her grip, feeling his tighten in return, supporting her, so that she was able to right herself.

'I—I thought we were both going to end up in the river just then!'

'I'm sorry. I should have expected that,' he said, the turbulence in his eyes turning to wry humour. 'Tarth is a devil for stopping in rivers and taking a drink whenever he feels like it.'

'He must be thirsty,' Rhianon said, as his gaze danced into hers and her stomach swooped in an altogether different way to how it had a moment ago. 'I've never seen a horse drink so deeply or make so much noise in the doing of it.'

Peredur grinned and, throwing his cloak back over one broad shoulder, braced his legs wide, the current flowing around his boots. 'Tarth's table manners leave much to be desired, although his many other virtues outweigh his few faults.'

'How does he breathe?' Rhianon asked, feeling far more off balance now than when her foot had been poised between one stone and the next. 'Drinking like that, I mean, with his nostrils underwater?'

Peredur's grin became a chuckle, the sound toppling her even more off a solid footing and onto unfamiliar and unsteady ground. 'They say a horse that buries his whole nose in water to drink is fearless.'

It was the first time she'd heard him laugh, a rich, hearty laugh…compelling, attractive. The breeze played through the wheat-gold hair, and his face was, for once, free of the frown of worry that usually lived there.

'And *is* Tarth fearless?' Rhianon asked, her mouth suddenly dry and her skin prickling, as if a thunderstorm had loomed up, though the sky was still clear blue overhead.

'Yes, he is.'

The next question was impulsive and out of her mouth before she could stop it. 'Like his master?'

'Some would say so.' He stared full into her eyes, his own unfathomable, if no longer turbulent, and definitely not amused any more. 'But then some also say I have no heart.'

Tarth raised his head then and shook himself, sending droplets of water flying. They spattered her face and spotted her clothing. Peredur's clothes didn't escape either but he paid no heed. A moment of utter silence fell, as they looked at each other, their hands still clasped tightly, the river flowing about them, also unheeding in its course to the sea.

And then, like his horse, he seemed to shake himself and the unsettling moment was severed, as cleanly as if he'd drawn his sword and sliced through it. 'We should carry on across,' he said, clicking his tongue to his stallion.

At the other side, he let go of her hand at last. Her fingers hot, and at the same time cold with the absence of his, Rhianon smoothed down her skirts. Then she touched a hand to her coif and straightened her braid, aware that he watched each movement minutely. And then they stood and looked at each other once more, without words, almost without breath.

Something in the air began to quiver, while the ripple of the river faded away. The reins dropped from between Peredur's fingers and the stallion wandered off, to crop at the grass at the side of the road, apparently as hungry now as he'd been thirsty a moment ago.

And Rhianon saw another kind of hunger light on Peredur's face. Hunger that began to roil in Rhianon's stomach too, as he lifted a hand and touched his fingers to her cheek. She started, despite the softness of the caress, and his thumb paused at the corner of her mouth.

'You had a drop of water on your cheek.'

The ground beneath her feet seemed to tremble, the river stop flowing, and the breeze stop blowing. The song of a blackbird somewhere nearby ceased abruptly and the whole world appeared to come to a halt, as if waiting for something to happen.

And her pulse pounding but her mind suddenly crystal clear, Rhianon made it happen. Lifting her hand, she stepped closer to Peredur and placed her palm deliberately over the left side of his chest.

'Why do they call you Peredur Galon Gudd?'

Peredur felt his heart turn a violent somersault. Not that she could feel it, of course, not there. His throat closed tightly as she pressed her hand firmer, her fingers splaying over his left breast, searching for the answer.

'Tell me, Peredur! Why do they say you have no heart when surely you must?'

His blood roaring in his ears, he brought his hand up and laid it over hers, pressing her palm harder still until the warmth of her skin struck through his tunic.

'You won't find it there,' he said, his words shaking on his breath.

Today he wore no gambeson, no thick leather jerkin to protect, not just his flesh from sword and arrow but his heart from far deadlier weapons.

But perhaps today was the time to tell her, since one day, sooner or later, she would discover it for herself. Better to get it over and done with, confront whatever reaction came, now rather than later.

And so, curling his fingers around her hand, Peredur moved it slowly from the left side of his chest and over to the right. There he pressed down upon it once more, firm and resolute now that there was no more hiding.

'It lies here,' he said. And waited.

She gasped and her eyes flew upwards to meet his. 'Your...your heart is on the wrong side of your body?'

Peredur steeled himself for the revulsion and the disgust that would surely follow the disbelief. 'As you see,' he said, simply, since there was no other way *to* say it.

'But...' She shook her head, frowning. 'How is that *possible*?'

'I don't know how—but it is.'

Rhianon was staring hard at the spot where their hands pressed, one over the other, as if she were determined to see through both skin and bone, right down at the thing they were talking about.

'Does it hurt...or hinder you?'

'No, it doesn't hurt nor hinder me,' Peredur replied, since it did neither, at least not in the way she meant.

'And...does it function as it should?'

He nodded. 'It works like anyone else's heart does.' Or did it? Beneath the pressing of her palm, his heart was beating erratically now, making his whole body quake as if an ague possessed him. 'It is merely in a different place.'

The explanation sounded so simple, so plausible, because that was how *he'd* explained it to himself, many times over, during his childhood, his youth, and on throughout the years. But he'd never had the courage to say it out loud to anyone else before.

'But why not speak of it?' she asked, meeting his gaze again, reading his mind, his fear. 'Why not explain it, instead of letting everyone think it doesn't exist?'

The question was so innocent that Peredur smiled. To those that knew—his adoptive parents, Maelgwn— he didn't need to speak of it. His parents accepted it as an inexplicable oddity, while his brother exploited it as a topic of malice and fun.

To his grandmother it had been a mark of his tainted birth, proof of his tarnished soul, the justification for her hate of him.

'Would *you* speak of it,' he countered, 'if it were yours?'

The words remained unanswered for a moment and then their double meaning hit him square in the gut. Perhaps that same meaning occurred to Rhianon too, for her eyes grew wide on his, but she didn't put it into the words themselves.

For how *could* it be hers unless he gave it to her? He couldn't even give his body, or take hers, less still his heart!

'I don't know if I would or not,' she said slowly, her frown deeper than ever. 'But I would hope I wouldn't be so ashamed of it as to try and hide it away completely, pretend it didn't exist at all.'

Peredur felt his face flame before the accusation. But he hadn't always hidden it, had he? Once, before he'd learned better, he'd offered it willingly, gullibly, and it had been thrown back at him in damnation and contempt by the woman who had raised him.

'Is that why you still sleep in the small chamber and avoid our bed? In case I might discover where your heart lies?'

Rhianon's questions came at him relentlessly.

'Are you so proud of your strong and fearless reputation then? Or are you afraid that you might be scorned for your weakness? Which is it, Peredur?'

Peredur didn't get the chance to answer, even if he'd known how to, as the next moment, the sound of cartwheels broke the silence. Hywel Felin Ddŵr was coming towards them, from the direction of the castle, returning from delivering the grain from last year's harvest.

Like lovers caught out in a tryst or a quarrel, he and Rhianon broke apart, their hands dropping to their sides and their heads turning toward the approaching cart.

The instant the miller saw them, his face changed and his stare became guarded, the scar on his cheek vivid in his red face. But astonishingly, for once, the surly man gave them a nod of greeting as the cart passed by, the boy at his side doing the same.

The dog, sitting in the lad's lap, however, began to back furiously, the sharp sound splintering the tense atmosphere and echoing loudly around the hills. It seemed to pierce Peredur's ears, burst in his head and sever the thread that strung his nerves tightly together.

The dog had barked at him twice before. What had the miller said? That he'd never beheld a Fleming and didn't know what to make of him! But then, nobody had *ever* known what to make of him, not even he himself.

And now he wondered…what did *Rhianon* make of him, now that she knew why exactly he bore the name of Galon Gudd?

Peredur watched until the cart disappeared around the bend, aware that Rhianon's eyes weren't on the retreating miller but on him, burning into his cheek until they seemed to melt the skin.

And his exposed heart cringed with shame and wanted to hide away again, deeper than ever before. But hiding would be impossible now that she knew where to look.

Spinning on his heel, he whistled to Tarth, who was grazing nearby, heedless of all the excitement. The stallion, instead of coming to him as he usually did, ignored him completely. So he strode over and, taking up the reins, wound them in his fist, silently ruing his horse's mood today.

When he turned back, Rhianon had followed behind and was standing as close as she'd been when her hand was pressed to his chest. She looked directly up into his eyes, the expression in her own thoughtful, and as penetrating as her questions had been before the miller came, questions that doubtless waited for another opportunity.

'It appears that Tarth is determined to defy you today,' she said.

Peredur stiffened, looked down into the intense blue gaze, waiting for her to lift her hand again, press it once more over his heart, ask him to explain the unexplainable.

How could he have satisfied her curiosity? Expound on all his defects and bear to witness the revulsion on her face? But she didn't touch him again and her hands remained where they were, hanging loosely at her sides.

'The day isn't over yet,' he said, his heart thundering all the same.

She shook her head. 'No, the day isn't over yet.'

In the distance, the dog barked again and the blackbird resumed its chatter in the nearby bushes, each seeing in that all-seeing way that every beast and bird possessed to mock him anew.

All of life closed in around him, the new grass, the crystal blue sky, the buds that sprouted from the earth, all of it joining in that mocking chorus. Announcing his defects, his shame, his unworthiness like a belated dawn song, loud and deafening.

But as he and Rhianon stood once more in silence, their unspoken thoughts sounded loudest of all.

'It is time we were back at the castle,' Peredur said pointlessly, but he didn't know what else to say, without giving voice to those thoughts, to his shame, his fear.

She nodded, said nothing and fell into step beside him. They walked homeward, their footsteps brushing through the grass and the river trickling quietly alongside a tranquil accompaniment to those thoughts that were far from tranquil, at least on his part.

No, the day wasn't over but the night would come all too soon. And tonight he wouldn't be sleeping in the small chamber as he had done, but in the lord's chamber, with Rhianon. And in that bed, she would have no need to ask any more. She'd see him and all his flaws for herself.

At the thought, his heart—the heart she'd been determined to discover—battered harder than ever against his ribs. It was as if now it was revealed, still flawed and unworthy, but no longer concealed or contained, it seemed resolved to defy him as well.

Chapter Ten

Up in her chamber later, after the midday meal was over, Rhianon paced back and forth. Where was that girl! She'd sent for Esyllt long since, her maid having disappeared after dinner without a word, let alone a request for permission!

Outside the walls, the clash of steel on steel as the men trained, accompanied by the never-ending calls of the *morloi*, made her head pound. And the request she had resolved to make of Esyllt burned like mustard on her tongue.

The crossing of the stepping stones at the ford, that unexpected discovery of Peredur's heart, the strange expression on his face when the miller's dog had barked at them, had all confused a matter that had been clear only a day before.

Then, when she hadn't witnessed any of those things, her plan to take the wimberry had seemed sensible, justifiable and imperative—but now? Now she didn't know.

At last, feet sounded, running quickly and lightly up the stairs, and Rhianon spun to face the door. It was flung open and Esyllt all but fell over the threshold, her hair awry and her face glowing.

'Where have you been till now, *forwyn*! It is well past noontide!'

Her maid started and then shrugged, her eyes dancing. 'I've been a-courting, my lady.'

Rhianon gaped. 'Courting?'

Esyllt closed the door behind her and floated into the room. 'With Guto Bren.'

'Who?'

'The *saer coed*! Don't you know the men of your own household, *meistres*?'

Yes, she knew the master carpenter, the same man she'd stopped that morning as he'd crossed the bailey with a plank on his shoulder. Big, gruff and red-haired, he was the last man she could ever imagine going 'a-courting'!

'Of course I do!' Rhianon retorted. She went to the window, intending to close the shutter and block out the noise, seeking quiet instead for what she had to ask of Esyllt.

Instead, she looked out. As if fated, the very man was hurrying through the gates, late for the battle training in the meadow beyond. With the threat of war looming, all the men—soldier, smith and *saer* alike—had to be able to wield a weapon as skilfully as they wielded hammer and chisel.

She saw Guto Bren spread his hands in a placating gesture as Peredur, overseeing the training as he always did, beckoned him forward. But she doubted the carpenter's explanation for his tardiness would come as candidly as Esyllt's had done!

From that distance, and because he wore a helmet, she couldn't see the expression on Peredur's face. But, as he levelled his sword and adopted a combative stance, it was clear he intended to give Guto a personal lesson in warfare.

Rhianon had seen him girded for battle before, on the morning he'd ridden out from Castell Llanbadarn with the Lord Rhys. But she'd never seen him with his sword drawn and now she watched mesmerised as the two men engaged. And, from the moment the steel arced and struck, Peredur's mastery was obvious and undeniable.

Man and weapon seemed forged as one deadly and destructive force, but skilfully held in check. So different, so deadly, compared to the tenderness and vulnerability he'd evinced at the ford that morning, like two different men entirely.

Her heart began to keep time with his movements, as he lunged forwards and back, thrusting and parrying. The heavy broadsword seemed to weigh nothing in his hands, as he outwitted his opponent time and again and with ease.

Esyllt had come to watch at the window too, her cheeks glowing with excitement at the spectacle. 'My lover is young and lusty enough but he is a far better carpenter than he is a soldier!'

Rhianon agreed. The *saer* was being driven backward now, his sword ineffectual against his lord's superior skill, his strength no match at all despite his being the size of a bear.

Then Guto slipped and fell, the point of Peredur's sword flashing to his throat. Rhianon's hand went to her own throat in alarm and even Esyllt drew a sharp breath as the scene stilled, the point held, the man on the ground waited.

And then, grasping Guto's arm, Peredur hauled him

to his feet, the lesson over and well learned. After taking a moment to demonstrate a different, better grip on the sword hilt, he matched the *saer* with another opponent and cast his gaze around for the next pupil.

Rhianon spun away and walked quickly from the window as steel rang on steel once more. A strange sort of exhilaration made her blood run hot and she wiped a bead of perspiration from her forehead as Esyllt voiced the very thing she herself was thinking but could never say.

'Your lord is truly magnificent, *meistres*!'

Yes, Peredur *was* magnificent. And when he came to her bed that night, she would surely be at his mercy, just as Guto Bren had been, though in a very different way. Which man would he be then? The strangely tender and exposed man of the ford, or the relentless, punishing warrior she'd just witnessed?

Esyllt spoke again, interrupting her thoughts. 'Better even than my father was in his prime, when he fought alongside Owain Gwynedd against the Normans.'

Rhianon crossed to the table and poured some ale, sipping it slowly as she recalled Peredur's suggestion that she might glean information about Hywel Felin Ddŵr from his daughter. She hadn't had an opportunity to do so yet and was denied one now, as Esyllt chattered on.

'I don't mind that Guto is a carpenter and not a soldier, of course. At least he's more likely to reach old age that way and not leave me a widow. I've got to get him to marry me first!'

She stared at the girl, her spirits dipping at the thought of losing Esyllt, an unexpected companion who, for all her cheek and irreverence, had made her feel less lonely.

'And who will be my maid if you marry and have children?'

Esyllt shrugged and began sorting out the soiled clothing on the coffer that was due for laundering. 'Oh, my sister Anest will soon be old enough.'

'I thought you said she was only eleven?'

'So she is, but she's a hard worker and is quick to learn. Anyway, I may not have babes for years yet.' Her maid winked. 'There's much bed sport to be had first!'

Rhianon shook her head, smiling at the irrepressible boldness, and bemused at the stolid acceptance of the lot of a woman. But Esyllt hadn't been wed like she had—not once, but twice. She might change her tune then.

Knowing Peredur was capable of tenderness, even of compassion, didn't mean he would always be so. People changed. Men changed. She'd seen her brother Rhodri—so sweet as a boy—turn into their father. Llywelyn had altered too, gone even deeper inside himself than *she* had done, in order to defend himself, even as he defended her from their father's brutality. And the more Llywelyn stood up for her, the harder Cadwgan knocked him down, until she'd cried and begged her brother not to. But Llywelyn had gone on taking the worst of it to protect her, until her heart had broken for him.

As for Peredur's heart…? Knowing that he possessed one didn't mean it would always be good and kind, that it would never be cruel, any more than it meant it was a heart that was capable of breaking too. And how could she know what sort of heart it was since she'd only just discovered its existence?

Rhianon drained her cup and put it down on the table. Then, not fortified at all, she walked to the bed and sat down upon its edge. She watched her maid sort through garments, putting those still clean back into the coffer, leaving the dirty ones in a little pile on the floor.

Then, having composed the words in her head, lined them up on her tongue, she chose her moment, between the rolling of one pair of stockings and the next.

'Esyllt, would you bring me some of your mother's red wimberry tomorrow?'

The girl's fingers stilled. 'What for, my lady?'

'Because I...ask it.' She almost said *I need it* but bit it back just in time. 'I will pay you, of course. But... this must be between ourselves.'

Esyllt nodded, her face suddenly cunning, as if the secrecy appealed to her. 'Ay, I can bring you some, *meistres*. What will you give me for it?'

Rhianon had already decided that. Rising and crossing to her little chest of jewels, she took out a silver clasp and returned to sit on the bed again. She held the trinket out on the palm of her hand. 'Will this do?'

Her maid laid the stocking aside and, taking the clasp, held it up into the light, her eyes as shrewd as those of any pedlar of gems. 'It's plain enough but it will suffice.' The clasp disappeared into the pouch at her belt and she recommenced her rolling. 'Is it to protect your lover, then, that you want the wimberry?'

'M-my lover?'

'Well, it's clear from the orderly state of the bed of a morning that Lord Peredur doesn't sleep there at night, so likely you have had to take another to satisfy your needs?'

Rhianon felt herself blush to the roots of her hair. 'I do not have a lover!'

Her maid giggled and, for some inexplicable reason, she felt the urge to do the same. 'More fool you then, *meistres.* Guto Bren is man enough to satisfy more than one woman, and he's not the only one here neither that would be glad to oblige!'

'Esyllt!' Rhianon's urge to laugh vanished and she leapt up from the bed. It was still unmade but, as the girl had said, it wasn't a bed where any sport had been had, willingly or otherwise. On impulse, she grabbed the coverings and hauled them off, shaking them out, then throwing them down on the floor.

Whirling round to Esyllt, she dusted off her hands, and then straightened her coif. 'I want some clean bedding put on, at once, *forwyn.* And then you can freshen my night shift and by then it will be suppertime, and you'll have gone before you've hardly arrived!'

Esyllt rose, deposited the clothing in the coffer and, shutting the lid, bobbed a curtsey, her bold gaze undaunted. 'Ay, my lady, and I'll be sure to bring the wimberry with me on the morrow.'

As dusk fell around him, Peredur stood on the northern parapet and stared at the bonfires on the other side of the estuary. There was one directly opposite, roughly between Pennal and the Dyfi crossing, and another to the east, on the border between Gwynedd and Powys.

Bonfires at night meant only two things. Secret messages being conveyed and interpreted, or beacons directing the bearers and recipients of those messages to nefarious nocturnal gatherings.

He chewed his lip, rubbed a hand over his chin, pondered. Meirchion should be back soon with news—unless he'd met with the builders of those bonfires.

The wind rose and a shiver ran over Peredur's skin. It had turned colder again, as if the night was determined to outdo the warmth and sunshine of the day. The moon was waning, a sliver of light in the eastern sky.

Below, the bailey was in darkness now, apart from the torches at the gates and at the door to the keep. The night was drawing in, supper was almost ready, the bedchamber waiting…

The strenuous training session that afternoon hadn't had the desired effect at all. Scrubbing his skin clean with a rough cloth and ice-cold water afterwards hadn't had any effect either. His blood still raced and his body, instead of being tired and satiated, ached not with fatigue but with anticipation.

Peredur stared at the bonfires. The air was so clear, the opposite shore so close, his eyes so keen that he could see the sparks that flew upwards. His senses were keener still, every nerve alert, so that his whole being seemed to quiver, as it did before a battle.

The voice of one of the guards on the main gates called out. Turning, he strode along the ramparts in that direction to see the gates swing open. Descending the ladder, he went down to greet Edwin ab Ieuaf who came through them, walking on his staff, Iago at his side.

'Lord Peredur.' Edwin greeted him first. 'I smell wood smoke in the air.'

Peredur fell into step alongside. 'Bonfires,' he explained. 'In the hills on the other side of the estuary.'

'That is ominous.'

'Yes, it is.' At the bottom of the steps to the keep, he let the other man ascend before him. 'Have you and your layman been all this time at the well, Edwin?'

'No.' The man hitched his robes with one hand and, planting his staff, ascended the stairway, his feet faultless. 'We visited the mill and took some ale with the miller and his family. The miller's wife, Elen, bakes excellent oatcakes so Iago and I require no supper,' he said. 'The miller, by the way, is not as intractable as he might seem, at first glance.'

'How do you surmise that?' Peredur asked, recalling the unexpected nod of greeting from the miller that afternoon at the ford. A nod to courtesy that, in the stupor of shame that had gone before when Rhianon had found his heart, he hadn't returned. 'Hywel has shown little evidence of loyalty thus far.'

'I may lack my eyes but there is nothing wrong with my ears, or my instincts.'

There was a pause and he wondered what else those sharp ears had heard, those keen instincts had sensed, that afternoon at the well. Had Iago not been present, he might have asked what exactly it was he'd interrupted.

'Loyalty, if not given willingly and at once, must be won instead.' Edwin reached out and, unerringly, touched his shoulder in farewell. 'I wish you and Rhianon a peaceful night, my lord.'

Peredur stood for a moment, at the doorway, looking up at the stairwell, the weighted inflection in that goodnight wish lingering even after Edwin and Iago had passed out of sight.

Had the holy man's decision to stay, so suddenly expressed, been deliberate? Had Rhianon actually confided to her uncle the sorry state of their marital life? And had they together come up with a strategy to resolve it?

He shook his head. Surely not! But the suspicion remained. In his mind's eye, he followed the men's movements above—the click of the latch on the door, the stoking of the fire and the fastening of the shutter across the window. Then the pulling back of the bed coverings and no doubt a moment for prayer before sleeping.

All the things he'd done in that same chamber the previous few nights. Tonight, whether by accident or by design, he would do them in Rhianon's chamber. And then, would his wife give willingly, and at once? Offer him her body even though she kept her heart from him? Or would she be as reluctant to give as he was to take?

After supper, Rhianon preceded her husband up the stairs to their chamber. She opened the door and stepped inside, leaving Peredur to shut it behind them. And then they were alone.

He walked past her and over to the far corner, to the little *prie-dieu* that stood there, and touched it lightly, running a finger over its simple wooden carving.

'Did you bring this with you from Uwch Aeron?' he asked.

She shook her head. 'No, I asked your carpenter to make it for me.'

Rhianon held her breath as he touched the devotional beads that hung there then picked up the book of hours that lay open. He leafed through the pages, the illuminated letters flickering in the light of the candle that burned above the *prie-dieu*.

Unobserved, since he had his back to her, she studied his tall form, wishing she could read his thoughts as easily as he was reading the pages of her breviary.

The book shut with a soft thud and he placed it down again. He turned and caught her watching him. 'And is this where you do your devotions?'

Rhianon nodded, her stomach beginning to turn far

faster than those precious pages had. 'There is nowhere else.'

The brazier hissed and smoked and the rush lights sputtered in their sconces. There was a creaking of floorboards as he walked over to the brazier and, picking up the poker, prodded the fire. 'Then I will see about the building of the church, soon,' he said.

Rhianon laced her fingers in front of her and felt perspiration bathe her palms. The room was too warm, her woollen jaune gown too heavy, her linen shift too thick. And, below all, her body had started to tremble with a mix of anticipation and apprehension.

'Esyllt mentioned today that her father once fought for Owain Gwynedd,' she said, clutching at conversation to stem her growing nerves. 'Against the Normans.'

Peredur glanced at her and nodded slowly. 'That is interesting…'

Silence reigned once more. 'The men at supper were talking of fires to the north, in Gwynedd?' Rhianon cleared her throat. 'Is there something afoot across the estuary?'

He put the poker down again. 'It may mean nothing. A hayrick burning on some farm, perhaps, or an accident.'

'But you don't really think it as innocent as that?'

'No.'

His gaze flickered to the curtain that concealed the bed and away again. Walking to the window, he tried the shutters, already fixed firmly in place by Esyllt. Then he spun around to face her.

'What were you and Edwin talking about at the well, before I came along?'

The question came without warning. Rhianon blinked

and snatched a breath. 'The building of a church,' she said, which was true, at least.

'That I know. I meant before.'

'I was asking my uncle about you,' she said, lifting her chin and trying not squirm like a guilty child who'd been caught out. 'Should I not have done?'

Peredur's eyes never wavered from hers. 'Why did you *need* to ask?'

'I suppose…' Rhianon began, forcing herself to breathe calmly, as her pulse began to flutter. 'I suppose because Edwin seems to know you better than anyone else.'

'I doubt that he does.' As he spoke, he took a step away from the window, a step closer. 'He doesn't know where my heart lies, for one thing…but you do.'

Another step and then he was standing right in front of her. 'What else is it you would like to know, Rhianon? Whether I am the sort of man your father is? The sort of man your first husband was?'

As if he'd thrust a sword, he penetrated to the root of her fear with deadly accuracy.

'Did you go further still, perhaps, and asked him whether I might be even *worse* than both of them?'

He was so close that Rhianon could see the flecks of silver in the grey eyes, bright around the dark pupil. So near that she could have counted the beats of the pulse at his throat, where it raced as fast as hers did.

'Why didn't you just ask *me*, Rhianon? Why *don't* you ask now?'

Rhianon *couldn't* ask, couldn't speak, couldn't breathe. She stood, her feet rooted to the floor, unable to run from what she sensed was coming even if she'd tried.

'You won't?' Peredur moved closer still until there

was hardly a gap between them. 'Then I will ask *you* something.'

Reaching for her hand, he took it up and turned it over in his, staring down at her palm until he seemed to study each and every line it contained. Then his eyes lifted to hers, locked on, held her so immobile that it was too late to run at all.

'What happened to you when you had eight summers? What changed your fear of Cadwgan to hate of him?'

Rhianon shook her head and tried to withdraw her hand but he held on, firmly yet with gentle fingers. 'Tell me.' His brows drew together. 'I need to know.'

'Why?'

'Because if this lies between us, we cannot lie together in that bed, tonight or any other night.'

She stared up at him. This was her chance, the opportunity to keep silent, keep safe, keep *him* from her bed, indefinitely, it seemed—if he meant what he'd said.

But suddenly Rhianon was ashamed. She'd wanted to know about him, she'd gone so far to ask others about him, listened and believed the tales that had gone before him. She'd let her fear blind her as surely as her father had blinded her uncle.

Why, as he'd said, hadn't she just asked him? And now…why shouldn't she tell him what *he* was asking *her*?

She drew a breath and, as she let it out again, the vision of that day—just one of many but worse than all the others—rose up before her. The day that had changed her irrevocably.

'It was the morning of my eighth birthday.'

And all at once the words came fluidly, willingly,

with no need to think them first. 'I went into my mother's chamber. My father had her pinned up against the wall, his hands around her neck.'

She paused, breathed again, as the fear of that day returned and closed with a cruel grip around *her* neck too. 'I ran to try and help her. I thought he was going to kill her. But he hurled me away and I hit the wall, became dazed. And when I opened my eyes... I saw...'

Peredur had listened in silence but, as her words finally faltered, his fingers tightened around hers, not imprisoning her, but encouraging her.

'What did you see, Rhianon?'

'Him.' Rhianon dropped her gaze away, stared at the floor. 'My mother told me, later when she'd crawled out of wherever she'd hidden herself, that she ran. When my father let her go and lunged at me, she just ran.'

Again, the terror of that day gathered hotly behind her eyes but Rhianon blinked it away, forced herself to go on. 'She just left me, there on the floor, with him standing over me. And so he took his rage out on me.'

Peredur still said nothing and his silence was a blessing. Because now he'd asked, now it was said, she felt the need to purge herself of it, all of it, once and for all.

'She cried afterwards, when she told me she was sorry for abandoning me like that. I cried too...but it was too late to say sorry. I never found out what she'd done to anger him that day, probably nothing, since it never required anything much to justify his violence.'

Rhianon looked back up into his face, met the eyes that regarded her so solemnly. 'But from that moment, I was never afraid of him again, no matter what violence he did to me. Because I learned, then and there, that nobody could protect me but myself.'

For a moment, Peredur made no comment, no judgement, and then he gave a slow nod of his head. 'Sometimes, the people who should care for us the most are the very ones to throw us to the wolves. It isn't right but it is so.'

He brought his other hand up, placed it so that hers was held between his two, just as he'd done at the altar on their wedding day. 'But I vow, here and now, that I will never hurt you, Rhianon. Nor will you ever have any need to run from me, as you mother did from your father, for I will never give you cause. I swear it.'

If she'd wanted to, she could have withdrawn her hand easily right then, just by slipping it out from within his. If she'd wanted to, she could even slide past his tall and imposing form and step away, out of reach altogether, run…

But Rhianon didn't want to run, not any more. Her whole being felt…free. As if now she'd spoken out loud of that day, spoken to him, her soul had been washed clean of an ugly stain. For wasn't hate as bad, and as awful a burden, as fear was?

Peredur spoke again. 'And I will do my utmost, always, to protect you, as a husband should.' His fingers loosened on hers but didn't drop away. 'However, that said, I will sleep in the chair tonight, and every night, if you prefer it?'

Rhianon hardly dared to believe her ears. Yet again, he'd given her an excuse, a reprieve, a choice, and now all she had to do was take it. Step away and go through that curtain, to sleep alone, undisturbed…safe.

'Do you *want* to sleep in the chair?' she asked, her heart beginning to thud in her breast.

He shook his head slowly. The pulse at the base of his

throat was beating too fast to count now and his chest rose and fell rapidly. Was *his* heart—the one she'd uncovered only that day—hammering as hard as hers was?

'No,' he said. 'I don't want to sleep in the chair.'

Rhianon swallowed as an overpowering response came in the wake of his words. A longing to feel his kiss, his touch, not just on her hand but on her body. On the breasts that had begun to ache beneath her bodice, at the womanhood between her legs.

'Then you don't have to,' she said.

Peredur's face changed. A flush mounted his cheekbones and his eyes grew dark. The fingers of his one hand locked with hers, while those of his other hand lifted and touched her cheek.

'Are you certain?'

She nodded, her limbs, instead of quaking with apprehension, now quivering with something very different. She wasn't *certain* of anything any more, only of what she was feeling. 'Yes.'

The curtain swished as he put out an arm and swept it aside. Then he led her through it and, his fingers still locked in hers, pulled the linen together, shutting the room out, shutting them in. Near darkness enfolded them, since there was only a candle burning low beside the bed.

Then, freeing her hand at last, he drew her plait over her shoulder and began to unbraid it, slowly and carefully. And with every gentle twist, every cord that unravelled, he unwrapped her defences, freed her from resistance and fear too, as easily as a bandage came off a wound.

'Do you remember the day I cut it?'

She nodded. 'Yes…of course.'

A smile played over his mouth. 'I wanted to unbraid it then too, very much. And then I wanted to do this…'

With infinite tenderness, he threaded his fingers into the tumbling hair, letting it flow between his hands, watching it cascade down to her waist, his gaze dark, hungry…

Rhianon's breathing quickened as his fingers undid the girdle at her waist, unlaced her kirtle, and drew her shift from her body. Dropping to his knees, he removed her shoes and woollen stockings and finally she stood naked before him.

As he rose again, a flush of colour swept along his cheekbones. He didn't say anything for a long moment, his gaze roaming with agonising leisure over every inch of her. Then, his eyes lifted to hers, darker than ever.

'You are…beautiful, Rhianon.'

'Am—am I?'

Rhianon looked down at the little pool of clothes around her feet, and at herself. The candlelight flickered over her naked body, lighting the slope of her breasts and belly. Was she beautiful? No one had ever said so…

She looked up again. The candle was casting light and shadow over his face too, though he was still fully clothed, and she saw he read the doubt hidden in her mind.

'Yes, you are.' He nodded slowly. 'You are the most beautiful thing I have ever beheld. But it is still not too late to say no, Rhianon, if you wish to.'

Rhianon wasn't sure why he was giving her a choice, when no one else ever had, any more than they'd remarked on her appearance. But *her* choice had been made the moment he'd shown her his heart. It didn't matter whether he found her beautiful or not, or whether she believed it or not. That was all irrelevant whereas *this* was inevitable now.

'No… I wish to say *yes*, Peredur.'

Chapter Eleven

Rhianon watched as, with visibly more haste than he'd undressed her, Peredur stripped himself down to his braies. Then drawing her down beside him on the bed, he propped himself up on one elbow, so near that the clean male scent of him rushed into her nostrils and dragged at her senses.

So near and yet not touching her at all. The candlelight flickered over his body too now, not just his face. They caught the ripple of muscle on his arms, chest and torso, delved into the hollows of his cheek and throat, and glinted on the strands of golden hair that fell over his brow.

Then, after a long moment of silent stillness, he dipped his head and touched his lips lightly to her naked shoulder. Rhianon snatched in a breath and his head lifted again at once, his eyes dark as pewter. His hand moved and she felt his palm, warm and heavy on her belly.

'You must tell me what pleases you, Rhianon.'

Her heart jerked against her ribs. What pleases her? She didn't know *pleasure* entered into the act of bedding. It certainly hadn't in her first marriage, when it was only thrusting, heaving pain, mercifully soon over, leaving only the bruises behind.

'I… I don't know,' she said, thankful that only the feebly flickering candle illuminated her embarrassment.

There was a pause, then his hand lifted to cup her face. 'Then you must tell me what does *not* please you.'

Rhianon nodded, although she didn't understand what he meant, not exactly, though the words themselves were clear enough. But surely a husband concerned himself only with his *own* pleasure in bed, not with any pleasure or displeasure his wife might experience?

His fingers trailed down her cheek, down her throat, so lightly they were hardly there. Then they travelled, still with a feather's touch, over her collarbone to the tip of her shoulder, then back to the hollow of her throat, where they lingered.

'Does that please you?'

Rhianon nodded again, said nothing, and his fingers moved on, down the valley between her breasts. His hand opened to cup her breast and she tensed, waiting for the bruising crush. But it didn't come. Instead, his palm cradled gently, his thumb brushing the peak until it hardened, making her gasp in delight as well as surprise.

She bit back a moan as his hand moved to her other breast and did the same. Then he bent his head and took the peak into his mouth, his teeth grazing gently and the swirl of his tongue making her back arch in response.

Immediately, his head lifted and his eyes found hers again. 'Does that please you, Rhianon?'

Nefoedd fawr! Rhianon didn't know *what* it was doing to her, what *he* was doing, or whether she should even be feeling the things that were happening to her. It went far beyond any pleasure she'd ever imagined.

But she nodded again. 'Y-yes.'

And it was like that all the way over her body as he explored, slowly, almost wonderingly, with his hands and with his mouth. His touch was still featherlike yet so powerful that her skin became hot and damp, her senses languid but quivering with heightened awareness.

His fingers stroked, caressed, delved, evoking responses that she'd never have believed she was capable of, reactions that came from both far outside herself and from deep within. And all the while, he asked, and she answered—or tried to, as speaking became almost as impossible as breathing.

His hand moved to rest between her legs, his palm cradling her womanhood as gently it had her breasts. Rhianon tensed, caught her bottom lip between her teeth, as a finger pushed tentatively inside her.

And then, instead of causing her pain, Peredur proceeded to stir her instead into a frenzy of sensation. Her body began to experience something that went far beyond pleasure to a sort of ecstasy that was so intense, that she could have wept.

She did cry out, then, and clutched his shoulders as she felt she was going to fall from a great height. Her soul seemed to soar and spiral, tossed around like a leaf in the wind, to plunge down again into a rippling river, a blissful drowning.

But even as she surrendered to the bliss, a part of Rhianon's mind clung on to reality, to stark realisation, even as she clung to him. He had given her pleasure yet he had still to take his own. And where there was pleasure, there could also be pain.

Unbidden, the memory surfaced of those nights with

her first husband, when her body had endured not pleasure at all, but only hurt, humiliating and lasting, even when the bruises had faded.

Perhaps that part was still to come.

Peredur felt Rhianon's fingers loosen on his shoulders where before they'd clung tightly, her nails scoring his skin. Her limbs went slack where they lay, entwined with his. He, by contrast, was tense from head to foot, like a rope twisted too tight or an arrow held too long.

When her eyes opened, a moment later, they were as dark as violet. Her cheeks were flushed, her skin damp with perspiration, and her hair fell wild and as black as midnight.

She was so beautiful that his chest heaved and his manhood became harder still. But he held himself in check, forced himself to breathe, as sweat beaded on his brow. It took all the mastery he possessed not to bring his mouth down upon hers, to cover her warm and limpid body with his and allow himself to drown in it, in her.

Instead, he cleared his throat. 'Did I hurt you, Rhianon?'

'N-no,' she said. 'No, you didn't hurt me at all.'

But there was a note of expectation below her words, one that was echoed in the shadow of apprehension that crossed her face. She would expect him to go further, of course. To complete the act of bedding as her first husband had.

'And did that truly please you?' he asked.

Her eyes were raking his face now, uncertainty evident. 'Yes.'

Peredur might never have lain with a woman before but he'd heard men talk, boast of their exploits and their prowess, feigned or otherwise. He didn't need to refer to tall tales or coarsely minute details. His own inherent and primitive instincts knew exactly what he should do next, what he wanted to do more than he'd ever wanted to do anything.

Thrust inside her, plunder that sweet womanhood that awaited, and release all his pent-up frustration at last. Spill himself deep in her womb, let desire master him, and then be free of it. Make her a wife in the fullest sense of the word.

But if he did…and then he lost her…this woman whom he'd grown to care for more than his own life…if he got her with child and then she died…no, it was impossible.

So, easing himself back a little, so that none of his flesh was in contact with Rhianon's, he drew the furs up over them both, hiding her lovely nakedness away.

'Yet you said, before, that you didn't know what pleasure was,' he went on, forcing his mind to supremacy over his body.

'Did I?' Her voice became wary. 'I meant… I hadn't thought it mattered.'

Peredur frowned. '*Not matter?* Did your first husband never ask you what pleased you and what didn't?'

She shook her head. 'Seisyll was…indifferent.'

Virgin he might be but even he knew that no man could be indifferent in the act of lovemaking. A man was either one way or he was the other—kind or unkind, selfless or selfish, adept or inept. Which had Seisyll been?

He stroked the back of his hand down over her arm and saw the quick flicker of surprise in her eyes. 'You mean he was not considerate to your needs?'

Her head turned away. 'No, Seisyll was *not* considerate.'

Peredur waited but she didn't say any more. Leaning on his elbow, he went on stroking her arm, even though the contact made his lust gnaw mercilessly in his loins.

'Then what *was* he?'

Her eyes came back to his but with obvious reluctance. 'He wasn't a lover, if that is what you are asking me. When he wasn't indifferent, he was…brutal. He took *enjoyment* from hurting me as he bedded me. Mercifully, it was quickly over and, after that, it only happened thrice more. A week later he was killed.'

'*Grist annwyl*, Rhianon!' Peredur drew in a breath, felt it stick in his throat, disgust and outrage choking him that any man could treat her thus. 'I never imagined…' His fingers clenched beneath the coverlet. If that man—that monster—had been here in this room, he would have used his fist on him.

Slowly, he uncurled his hand and returned to stroking her arm. 'I can understand, now, why you were so reluctant to be betrothed to me so soon afterwards.'

She shook her head, as if shaking those experiences she'd suffered far away. 'Instead of to your brother, Maelgwn, as you told me, on our wedding night.'

'Yes.' Peredur let the subject of her first husband alone—for now—as she seemed to wish it. 'Are you sorry that I did?'

'No, not any more…but I've never understood…' Her brow creased and her gaze searched his. 'Why did you *do* that? Why did you want me?'

'I told you. I would not wish to see even an enemy suffer Maelgwn's cruelty.'

Though he'd not told her all, on their wedding night,

and that omission now covered him with shame. If he had to go on denying himself, all the days of their marriage, he could at least be honest. Assure her that it wasn't out of indifference to her, or lack of consideration, but quite the opposite!

'Though it wasn't only that,' Peredur went on, choosing his words with care. 'From the day I first saw you, ten years ago, I've never forgotten you.'

'Because I was kind to a horse?'

He nodded. 'But much more besides.'

'Such as?'

'Your beauty, your spirit, your courage, your integrity, all those things I saw in you then, in that brief moment, and they are still there in you now. Maelgwn would have destroyed all that, as he destroys everything.'

As he said it, the truth of that statement made the sweat on his brow turn to ice. Lying as she was in his arms, she seemed more fragile than ever, so vulnerable. 'But you would have been wasted in a convent too, Rhianon.' A little trickle ran down his temple, over his jaw, and pooled at his collarbone. 'You would have been destroyed there too, if not quite in the same way.'

Rhianon was looking at him in amazement and he smiled, to himself as much as to her. 'You stare at me as if you've not understood a word I just said.'

Her lashes fluttered and she shook her head. 'I understood them. I just didn't expect to hear them.'

Peredur didn't dare move, even though the arm he leaned on had gone numb. He longed to gather her to him and show her that not all men were alike. But if he did…would his lust, so powerful that it pained him, make it a lie?

Because he might end up possessing her completely and hurting her far more than Seisyll had done, destroying her even as his brother would have done.

Dduw annwyl! Springing from the bed, he dragged the curtain open and lurched out into the room, closing the linen again behind him. Dropping his hands to his knees, he drew a deep breath into his lungs, and then another. And another.

Then he crossed to the window. Taking the shutter down, he pressed his hands to either side of the frame and drew the cold night air deep into his lungs in yet more breaths.

Across the estuary, the bonfires still burned, as he still burned, for her. But there was a difference. Those fires would die down, and eventually go out, whereas the fire within him would only flame higher and higher.

For a long time, Peredur stood and looked out into the dark, letting the cold air envelop him, chill his skin, cool his blood, kill his desire. But, even if he'd mastered himself this night, what about tomorrow night and the night after that, and all the nights of their married life together?

What if, on one of those nights, he failed to control his desire, planted his seed in her womb, and made a babe there? What if…

Bedding almost always led to birthing. And birth didn't always mean a new life. Sometimes it meant death and that was something that he would never allow to happen.

The cold from without began to penetrate so deeply that his senses iced over and a dull ache filled his head. Still he stood, letting the moments pass, allowing the bitter night air to bite deeper still, until his limbs began to shiver, his skin became numb and the very marrow of his bones froze.

Only then did Peredur close the shutter. Dousing the rush lights on the walls, he went back through the curtain again. Rhianon was still awake, lying as he'd left her, her hair like midnight on the pillow, her face like pale cream in contrast. Waiting…

He slipped in beneath the covers, aware he was bringing the cold with him, and before he could grow warm again, before his lust could kindle once more, he took her hand and pressed his lips to her palm.

'Goodnight, Rhianon.'

Then he turned away and, extinguishing the candle beside the bed, pulled the covers up over him. Facing the wall and shrouded in darkness and desire and fear, Peredur shivered and prayed for sleep and for oblivion.

Rhianon stared at Peredur's back, the chill from his body bathing her skin and making her shiver too. He didn't speak again and, as long moments passed and the quaking of his limbs grew still, it became clear that he wouldn't.

Nor would he look at her or touch her again or kiss her again. Or ask any more about her former husband. Why had he done that? Why had he listened so patiently to the whole sorry tale, as if he really wanted to know, to understand, as if he even sympathised?

And why hadn't he taken her as she'd expected him to?

Rhianon pressed her fingertips to her mouth. He hadn't kissed her there, however, on her lips, even if he had touched her, kissed her, everywhere else, even in her most intimate places. That kiss he'd bestowed on her palm before saying goodnight had been strangely chaste, as if none of what had gone before had happened. As if she'd dreamed it all.

But she *hadn't* dreamed it. It had been *real*, the most real thing she'd ever known. He'd evoked such sensations within her, such responses, that it seemed impossible to extinguish them now, as easily as he'd extinguished the candle.

And yet, he had kept himself apart the whole time, denied himself the pleasure he'd given her. *Why?*

Rhianon turned over on to her side too and stared at the opposite wall. And as she listened to the fire hiss and burn low, her mind searched the darkness for the answers to all those questions but found none.

'I've brought you the wimberry, *meistres*.'

Rhianon, sitting next to the brazier after the midday meal the next day, put down her cup of ale and took the small clay vessel Esyllt held out. Untying the parchment that covered its opening, she sniffed at its contents then peered inside at the thick, sweet-smelling conserve.

'My mother says you are welcome to as much as you like.'

The pot almost slipped to the floor. 'You…you told your *mother* about this? But asked you to keep it a *secret*, Esyllt!'

'I *had* to tell her, *meistres*. She has eyes everywhere! And if she found out that I'd stolen it, she'd have the skin off my back in no time.'

Rhianon's heart fluttered in panic. What if Elen Felin Ddŵr was a gossip as well as eagle-eyed? And what if her deception came, in due course, to Peredur's ears?

'Well, I trust your mother will tell no one else!' She

stared down at the pot in her hands, not at all sure about her plan now that she had the means to implement it. All the same, curiosity won out. 'What does it taste like?'

'The berries have a sharp flavour, but when they are boiled and honey is added, it is very sweet.'

'How often should I take it?'

'My mother takes a goodly spoonful thrice daily.'

'And do the virtues of it have certain effect?'

Her maid shrugged. 'That I don't know, *meistres*, though it has never failed my mother.'

Rhianon peered into the pot again, almost expecting its magical contents to leap out at her. 'So…should I take a spoonful immediately?'

Esyllt nodded. 'If you intend to use it, then it might as well be at once.'

Was that a note of disapproval? She glanced up at her maid. 'You think I am doing wrong in this, Esyllt?'

The girl shrugged again but her face had lost its usual carefree expression. 'I can understand why my mother takes it, *meistres*, but….' With characteristic irreverence, Esyllt sat down in the chair opposite. 'But you are young and newlywed. You deny that you have a lover, and so you have no need of deception. I can't understand why you would not want a babe at once.'

'I have not been wed a month yet!'

'Mayhap not, but what difference does that make?' Her maid shook her head. 'Children come when they are ready to come—but the coupling needs to come first, of course.'

Rhianon felt her cheeks turn even redder than the wimberry. 'I have my reasons, Esyllt, and I'll thank you not to be so bold in your opinions.'

Her maid tossed her mousy brown plait over her

shoulder. 'It was *you* who asked me for my opinions, my lady.'

Yes, she had, hadn't she? Why was she so offended then to hear them, plain and to the point, as was everything that came out of Esyllt's mouth? But the next remark was bold, even for her maid.

'And now that your lord sleeps in your bed, is it not because he has a mind to get heirs?'

Rhianon stared over at the unmade bed. It still looked orderly, no bedding in disarray, no crumpled and discarded pillows to show any passion had taken place there. Even Esyllt didn't see everything.

Her maid couldn't know what had happened to her in that bed last night, the pleasure she'd been given, the sensations that had woken her from a slumber deeper than sleep. Esyllt couldn't know either that Peredur hadn't taken *his* pleasure. That he'd slept until dawn, or at least appeared to sleep, and then risen, dressed, fed the fire, and left.

What would happen this coming night? Was last night the prelude? Tonight, would he take her, and his pleasure, and his due? And, if not tonight, what about the night after that, and all the other nights that would follow?

But Esyllt had been right in one opinion, at least. Peredur would surely want heirs, as all men did, be they high- or low-born. And her purpose as a woman and a wife was to provide him with those heirs.

Abruptly, Rhianon got to her feet and tying the paper back over the pot, put it down next to her wine cup. 'Fetch my cloak, Esyllt. I wish to take a walk.'

'Walk?' Her maid got to her feet too, her face astonished. 'Walk where, *meistres*?'

'I don't know! Anywhere.' She placed a coif over her hair. 'What is so strange about wanting to walk anyway?' she snapped.

'But why would you walk when you can ride?' Esyllt rolled her eyes and pouted. 'I suppose I will have to walk too?'

She should be annoyed at the girl's truculence, but somehow she never could be annoyed with Esyllt, no matter how much she deserved it at times. But she didn't want company this morning. She wanted—needed—to think, and she had to do that alone.

Peredur might have slept but *she* hadn't. Her body had ached, not just with the lingering echoes of pleasure, but with a strange lack of fulfilment that left her hollow inside, her mind restless…adrift.

'No, there is no need for you to accompany me,' Rhianon said. 'I will go on my own.'

'Then where do you intend going?' Esyllt's relief was as candid as her opinions had been. 'If anyone should ask after you.'

'Down to the beach.' The idea came out of nowhere, though she felt the need to justify it all the same. 'I've always wanted to walk along the seashore.'

She had trusted Peredur last night with more than her body. She'd trusted him enough that, when he'd asked her things she'd never said to anyone, she'd told him.

And now was she betraying that trust, revoking it altogether, by taking the wimberry?

'Then you'll need something sturdy on your feet. It's more mud than sand this time of year.' Her maid went to the coffer and took out a pair of leather shoes. 'But be sure to watch out for the *morloi, meistres*. And, if you see them, don't approach them for your life!'

* * *

Outside the main gate, Peredur watched for the return of Meirchion ap Dafydd. But the road north into Gwynedd was empty, with no news, good or bad, on the horizon.

If he could have done, he would have ridden northwards too, yesterday. Not because he would have personally liked to catch his brother in the act of treachery, but because it would provide an escape from Abereinion.

And from Rhianon—or rather from the lure of her, and the desire that was fast overleaping his boundaries, as a stag leapt clear and free of the hounds on its heels.

How in God's name would he be able to master himself again this coming night? Lie with her and give her pleasure but take none for himself? How, when his whole body was already imagining hers, pressing close, warm and inviting? His arms already about her, drawing her even closer, too close…

With a curse, Peredur turned and went in through the gates. Within, everyone was hurrying about the task of reinforcing the castle. The sounds of weapons, shields and armour being cleaned came from the armoury. In the stables, the horses stood, ears pricked and nostrils flared, as if they already scented war in the air, and not merely waited for their midday corn.

But there was more than one kind of war to be fought and, while he had no fear of the sort of battles he'd fought before, against enemies he knew he could defeat, the inner battle against himself now seemed insurmountable.

Rhianon's maid was crossing the courtyard, a bundle of dirty linen in her arms. She saw him, dipped a curtsey, hesitated, and then changed direction and came over to him.

'Good morn, my lord.'

Peredur looked down at her. She was a pretty girl, bold too, who'd already caught the eye of more than one of his men, and the eyes of Guto Bren, in particular. The thought crossed his mind that he should have a quiet word with his master carpenter. Since Rhianon hadn't appeared to have discovered anything further, mayhap Guto could glean from the girl any information about the treachery, or otherwise, of her father.

But, as he nodded in return to her greeting, making up his mind to do just that, her next words drove all thoughts of garnering information out of his head.

'I thought you should know, my lord, that your lady has gone for a walk on the beach. I did warn her about the *morloi*, but…'

Peredur didn't wait to hear any more. Turning, he ran for the postern gate, fear gripping his throat, while beyond the walls the calling of the *morloi* grew louder in his ears.

Chapter Twelve

Rhianon strode along the beach—which turned out to be more of a mudflat after all—her spirits lifting with every stride. The day was a breezy but lovely one. A cloudless blue sky reigned overhead and the morning sun was warm, even though January had yet to give way to February.

The cries of gulls, the gleam of the water, the sting of the air on her face, the salt in her nostrils, all of it was refreshing, invigorating. She'd never walked so freely into such an open landscape before, never felt so liberated in all her life.

Behind her, the castle, its lord, the red wimberry, the unexpected and tender pleasure of the previous night, and the uncertainty of the coming one, receded somewhere far away, for the moment at least.

The calling of the *morloi* became deafening. She'd grown used to it now, their sound as familiar as the breaking of waves. She smiled as she remembered the day they'd arrived, the night Cristin had sobbed with fear of them, convinced they were demons.

The mottled grey bodies seemed harmless now, as they lay on the shore opposite, so near it seemed she could touch them. Some were basking on this side too, but much further down, a long way away. She wouldn't go near them, of course, she wasn't that foolish! But there was no harm in walking a little farther, to the edge of the water, to find out if seawater really was salty, as she'd heard it was.

And it was! Crouching down at the estuary's edge, Rhianon put her fingertips into the water and then touched them to her tongue, her senses delighting at the pungency of taste. But it was more than just salty. It was primitive and ageless, seeming to contain all of life, visible and invisible below the surface.

Esyllt had told her that people sailed across the estuary often, to the southern edge of Gwynedd, to trade or sometimes to raid. They fished in it—although there were no fishing boats to be seen today—and in summertime, some even bathed and swam in it. Peredur himself had done so, as he'd told her that day on the battlements.

Rhianon had no intention of bathing, let alone swimming, not that she *could* swim. But she felt a sudden urge to just put her feet in the water, to find out what it felt like, to dip into that hidden life and feel a part of it, for a moment at least.

Her fingers were reaching to take off her shoes when a cry caught her attention. She straightened up and looked down the beach to what she'd first thought was a piece of driftwood or a small boulder.

Now the object was moving and it was coming straight towards her. She recognised it at once for what it was, since it couldn't be anything else. One of the *morloi*!

Rhianon froze, her hand flying to her mouth to stifle a scream as the creature came bowling along the sand towards her. Two bright black eyes stared back at her, oddly human in its round furry face.

She began to back away, one foot at a time, but to her horror, the creature followed her. It shuffled faster than ever, its head bobbing up and down, and weaving from side to side. And then it opened its mouth and gave another cry, piteous and pleading, as if it was asking for help.

Rhianon stopped in her tracks. It was only a pup, after all, not a fully grown beast, and therefore surely harmless. Was it hurt? Lost? Abandoned by its mother? It cried again, a heartbreaking sound, and she could almost read the entreaty in those dark expressive eyes.

Out of nowhere a rush of compassion swelled up inside her, banishing her fear and leaving her only with the urge to help it. Reaching out a cautious hand, she began to walk slowly towards the creature, making soft incoherent sounds of her own to show it she meant it no harm.

But when she'd gone as near as two or three yards, a shout rent the air, loud, imperative, severing through the barely formed thread between her and the pup.

'*Uffarn dân!* Rhianon! Come away from there!'

Peredur was running towards her, arm and legs working fast, his cloak streaming out behind him. His yelling frightened the pup and it began to back away with a flapping of tiny flippers. At the same time, there was a mighty splash and a head broke the surface of the water. A bigger head with eyes that were not helpless or entreating at all, but filled with the furious intent to attack.

The way a mother will attack to defend its young.

Rhianon screamed and turned to flee but, even before she'd taken a step, Peredur's hand had closed fast around hers.

'Run!' His voice was louder even than the roaring

of the female, out of the water now and propelling itself with incredible speed towards its young. 'Run as
fast as you can!'

Together they flew up the beach, Peredur's hand clutching hers, urging her feet faster. Her gown got tangled in
her legs, making her stumble more than once, and sand
rose up to choke her. The wind snatched her coif away and
her hair blew around her face so that she could hardly see.

But Rhianon didn't care. Perhaps it was the urgency
of the moment, or the freedom of the beach, or her
worry that had grown so large, her deception so huge,
that it needed to be vented. Whatever it was, a sense
of excitement had gripped her, bubbling up inside her
like broth boiling in a pot, until her eyes filled and she
began to laugh helplessly.

She was still laughing, the tears running unchecked
down her cheeks, as they crested the grassy bank to
safety. There, at last, they stopped, both of them gasping for breath, and her knees so weak that she had to
clutch at Peredur's sleeves to stop them from buckling.

'*Er mwyn Duw!* What were you *thinking*, Rhianon?
Didn't I tell you the *morloi* could be dangerous, that
they've been known to attack?'

Rhianon looked up into his face and her heart
seemed to fly, faster even than her feet had. 'Yes, so…
so you did.'

She nodded, tried to stop laughing, but the look of
consternation on his face only made her laugh all the
more, until her whole body shook helplessly. 'Oh, but that
was the most fun I've ever had in all my days, Peredur!'

Peredur stared down at her, dragging air into his lungs,
his heart in his throat. Tears were running down her face

and her fingers dug into his arms as she laughed as if she'd never stop. He, however, couldn't have laughed even if he'd wanted to. His blood pounded in his head, and his chest heaved from running, faster than he'd ever run in his life, down the beach, to reach Rhianon before the *morloi* did.

And she thought that *fun*?

'Are you hurt?' he asked, shaking his head in disbelief and wracked with fear at the thought of what might have happened. 'Did the creature touch you?'

She blinked the tears of laughter from her eyes. Beautiful eyes that danced into his, bluer than the sky, brighter than the sun. Her coif was gone, carried away on the wind, and her hair cascaded, loose and wild, down to her waist.

'No, I'm…not harmed,' she said, between gasps for breath, her laughter subsiding into stifled giggles. 'But thank you…for coming to my rescue…all the same.'

Peredur brushed a strand of hair back from her cheek, his fingers trembling, not just with fear now, but something just as powerful. 'When Esyllt told me you'd come down to the beach… Rhianon, don't you realise what might have happened?'

She nodded and then succumbed to another burst of laughter. 'Of course I do!' Her breath was steadier now, and she loosened her grip on his arms as she recovered herself. 'But I thought…that the pup was hurt and I wanted to try and…help it.'

'Help it! And risk your *own* safety in doing so?' Peredur bit his tongue. Admonishing her recklessness would serve for nothing and she was safe now, though he badly wanted to shake some sense into her. 'And help it how, pray? By bringing it indoors and wrapping it in furs before the fire!'

His comment brought forth another burst of laughter and, this time, he found himself struggling not to laugh too. He shook his head in despair. It truly was no matter for amusement and yet her laughter was infectious, seeping through his skin and eating away at his whole being.

'Commendable but foolish,' he said. 'Don't ever do it again, Rhianon…please!'

Her laughter vanished in an instant and silence fell like a stone between them. Above their head, gulls wheeled and shrieked and, low over the water, a sea eagle glided, looking for fish, its shadow darkening the water where it passed.

'Perhaps it *was* foolish.' A shadow darkened Rhianon's eyes too and her words came, not breathlessly now, but slow and deliberate. 'But I think *you* would have done exactly the same as I did.'

As she spoke, she moved closer to him. Her gaze locked firmly on his, serious now, and penetrating right down inside him. 'Wouldn't *you* help a creature in distress too, Peredur, bc it foolish or not? Be it dangerous even?'

Peredur shook his head as the tang of salt on her skin and her hair invaded his nostrils and stirred his senses. 'No,' he said. 'I wouldn't.'

'I don't believe that.' She tilted her face upwards, her mouth close to his, her words soft, challenging, inciting. 'A week ago, a day ago even, I might have believed it, but I know you better now.'

Her breasts rose and fell against his chest and he balled his hands into fists to stop them reaching for her. But it was too late. His arms were already around her waist, drawing her nearer still until her hips slotted into his and his loins sparked into pulsing, ardent life.

'You think because you have discovered where my heart lies that you know *all* of me?'

'Perhaps not *all*…not yet.' A smile played over her lips as she placed her palm over his right breast, where his heart hammered like iron on an anvil. 'Is there *more* I should yet know, Peredur?'

Her lips parted and her breath came quick and hot against his face. His blood surging, Peredur lifted his hand to the back of her head and threaded his fingers into her hair, gently gathering the silken strands into his fist.

Then desire eclipsed everything around them—the *morloi*, the birds, the wind, the water—and the ground seemed to shift beneath his feet as he brought his mouth down upon hers.

He didn't kiss her fleetingly, as he'd done at the altar in Llanbadarn Church. He didn't touch his lips lightly, and with agonising restraint, as he'd done the previous night, everywhere except on her mouth, where he'd wanted to kiss her most of all.

Peredur kissed her long and slow, searching and yearning, consuming and devouring. He kissed her with all his heart, with his whole soul, the way he'd wanted to kiss her since the moment he first saw her.

Her lips tasted of sea salt and her own sweetness and, as he drove his tongue between them, tasting the wild and heady essence of *her*, he marvelled that he'd resisted kissing her like this for so long.

It was Rhianon's gasp, moments later, that made him lift his head. She was staring over his shoulder, her eyes wide with shock, her arms slackening where they'd lifted and wrapped around his neck. Slowly, Peredur turned to look where she did and his blood went from fire to ice.

A boot was sticking up out of the sand, a few yards away, in a deep ditch overhung with tufts of grass and half filled with brash. At first sight, it looked like a young tree stump, shorn and withered by winter, or a broken-off branch, carried on the wind and buried under windblown sand. But it was neither.

'Stay here,' he said and, tearing himself away from her, crossed quickly over to the place. Leaping down into the ditch, he swept away the brash and began to scoop the sand from around the boot. Bit by bit, a hosed leg was revealed, then a tunic-covered torso, then the shoulders, head and face of a man, his hands bound and his throat slit from ear to ear.

Peredur sat back on his haunches, his elbows resting on his thighs, his fists clenched. A yard or so away from the first body, the tethered hands of a second corpse was sticking up between the brash.

'O Dduw annwyl!'

Twisting around, he saw Rhianon standing behind him, her hand over her mouth, her gaze wide with horror. Swiftly, he rose and, taking her elbow, led her out of the hollow and away from the grisly discovery. There, he cupped her face with his hands.

'Why didn't you stay here, as I bade you, Rhianon? Must you *always* ignore my advice, *ddynes*!'

She nodded, the colour ebbing from her cheeks as she attempted a thin smile. 'Yes.'

Peredur's heart heaved and he pulled her to him, resting his chin on the top of her head. 'It seems you must... but next time *please* do as I ask.'

She said nothing but pressed her head close to his chest, her fingers curling into his tunic. For a long moment, they stood there in silence, the sounds of the gulls and the curlews and the *morloi* filling the air like a lament.

Then her voice came, muffled in his cloak. 'There can be no doubt about you possessing a heart any longer, Peredur, for it is beating even faster than mine is.'

Placing a hand under her chin, Peredur tilted her face up and his gut twisted with a searing, aching longing to kiss her all over again. 'Shock does that to one,' he said, touching a finger to her throat and feeling her pulse beating fast, but thankfully, strong and steady. 'It will pass.'

He looked back to the hollow in the sand. There was nothing definite to be seen now, only the top of the boot that looked, from here, nothing more than a twisted piece of driftwood.

'At least we know what become of the men of the garrison,' he said grimly.

Rhianon had turned to look too. 'Are they…all there, all five of them…dead?'

Peredur nodded. 'I suspect so, though I only saw two. And judging from the decomposition, they've been dead for several weeks. The snow must have covered them completely, which is why they've lain undiscovered until now.'

He glanced up at the castle battlements, not a hundred yards distant. 'Even if you leaned out from above, you still wouldn't see them, lying in the lee of the hollow like that, hidden by the scrub.'

'How did they die?'

'That poor wretch, at least, was slain by the knife, as

you saw.' Peredur looked back at Rhianon, and the ache inside him pulled tighter than before. 'I won't know for certain about the rest until we dig them out.'

Her face blanched. 'You mean they were *murdered*?'

He nodded, the ugly word bringing a surge of disgust into his mouth. 'It appears they were bound, dragged out here, then killed. And then the bodies hidden in the ditch and covered over.' But why? And by whom?

Rhianon's gaze was searching his, as if she too asked those last two questions he'd not uttered out loud. Horror still shadowed her eyes, eclipsing the desire he'd seen there before, the desire that he'd known had filled his own eyes. Perhaps it was just as well that the discovery had been made before he'd gone further and done much more than kiss her.

Before he'd laid her down in one of those hidden, sandy hollows, peeled her clothes from her body, given in to that desire and possessed her wholly, all resistance futile, all his restraint undone in a moment of madness.

Peredur took her hand and locked his fingers in hers. 'Come,' he said. 'Best not linger here. I'll see to it these men are dug out at once and laid to proper rest.'

As they waited for the postern gate to open, Rhianon's stomach still churned. The sight of that poor dead man in the sand would live with her for ever. But stronger even than horror was the echo of Peredur's heartbeat in her ears as they'd stood and stared.

And before that, the taste of his lips on hers, the warmth and strength of the arms that had wrapped about her. The desire that had flooded her whole being with fire, then the cold and the loss when he'd left her and gone to investigate the grisly thing in the sand.

From within the walls, footsteps came running and the gate was opened, Peredur sending the guard a curt reprimand for his tardiness. He was worried, though, more than angry. She could see that from his face, which was set into a grim mask, the knit of his brows deep.

He escorted her to the steps of the keep and there he relinquished her hand at last, though he made no move to leave her. Rhianon placed a foot onto the bottom step, then paused, not willing to leave him either.

'Where will you lay the bodies?' she asked, holding on to their new-found bond that had been forged, out there, when they'd kissed and he'd held her as if he'd never let her go.

'They can rest in one of the barns tonight,' he said, his eyes delving so deeply into hers that they seemed to reach right down inside her. 'Until they can be buried with dignity tomorrow.'

The afternoon was fast fading into dusk and the dying rays of the sun slanted over the palisade wall, glinting like bronze instead of gold on his hair. And suddenly, out of nowhere, came a startling and certain realisation.

Discovering where his heart lay was almost irrelevant, since she'd known all along he must possess one. It was the true nature of that heart, the indisputable truth of his nature, of *him*, that knocked all the breath from her body.

'Perhaps they can be buried at Non's Well,' she said, her thoughts somehow working with reason while her senses did anything but.

He nodded, his gaze dark as it bored into hers, just as it had done on the beach. 'That would be a fitting place.'

At that moment, the main gates opened and Meirchion ap Dafydd rode in, returned from Gwynedd. Peredur glanced over his shoulder, a muscle moved in his cheek, and then his eyes came back to hers.

'I must go.'

He bowed and, with a final blistering stare, strode swiftly away to speak with his captain. Rhianon stared after him, her revelation coming back to her, louder and clearer than before.

Peredur had saved her from harm when the *morloi* had come out of the sea, putting himself in danger without hesitation. Her father would *never* have done that. Last night, he'd given her a pleasure she'd never known existed, yet had taken nothing for himself. Seisyll would *never* have done that.

And, as she climbed the steps and upward to their chamber, those contrasting truths whirled around Rhianon's mind, even faster than her feet had flown as Peredur had led her to safety.

Desire now, on both their parts, was impossible to ignore or deny. She didn't want to ignore or deny it any longer. She wanted to embrace it, clutch it as close as he'd clutched her earlier, never let it go.

But did the fact that he possessed a heart mean it was the *right* sort of heart? Could Peredur's heart feel passion as well as compassion? Could it feel love even?

At the table in the hall, Peredur sat with Meirchion as his captain confirmed what he'd suspected from the moment he'd learned his brother had ridden northwards for Gwynedd.

'Lord Maelgwn's party crossed the Dyfi river, as you know, and I followed their tracks to the *llys* at Pennal.'

Leaning forward on his elbows, Peredur cradled his

cup of ale, discovered a trickle of sand in his sleeve, and shook it out. 'Was the Prince in residence?'

'Ay, my lord.' Meirchion leaned forward on his elbows too. 'I saw him with my own eyes within the walls.'

Peredur cursed softly and, with his forefinger, traced a pattern in the little spot of sand on the tabletop. 'It seems certain, then, that Maelgwn is plotting something with Owain Gwynedd, quite possibly an attack on the Lord Rhys.'

His captain took a swig of ale. 'It looks that way, my lord, though whether the Prince will attempt it, who knows? By all accounts, he has his hands full with his disgruntled brother, Cadwaladr, as well as his own sons.'

Peredur sat back, flexed his fingers, and cursed the greed and ambitions that set son against father, brother against brother. The disunity that splintered the dynastic families of Wales instead of binding them together against their common foes from beyond the border.

'And there is more, my lord.' Meirchion went on. 'After passing one night at Pennal, your brother turned east into Powys. I didn't follow as I thought it prudent to return here with the news.'

'East to the *llys* of Tafolwern, then…perhaps to embroil the Prince of Powys too in this plot.'

His captain agreed. 'It would seem that way.'

Peredur nodded. 'That, at least, grants us a little more time to act. We may yet be wrong about Maelgwn's intent. I hope to God that we are,' he said. 'But better to prepare for the worst than to be caught off guard, as that wretched garrison must have been.'

He refilled his cup, his mouth dry with the distaste of treachery, the vision of those murdered men lying shrouded in his barn unsettling even now. Did his brother have a hand in *that* too? He wouldn't put *any-thing* past Maelgwn.

As if Meirchion had seen into his mind, his captain voiced the inevitable question. 'What do you intend to do, my lord?'

'Tomorrow, I will ride to Llanbadarn to alert my father of Maelgwn's actions and bid him send word south to the Lord Rhys at once.' Peredur pushed his cup away. 'If an attack from Gwynedd or from Powys *does* come, this is where it will be, here at Abereinion. We must be ready.'

His captain got to his feet. 'I will alert the men and see to the defences.'

'And double the watch, day and night, the seaward side too, Meirchion, lest they come by boat across the estuary. I will only be a day at Llanbadarn but, in the meantime, no one is to leave the safety of the castle.'

After the man had gone, Peredur rose and went to stand by the hearth. Sand still scratched at his skin from where he'd helped to disinter the bodies, his men and himself working quickly before night fell to dig them out.

As he'd feared, they'd all died the same way, by the murderer's knife. But by *whose* knife? Murder was the coward's way of killing. Would his brother really stoop so low? And, if so, how much lower would he sink to get what he wanted?

He looked upward to the ceiling, his imagination passing through the wooden planking and up to the top level. Rhianon and her maid would be up there now, in their chamber, preparing to come down to supper. Was she naked in her bath, her clothes in a heap on the floor ready to be washed clean too, as her body was being cleaned?

Or was it cleaned and fragranced already, her maid drying her soft skin with a cloth before the brazier? Rubbing the salt from her hair then combing out the tangles until it hung to her waist like spun silk?

Perhaps it was all to the good that he was riding to Llanbadarn tomorrow. A day apart might help to clear the sand from his mind too and cool the desire that raged every time he thought of Rhianon, let alone saw her, held her, touched her, kissed her.

And, if war should come, who knew where the battle would take him. He just had this one night to get through. This night, when he had to lie next to a woman he desired more than he'd ever imaged. Give her the pleasure he wanted to give her and take none for himself.

Peredur grimaced. Facing Maelgwn's treachery, and all the might of Gwynedd, and mayhap Powys too, suddenly seemed a far easier task, and one he was fairly confident of winning, or at least putting up a good fight.

Tonight, on the battlefield of that bedchamber above, he already knew himself to be lost. He'd been lost from the moment he'd held her to his heart that afternoon and kissed her.

Chapter Thirteen

After supper that night, Rhianon opened her coffer, dug her hand down to the bottom, beneath all the clothing, and pulled out the jar of red wimberry. Opening it, she peered inside, the sweet tang of the conserve rising to her nose, the tang of deception bitter.

She'd almost told Esyllt to take the wimberry away with her again, when her maid had left to return to the mill earlier. But she hadn't and now she didn't know what to do.

Should she take it just in case what had happened at the ford yesterday and on the beach today proved false after all? In case this night would not be like last night and tonight he would go further....

Or should she have faith that when Peredur had revealed his heart, he'd revealed all of him? Shown her the real man beneath the warrior's reputation? Trust that the shock and disgust she'd witnessed on his face when she'd told him about Cadwgan, about Seisyll, meant he was not like either, and never would be?

There was a knock at the door and Rhianon almost jumped out of her skin. Quickly the shoved the jar to the bottom of the coffer again and spun around.

'Come in.'

The door opened, and Peredur crossed the threshold. Their eyes met, held for a long moment, and afraid he might see her deception written there plain, she looked downwards, fixing her gaze instead on his body.

He looked tired and his arms hung loosely at his sides. His hands were un-gloved, the dun-coloured gauntlets tucked into his belt. His clothes were stained with dirt and sand had dried on the bottoms of his boots.

'Forgive me,' he said, his gaze following hers down the length of his body. His voice sounded weary too. 'I have had no opportunity to change or bathe.'

Shutting the door, he came into the room and crossed to the brazier, holding his hands out to warm them. 'We had to work quickly to recover all five men before the sun went down.'

'Did they all die…the same way?' Rhianon asked.

He nodded. 'Yes, murdered, every one of them, and judging by the absence of any other wounds, taken by surprise.'

The faraway cry of a wolf broke the stillness of the night, perhaps even the same one that had howled the night she'd comforted Cristin. That night seemed a lifetime ago now, not just a fortnight. The uncertainties, the doubts, the fears remained but they weren't the same now.

Tonight she felt she faced something far different to anything outside the walls, that now the danger wasn't out there, but here in this room, inside herself.

Peredur lifted his head to listen as the creature howled again. 'It was a miracle that the bodies had lain undisturbed all this while,' he murmured. 'Wolves are known to scavenge on the unburied bodies of the dead.'

Rhianon shuddered and moved closer to the fire, closer to him. 'At least their souls are salvaged too now, as well as their corpses. Edwin is doing vigil for them?'

'Yes.'

But she didn't want to think of those murdered men any more, nor envisage them lying shrouded and silent in the barn, her uncle watching over them. 'What news did Meirchion bring?' she asked.

'All bad.' He looked down into the flames, rubbing his palms together. 'It seems my brother's ambition has flown high indeed or else his treachery sunk to the very depths. Either way, tomorrow I must ride south to Llanbadarn. My father will take the news hard.'

Turning abruptly, he crossed the room, took off his cloak and hung it on a peg. Then he paused, his face in profile solemn in the torchlight, as if he were already relaying those ill tidings to Eilyr ap Bleddyn. It would indeed pain the old man to hear his youngest son was a traitor.

And as for his eldest son… Rhianon studied Peredur, standing with his hand still on the peg, deep in thought. She might have doubted the existence of his heart but she'd never questioned his loyalty, to his father, to his overlord, to his *gwlad*, his country.

'How long will you be gone?' she asked, feeling his absence even though he was still here with her.

'One night, no more. Llanbadarn is only half a day's ride. I'll return before noon tomorrow, sooner if I can.' But as he voiced it, one night seemed an age to Rhianon, the distance he would ride a threat to the closeness that had formed between them that day. 'Can you not send Meirchion?' she suggested. 'Or someone else?'

He shook his head. 'No, the news must come from me.'

'Yes.' She nodded but a part of her was already riding out with him, not wanting to let him go. 'Yes, I understand that.'

Going to the table against the wall, Rhianon poured water from the pitcher into the basin. She'd been a wife, she'd undressed her former husband at the end of the day, even though it was done unwillingly, at his command, instead of any wish or desire on her part.

But it was desire now, not duty or command, that made her hands tremble and a blush creep into her cheeks. Intense and irresistible desire that she'd never felt before that overpowered even the most persistent of her doubts.

'The water is not warm but it is not quite cold either,' she said, keeping her gaze fixed on the ewer and basin, her voice fluttering along with her heart. She didn't have to see Peredur's face to see his astonishment, for it was there in his voice.

'You wish me to wash?'

Rhianon's cheeks grew hotter still as she turned and met his eyes. But now, after that kiss that afternoon, modesty seemed pointless. 'You can hardly come to bed as you are. It would not be comfortable…all that sand.'

He looked down at himself and then dipped his head in agreement, a wry smile touching his mouth. 'Then, if you will withdraw beyond the curtain, I will send for my body servant.'

'There is no need to send for him.'

Her heart lurched from a flutter to a thudding as he came over to her side, his gaze delving into hers, as if he wasn't sure she meant what she had. *She* wasn't sure either but, as irrational and unbelievable as it was, she ached to touch him, to see him naked, to know him.

'Besides which,' she went on, turning back to the basin. 'I imagine he has already retired for the night. Why disturb him when I can do what he would do?'

Her pulse pounding, Rhianon took up a cloth and soap and plunged them into the tepid water, swishing them vigorously around, too vigorously, as if her desire was determined to make itself heard too.

Then, drying her hands, she stepped purposely towards him. 'You will need to…disrobe first of course,' she said.

He stared down at her, his expression unreadable, and her stomach clenched hard. Had she mistaken that moment on the beach earlier, misinterpreted his kiss, his touch, the desire she'd seen in his eyes, and made them mean something they did not?

There was only one way to find out and, now she'd come this far, she could hardly go back again. So, with trembling fingers, she reached out and undid his belt, feeling the flinch of his body against her hands.

'What are you doing, Rhianon?'

Rhianon stared at his throat and, avoiding his eyes, let the belt drop to the floor. 'I am disrobing you.'

He made no reply but he flinched again as her fingers went to his collar to unlace his tunic. Standing on her tiptoes, she pulled it over his head, her breasts brushing against him, making the flesh beneath her bodice quiver.

And then she did the same to his undershirt, dropping it to the floor with the other garments, before stepping back to look at him, more boldly than she'd ever dreamed she could look at any man.

But this wasn't just any man. Esyllt had called him magnificent, the day they'd stood together at the window and watched the mock battle on the training field. Peredur *was* magnificent and so much more.

For he was beautiful. The height and the breadth of him filled her whole vision. His skin was like burnished bronze, his flesh firm and hard. The muscles of his arms, the sculpted ridges of his torso, every line of his body seemed to be cast from iron—tensed, primed, a latent and fluid power tightly leashed.

From his collarbone a scar ran downward and across his chest, where a sword had dragged. It cleaved through the fine dusting of golden hair, from left to right, from where she'd tried to find his heart to where it actually lay.

Rhianon reached out and touched her fingertips there, feeling his flesh quiver in response. 'A battle scar?'

He nodded, his eyes dark as they bored down at her. 'One among many.'

She traced her fingers from its leftward, and deepest point, down and across to the right of his chest. There, beneath the taut flesh of his breast, she felt it, like thunder. The beat of vital and ardent life, like a storm in the palm of her hand, ready to break or else pass by, or yet to hover, contained, waiting…

Clearing her throat, Rhianon took up the cloth and soap and rubbed them vigorously together until she'd created a thick lather. Then, she began to wash the sweat and the toil from his body, beginning there, where the scar met his heart.

For several moments silence filled the room, the sound of the fire and the rubbing of linen on flesh louder than they should be. Peredur's breath came now as fast and as shallow as hers did and wherever she touched the cloth, his skin shuddered and his body grew hard until every inch of him seemed to be pulled tight to the breaking point.

'Yesterday…' she said, her eyes fixed once more on the pulse that beat strong and fast at his throat. 'When we were at the ford, before the miller came, you didn't answer my question.'

'Which question was that?'

With hands that had become braver now, more sure in their task, Rhianon washed the broad shoulders, then down his arms, his wrists, his hands. Then, pausing only to muster more lather, she drew the cloth across his flat, hard stomach, feeling the skin below tighten as he snatched a sharp breath.

'Why you have never told anyone where your heart lies,' she said, her voice a-tremble, both with the intimacy of what she was doing and the boldness of her questioning.

Dipping the cloth and the soap in the water again, Rhianon moved behind him. The air grew quieter still, with only the creak of a floorboard, the rustle of the rushes, the hiss of the torches sounding in the silence.

There, as she washed his back, she discovered other scars, marks of violence that didn't mar the overall image of beauty at all but only added to it.

'Whether you are so ashamed of your heart that you have hidden it away all your life,' she went on, after a moment. Between her words, she inhaled the male scent of him that emerged as she scrubbed the grime and the sweat from his skin. 'Or if you are afraid of what people would think of you if you revealed it.'

There was a sudden heightening of tension but no answer came. Silence reigned once more but the storm that was building overhead seemed more threatening than ever.

Returning to the table, Rhianon took up the basin and placed it down on the floor, the soap and cloth beside it. Then she reached for the fastening of his hose, intending to wash his legs and his feet.

But then Peredur moved, with startling swiftness, placing his fingers around her wrists and putting her away from him. Dragging a low stool forward, he pulled off his hose and, leaving his braies on, sat down.

'I will do the rest,' he said, not looking at her, the words gruff and his cheeks scarlet.

Rhianon nodded, her cheeks scarlet too. She dried her hands on her skirts and then stooped to pick up the discarded clothing. Going to his coffer, she began to separate the clean garments from the soiled, watching from the corner of her eye as he washed the lower part of his body.

She was folding his undershirt when Peredur spoke again, many taut moments later. And his voice, muffled though it was since he was bent double on the stool, sent a thrill down her spine.

'I didn't always hide it…my heart…but…'

Rhianon's hands stilled for an instant, then she laid his shirt down upon the coffer and turned slowly around. 'But?' she prompted breathlessly.

'But I learned that it was better…wiser…to do so.'

His head was still bent downwards, his hair falling over his brow, the muscles of his arms flexing as he went about the task of drying his lower legs. There was a knot in the bone of the left ankle, Rhianon saw, indicating that it had once been broken.

The words of his brother, Maelgwn, came back to

her, how he'd called Peredur ill-formed and unnatural, a base-born mongrel.

'That must have been a harsh lesson to have such a dire and lasting result,' she said.

Maelgwn had spoken harshly too, and false, she knew that now, even if she'd half believed him on their wedding night. For none of those things were true of the beautiful man who sat before her, his body bearing the marks of his valour and courage. His soul marked with the compassion that she knew he had for both man and beast. And as for being a virgin....

The thought brought a smile to her lips. For the skill with which he'd pleasured her last night in bed revealed his brother's slur for what it was—an insult doubtless born out of his fury at being thwarted, the enmity that existed between the two men. It was not a fact.

'Perhaps it *was* a harsh lesson,' he said, standing up abruptly, the work of drying complete. Picking up the basin and linens, he placed them back on the table, and stood for a moment facing away from her. 'But did you not learn the same lesson, Rhianon, growing up with a father like Cadwgan? Then becoming the wife of a man like Seisyll?'

Rhianon watched mesmerised as he bent and plunged his hands into the water. He scrubbed them over his face and ran long fingers through his hair, making it gleam like wet gold.

And, as she watched, her eyes drinking in the beauty, the strength, the nobility of him, a chasm of yearning opened up low in her belly and a different sort of wetness pooled between her thighs.

'Just because the lessons we learn as children are well taught,' she said, her voice trembling as her throat constricted with desire, 'that doesn't mean they are always right or true lessons, Peredur. And when we are grown and know better…we might even *unlearn* them… if we try.'

Peredur threw down the cloth and turned around. His heart jerked against his ribs and his manhood became harder still beneath his braies. There was no point in trying to deny how much he desired her. The evidence was right there, blatantly visible, and utterly impossible to hide.

He hadn't been able to hide it from the moment she'd begun to wash him. Instead, it had kindled ever hotter with each touch of the cloth on his body until now even his bones ached for her.

The same aching need that he saw reflected back at him from Rhianon's eyes. The same desire that showed in the parting of her lips, in the way her body called to him, even though she didn't move or lift a hand to beckon him to her.

But he went all the same. Striding across the floor to where she stood, he cupped her face and brought his mouth down upon hers. She gasped but her arms wound around his neck and she pressed her body into his. Warm, pliant, inviting, she returned his kiss with the same fervent hunger, the same insatiable need.

Pulling the coif from her head, Peredur loosened her hair, his hands threading through the heavy silken curls as they fell to her waist. Between urgent, hungry kisses, he removed her clothing, item by item, as she'd removed his earlier, his eyes devouring every piece of flesh as he laid it bare.

Then he picked her up and carried her through the

curtain to the bed. Lying down beside her, he looked, touched, tasted. From her brow, to her throat, to her breasts, down over her stomach, to the swell of her abdomen, and lower, between her thighs, Peredur kissed and looked, touched and tasted his fill.

Just like the previous night, he asked and he listened, discovered which of the sounds she made indicated the places of most pleasure, the sort of touch she liked best, the stroking and teasing that made her sigh and gasp, and slick her limbs with sweat.

And, just like last night, though even more difficult now, Peredur drew fiercely on all the strength of will he possessed, reining in his lust just as he would a rearing steed, fighting it for mastery.

His hand moved to her womanhood, his fingers slipping inside her, stroking and teasing her. He watched her face, saw the pleasure in the flushed cheeks, heard it in the shallow gasping breaths, the deep primeval moans, as ecstasy claimed her.

Finally, when she arched and cried out, he took her mouth again, sharing in her fulfilment that way since he could not give himself the same release. And when she began to grow quiet again, her breathing slowing, her skin start to cool beneath his, Peredur took her into his arms and held her tightly.

Many moments later, her eyes fluttered open and her gaze fell into his. They were lying face to face, skin to skin, limbs entwined, his manhood pressed firm and ardent against her thigh. And he knew she must be wondering if now, unlike the previous night, he would possess her at last.

'Did that please you,' he asked, though now he hardly needed to.

She nodded, her reply nothing more than a breath. 'Yes.'

Outside, in the upland forests, a wolf howled again, like a lost soul wandering through the unearthly hours. When it died away, her gaze was puzzled, as if she was looking for something that was lost too. From its depths, questions surfaced, ones he could not answer now any better or more willingly than before.

'Good,' he said, instead. 'I will *always* try and please you, Rhianon.'

Releasing her only for a moment, Peredur snuffed out the candle and gathered her into his arms again. In the dark, they lay close together, their arms around each other, as if neither wanted to let go.

A long time passed, hours perhaps, before he felt Rhianon relax against him, her limbs growing limp as sleep claimed her. But he lay awake, his body aching, his *soul* aching, as darkness encroached, pervading from without to gather deep within him. And then the wolf howled again, much nearer, right outside the castle walls judging from the shout that went up from the guard over the gate to frighten it away.

Rhianon stirred and she moved closer, the palm of her hand coming to rest on his right breast, over his heart. And Peredur knew, as the night pressed down upon him, more dangerous than any nocturnal predator, that he could no longer scare away the truth as easily as the wolf had been driven off. He *had* to speak it, he *wanted* to speak it, to her.

He touched her hair, gently, lest she still slept after all. 'Are you awake?' he whispered.

The reply came at once. 'Yes.'

'It was my grandmother, Mallt,' he said, dropping his

hand from her hair and letting it rest on the dip of her waist. 'It was *she* who I offered my heart to.'

He felt the start that she gave, sensed her eyes were wide open now and searching his keenly. 'Why didn't she want it?'

'For the reason I spoke of that night we sat at table in the hall.'

'That she rejected you because of the manner of your begetting?'

Peredur nodded, glad of the dark now, so that she shouldn't see the pain he knew would be there on his face. 'Now I realise it was her grief that made her hate me. Then I was too young to understand that but eventually I stopped looking for love or anything else from her.'

'Yet she housed you, fed you, clothed you…could she *really* have been so unfeeling, Peredur?'

Beneath her palm, his heart drummed so loud he could almost hear it. 'While Letard was alive and he paid her, yes, she did all that, but not out of any sort of feeling, or even duty. And then, when he was killed…'

The words died in his throat as that day flashed back, like a bolt of lightning from a storm cloud, illuminating the darkness inside him with terrifying brightness.

Beneath the furs, she inched closer. 'Tell me,' she whispered.

'The day of the attack on Pebidiog was the day I finally realised the depth of her hate for me.' Peredur drew in a deep breath, felt it burn his lungs like quicklime. 'Anarawd hadn't even wiped his sword clean of Letard's blood before she dragged me forward, exposing me as the Fleming's bastard and screaming at him to kill me too.'

Her hand on his chest twitched and curled into a ball. '*O nefoedd*, no!'

Perhaps it would have been better if he'd left the candle burning, after all. At least then he'd know whether it was horror, or pity, or disbelief, or all three that had echoed in her exclamation.

But then she whispered, her voice instead soft, reassuring, understanding. 'Surely, she must have been so demented that she didn't know what she was doing...'

'Perhaps,' he replied, 'but she did it all the same.'

There was a little silence and then she spoke again, her words a warm breath at his throat. 'Do you remember what you said to me when I told you what happened on my eighth birthday?'

'That sometimes the people who should care for us the most are the ones who, instead, throw us to the wolves.'

'Yes, and it is as true of your grandmother as it is of my mother.' She laid her cheek into the hollow of his shoulder. 'It isn't right, Peredur, and neither is it an excuse...but sadly, it is so.'

Peredur nodded. 'I know that now. And in a way, I understand why she wouldn't, or couldn't, accept what I offered her.'

And all at once it had to be said. He *wanted* it said so much it was bursting out of the very depths of his soul. His voice shook, his entire being—body, soul and heart— was shaking with the *need* to say what couldn't be suppressed or denied or feared now.

And, no matter what the result might be once it was said, there would be no way to unsay it. It didn't matter if Rhianon didn't really care to hear it. Nor even if all the understanding, and sympathy and compassion she'd spoken just now proved to be only that and no more.

'But I'll offer it to you now, Rhianon.' And, closing his fingers over hers where they lay on his chest, Peredur said it at last. 'My heart is yours, now and for ever... if you want it.'

Chapter Fourteen

Sudden tears filled Rhianon's eyes. Had he really said that? And meant it? Or had she imagined it because she wanted to hear it so badly, more than she'd ever realised until now when it was said.

'Will you?' she asked, her voice a whisper, because all her breath was stuck in her throat. 'Will you really give me your heart?'

'I will.'

A surge of joy rose up and engulfed her, like a fountain that had burst up out of a well that she'd thought empty. Or perhaps if not empty, then firmly lidded down, suppressing things like happiness and love, while she'd grown used to the other feelings that had dominated her life—fear, pain, mistrust, even hate.

But now, all at once, it was as if all those bad feelings were swept away, like autumn leaves, dead and withered, before the arrival of a long-awaited springtime.

'Yes,' she said, lifting her head, her joy making her smile. 'I want it.'

His arms gathered her close and he kissed her forehead, then her mouth. Rhianon could feel the ardour in his kiss, the pounding of the heart he'd just offered, the strength of the magnificent body that housed it.

When he relinquished her lips again, she moved her hand from his chest and touched his cheek, then his mouth with her fingertips. There was more yet to burst up from that well before her joy was made complete.

'But I want everything else too, Peredur.'

Even though they were still lying close together, body to body, flesh against flesh, except for where he wore his braies, she felt him withdraw slightly.

'What else is it that you want of me, Rhianon?' he asked after a moment.

Rhianon blushed, grateful for the darkness that hid it, because she didn't just want, she needed. She *craved* him, all of him—his heart and his love, his soul and his body. But how could she voice it, especially now, after all her excuses and deception, after what she'd said about Seisyll's brutal lovemaking?

She drew a breath and formed the words in her head carefully before letting them come to her tongue. 'You have given me so much pleasure these last two nights. I never knew such…feelings existed, or were possible. But…why is it that you haven't yet taken your *own* pleasure?'

Rhianon waited but still he didn't speak so, her heart pounding, she moved her palm down to his stomach. As she explored the ridges of his ribs, the taut muscles, the hard firm flesh, she felt him quiver and draw his breath in sharply.

'I have been married, Peredur,' she said, her eyes fastened on his, even though in the dark their expression was impossible to read. 'I have lain with a man before…

even if it was only a few times. So I am not completely ignorant of a husband's needs.'

She paused then, her heart rattling so hard that it shook her whole body, went lower still and traced her fingertips along the band of his braies, rolled low on his hips. 'Needs that you must have…needs I *know* you have.'

Peredur gave a groan and his head moved on the pillow, his forehead coming to rest upon hers. 'Rhianon… don't…'

'Why must I not?' she breathed. 'Isn't it what you *want*?'

He made no answer but his breath came ragged on her face and his brow grew damp against hers. Rhianon knew what *she* wanted, however. She wanted the braies gone. She wanted to know what he looked like, what he felt like. She wanted him to take the same pleasure he'd given her. So, slowly, she slipped her fingers inside the linen, her knuckles touching the taut flesh of his belly.

'Stop…'

Peredur gave a groan and his loins jerked violently. And then his fingers wrapped around her wrists, bringing her hands away and pressing them to his chest.

'You shouldn't…you mustn't.'

Should not? Must not? Why not! Moving her head back a little, Rhianon tried to see his face, read his mind, understand his reasons. He desired her, he *must* do. She could *feel* it in every line of his body, in the sweat that beaded his brow, in the hardness of the loins that pressed against hers.

So *why* was Peredur containing his lust, with no small effort, but at great cost to himself? Unless…he didn't desire her at all! Unless, in her ignorance, and her innocence, and because of her need, she'd misread all the signs. Unless he'd given her pleasure in bed out of a husband's duty only!

'Why not, Peredur?' she asked, her voice a-tremble. 'Are we not husband and wife?'

There was still no reply and the silence extinguished her joy as completely as he'd snuffed out the candle earlier.

Yes, they were man and wife, but desire didn't necessary exist within marriage. And yes, she might have been married and bedded before, but she'd never been truly *desired* before. Seisyll hadn't desired her, not for herself. He'd only dominated her, bedded her, *used* her because she was his property to do with as he pleased.

Colour flooded her cheeks. Not the same carnal heat as before but the flush of hot humiliation. Her blood turned to ice in her veins and her heart seemed to stagger to a halt. How foolish she must seem to him, how ridiculous, how…wanton!

'Do you not…want heirs, Peredur?' she challenged, clearing her humiliation from her throat, and saying the words she'd never envisaged herself speaking. But it was the only possible way to ask without making even a bigger fool of herself—the biggest fool of all! 'Surely that is part of the reason you married me?'

'*Uffarn dân*, Rhianon!' His head drew back. 'Why do you ask that *now*?'

Why *did* she ask? And why did she yearn to feel his naked body over hers, *inside* hers, when she'd dreaded it so before? Why *did* she long to be possessed by him, to have this aching, yearning emptiness fulfilled, when before she'd feared it?

'Isn't *now* the appropriate time to ask?' she countered. 'Now, at the beginning of our marriage.'

His arms around her slackened, a cold space opening up between them where before there had been warmth, closeness, communion.

'This is not a place to bring a child into, Rhianon.' His chest heaved and a heavy sigh came from him. 'Abereinion is a frontier post, not a nursery. It is not safe here for either you or a babe.'

Rhianon felt the gulf open up even wider, though neither of them had actually moved apart. And his words, brutal in their common sense, pierced all the way through her, bursting the dreams she hadn't even realised she'd dreamed.

'Then you don't intend to…consummate our marriage?'

There was a long pause and then, 'No.'

That short single word came most brutal of all. Yet once she would have rejoiced to hear it, because that had been what she'd *wanted* to hear from him.

That he had no intention of bedding her proper, nor getting her with child, nor any wish for an heir. Just as she'd had no wish for it either, before…

'I see,' Rhianon said, feeling tears gather behind her eyes and begin to blind her. Though it seemed she'd been blind all along, deluded even, just as she'd planned to delude him! 'I suppose, with everything so uncertain at this time, mayhap it *is* foolish to want more…'

But she *did* want more, she *did* want all. She wanted to be a wife to Peredur, to be the mother of his children, their children. All the things she hadn't realised she'd wanted until now.

She wanted to be desired…loved…

Rhianon felt her heart crack in two, for there was the one thing she *hadn't* seen at all, until now. Something that had crept up, invisible yet completely present, and now stared her right in the face, more terrifying than anything she'd ever known.

When he'd fed the fire that first freezing cold night so she should be warm. When he'd guided her safely across the stepping stones at the ford and then shown her his heart. When they'd raced, hand in hand, up the beach from the *morloi*…

All those times, and countless others, when Peredur had shown her he was nothing like her father, nothing like Seisyll, she'd been falling in love with him.

His arms tightened around her again and his chin came to rest on the top of her head. A sigh, heavier than the last, stirred her hair. Rhianon waited, absorbing that realisation and all it meant, and all it could not mean, not ever.

But he said nothing, and she knew he wouldn't speak again if she didn't.

And then, abruptly, he threw the covers back and got out of bed. A moment later she heard the splashing of water, as if he was washing himself again. But the water in the ewer would be cold now…

Rhianon lay on her back and stared up at the ceiling. There was a long quiet from without, as if he was just standing in the dark. Then the fire hissed as more peat was placed upon it. The water splashed again and, a moment later, the curtain moved and Peredur stepped back through it.

The bed dipped a little, the hay rustling in the mattress as he lay down beside her and drew the covering up. He reached for her but instead of turning her towards him, he turned her away from him, and then fitted his body snugly into hers.

Then he kissed her neck. 'Sleep now, Rhianon.'

He sighed again, as if all the sorrows of the world had descended on his shoulders. But it was only the sigh of fatigue after all, for a moment later, Rhianon sensed him fall into a deep sleep, his arms still around her, his cheek resting on her hair.

The hours slipped past. Rhianon closed her eyes but didn't sleep, though Peredur slept soundly, not moving once. All night long, he held her, his body warm against hers, his breathing soft, his heart beating strong and steady.

Tears welled behind the eyelids she squeezed tightly shut. Not the hot tears of joy that had come when he'd offered her his heart but the cold, stark, terrible tears of rejection. Because, without love, a heart was nothing.

Sometime before dawn, Rhianon fell asleep too. When she awoke, with the first light and the song of a blackbird outside the window, the bed beside her was empty.

However, Peredur hadn't left, the way he had the morning after their wedding night. She could hear him beyond the curtain. The opening and closing of his coffer, the chink of a cup being placed down on wood, the rasp of steel as he girded his sword at his belt.

But just as she got out of bed to dress too, to bid him farewell, the door opened and closed again, and there was quiet. A dreadful chill of foreboding settled over her, seeped down into her belly, seeming to freeze her womb, until it felt dead inside her.

But it didn't matter since she would obviously never have need of it.

Peredur might not be the man his reputation said he was. He might not be cruel like her father, or brutal like her first husband, but Maelgwn had been right after all. It was clear that her husband knew even less of love than either of them. He couldn't even recognise it when it was right there beside him, lying in his arms.

He might have given her his heart but it was an empty gesture, made even emptier because she'd given him not just her heart, but everything she possessed—her heart, her soul, her body and her love.

At the gates, Peredur halted Tarth a moment and cast his eyes about him, as if taking a last look at something he might never see again.

The bailey was empty, no one yet about their tasks, since dawn had hardly broken. There had been a frost in the night and the ground was still white, since no sun peeped over the walls yet. Perhaps there would be no sun today.

Abereinion looked almost as desolate as it had the day they'd arrived. But he knew that feeling wasn't inside the castle walls—it was inside himself.

It was a force too strong to resist that drew his eyes up to the window of the chamber he'd left, not half an hour since. Rhianon was there, looking down, straight at him, her black hair loose and lifting from her shoulders in the morning breeze.

She didn't call down to him—she didn't even lift a hand in farewell, and neither did he. They just looked at each other. And even from the distance, and through the dim dawn light, something powerful seemed to flow along the beam of vision.

Something that drew him as surely as if she'd let down a rope and wound it around him, reeling him in, like a fish floundering on the end of a hook. Pulling him back to her. But he couldn't go, not now that he'd lied to her because he was too much of a coward to tell her the truth.

I love you.

The word thudded into his throat, like an arrow flying from a bow. Tarth's ears pricked, his head lifting and his nostrils sniffing the air, as if even his stallion scented his deception. Or perhaps he'd spoken the words out loud, as loud as he'd spoken his lie last night?

And now he would have to go on lying to Rhianon and to himself for the rest of their life together, until the end of their days. And with every night that came, he would have to ensure that lie became the truth.

But, surely, even a lie was permissible, necessary, *vital* if it was said for the right reason? Meant to protect and not cause harm, or worse, inflict terrible suffering and loss, perhaps even agonising death?

So, he would go on resisting the arms that drew him into her embrace, refuse the body that called to his, master the longing to possess Rhianon, make her his wife proper and the mother of those heirs he'd so vehemently denied he wanted.

There was no turning back, no taking that denial back either, no matter how much he longed to. With a nod of his head that went unreturned, he trotted through the gates and took the road to Llanbadarn.

But as he galloped out into the dawn, Peredur knew himself a man torn in two. His mind and his body might be following the road south but his heart would never be his again. He'd given it to Rhianon, for what it was worth, and that was a truth that could never become a lie.

The next morning, the eve of Candlemas, Rhianon climbed the battlements and looked southwards. Her eyes scoured the road that led to Llanbadarn until it disappeared over the first hill and into the trees.

It was empty. The bailey was deserted as well, everyone at table except the two guards on duty—one over the main gate and the other over the postern—and she herself.

It was so quiet, the air so still, that Rhianon could almost hear the thoughts in her head, the clarity so stark that her skin began to prickle. A shiver ran down her spine and she drew her cloak tighter around her, her nerves alerting to something very strange.

And then she knew what it was.

Spinning around, she looked out over the northern wall and a gasp filled her mouth. The beach was completely bare. The *morloi* were gone! It was as if they'd never been there at all.

And amid all that emptiness, that raw act of desertion, a sob of utter loss rose up to choke her. But how could she miss the grotesque creatures that had first puzzled, then frightened, and then fascinated her? Miss the endless calling of the pups for their mothers that had deafened her ears and haunted her soul?

But it wasn't the loss of the *morloi* and their cries that caused this unbearable ache inside her. She missed Peredur. She wanted her husband. She ached for the man she loved. The man who had given her his heart, in words only, and hadn't asked for hers in return, any more than he'd asked for her body.

Rhianon gripped the edge of the parapet and dug her nails into the wood, as that truth finally dawned. It was cruel in its irony. Peredur had given her the very thing she'd wanted and now she found she didn't want it at all. All her efforts, all her deception, all her fears had been for nothing.

What was so *wrong* with her? *Why* was she so undesirable to him? Was it a punishment from God for not *wanting* to be desired, for being afraid of the consequences even more than the act? For planning to break His laws by preventing a babe from being made?

A babe that wasn't going to be made anyway, it seemed!

Turning slowly, the silence ringing loudly in her ears, Rhianon made her way back down to her chamber. There, she took the jar of red wimberry out of her coffer and held it in her hands. For a long time, she stared down at it and then a wave of anger engulfed her from the crown of her head to the tips of her toes.

'T'r diawl iddo!'

Grounding a scream out through her teeth, she lifted her hand high, to hurl the jar away, to see it smash against the wall, as *she* had been smashed the night before, into tiny and irrevocable pieces.

She almost *did* throw it. How she resisted, she didn't know. But accursed a reminder though it was, she wouldn't smash it. Destruction wouldn't change anything, nor heal the cracks, not in the jar but in *her*, wounds that could never be repaired.

But she would get rid of it and, with a nod of decision, Rhianon went out through the door, the jar still in her hand. When she emerged into the bailey, her uncle was coming towards her, returning from his morning devotions at Non's Well, Iago at his side as always.

'Good day, Rhianon.'

She didn't even try to smile. 'Good day, uncle. Did you happen to meet Esyllt on her way from the mill?'

Edwin shook his head, his brow furrowing, as if he saw the misery on her face. 'No, we met no one. Are you seeking her?'

'Yes, she is late this morning, as she is every morning, so I mean to walk down and remind her of her duties.'

The realisation that she'd lied to her uncle brought a blush of shame into Rhianon's face. And the fact that he would know she was lying made it worse.

'And there is something I wish to return to her mother, Elen,' she added, undoing her lie, in part at least. 'I don't need it…now.'

Her uncle's head tilted and his sightless eyes dropped to her hands, where she clutched the wimberry so tightly that her knuckles hurt. And it didn't make any difference he couldn't see, he knew what she was about all the same.

'Then best take a man with you, Rhianon, just in case. I believe Peredur has left orders that no one ventures outside the castle walls while he is away.'

'Yes, he has…and yet you have been down to the holy well?'

Her uncle nodded. 'The guard could not gainsay a monk, so he said, even though I am not one.' His face sobered. 'But do not go alone, Rhianon. Iago here will accompany you, if you wish?'

Rhianon shook her head. What she had to do was

better done without witnesses, even though had her uncle asked she would have confessed there and then.

Told him everything of her pointless and humiliating deception, even of her love, which was even more pointless. A love that hurt as well as humiliated, inflicting a pain greater than any she'd ever suffered on her body.

'No,' she said. 'I would *sooner* go alone.'

Bidding them both farewell, she ordered the guard to open the gates and, since the man could not gainsay the lady of the castle any more than he could a monk, he let her pass.

Briskly, Rhianon made her way to the mill. She crossed the stepping stones without fear of slipping today, her feet sure in their course. The robin still sang in his tree at Non's Well, though he had a mate with him now. A cruel taunt! With the coming of spring, she and *her* mate wouldn't build a nest together as those two birds would do. Never make a babe to be raised and loved over a long and blissful summer.

In the verges, early flowers bloomed brightly but Rhianon paid them no heed, nor did she feel the sun on her back as she walked purposely along the road. Instead, it felt like winter had returned, that the thaw had only been temporary, as deceitful as her own deception had been.

Perhaps it was divine justice, after all, and now she would have to do the proper penance. Remain undesired, unloved and childless all her days.

Rhianon was nearly at the mill when she saw Esyllt coming towards her. The girl lifted a hand in greeting, her face all smiles, completely unabashed at having to be chivvied to her duties.

She quickened her pace, a reprimand and not a smile

in return poised on her lips. And then Esyllt's eyes flew wide and looked past her to the road that led north into Gwynedd. Then her maid turned and fled back towards the mill house, calling for her father.

Rhianon spun around to look northwards too, to see what had alarmed her maid, and the pot of wimberry slipped from her fingers and smashed on the ground.

Maelgwn ab Eilyr was riding towards her, his green eyes gleaming with intent.

Chapter Fifteen

Tarth leapt the stream of the Cletwr, the stallion not even attempting to stop and drink, as was his wont. It was as if he too sensed the need to make haste and, on the other side, he broke into a gallop without being asked. Peredur gave him his head, his heart drumming louder even than Tarth's hooves.

He'd imparted the news of Maelgwn's treachery to his father as gently as he could, although the anguish in Eilyr's old eyes had been palpable, and painful to behold. Word had been sent south, on a swift horse, to the Lord Rhys at his *llys* of Dinefwr.

Now all that mattered was to get home and thwart any threat from Maelgwn and the Prince of Gwynedd should it arrive at the gates of Abereinion. And, even more vitally, protect his people…and his wife.

But as he finally rounded the bend in the road before the mill, Peredur discovered he was too late, for all his speed.

Outside the mill house stood Hywel Felin Ddŵr, a broadsword in his hand, aged, yet its blade glinting sharp in the sunlight. At his side, his eldest son held a vicious-looking pitchfork, while the rest of the family crowded within the gates.

Beyond the wheel, at the other side of the bridge, were two men-at-arms, mounted, mailed and with weapons drawn.

And in the middle, on the bridge itself, were Rhianon and Maelgwn. His brother had her by the wrist, dragging her to his horse. She struggled fiercely to free herself, her body twisting and her feet digging into the ground. But she was powerless against his strength and, then, as he closed his arms about her and attempted to lift her into the saddle, she screamed.

Peredur's blood ran cold. With a roar that came from somewhere deep inside him, he pulled Tarth to a skidding halt and leapt down from the saddle. Drawing his sword, he dashed past the miller and onto the bridge, his footstep resounding on the wooden planks.

At the same time, Maelgwn turned and saw him and his face, red with exertion, went white. In his surprise, his hold on Rhianon loosened a little and, with another desperate twist of her body, she pulled away from him.

And then Peredur was at her side, his arm going around her waist and drawing her close.

'Are you harmed?' he asked, searching her face urgently.

'No…no,' she gasped between breaths, steadying herself against him, 'but take care, Peredur!'

Maelgwn had recovered himself quickly, his hand going to his sword hilt and his eyes blazing with a mix of fear and fury. 'Not a very brotherly welcome I must say, but one that might be expected of naught but a Flemish dog!'

Peredur put Rhianon safely behind him and, as she

stood composed now at his shoulder, he eyed his brother. As he did so, he cast his mind about him, assessing the situation with the experience of old. 'I could say the same of you, Maelgwn.'

But an icy feeling of dread was sliding down his spine and his heart beat harder than it had ever beaten before. Four men against one were unfavourable odds at the best of times, but now they were almost impossible. How could he fight them all and protect Rhianon at the same time?

Maelgwn, with renewed bravado, took a step forward, his fine nostrils flaring as if he'd assessed the odds too and already scented victory. 'But, welcome or not, your appearance is indeed timely…*brother*!'

'More timely than you think,' Peredur replied, his tone deadly calm despite the knowledge that there was very little chance he'd get out of this alive. 'I have just returned from Llanbadarn.'

A swift flash of uncertainty crossed Maelgwn's face and then his mouth thinned, ugly now, not beautiful. 'And how is our dear father?'

'Much improved and a lot wiser now than he was when you left him.'

His brother laughed but it was a forced sound. The green eyes wavered and then moved to Rhianon, standing quietly at his side.

And it was that look, the way it lingered and narrowed with lust, even now, that made Peredur afraid. If he died here today and Ceredigion was lost…that would be disaster enough. But if he died and Maelgwn took Rhianon—the bride he'd wanted all along, and clearly still wanted…

Dipping his head, Peredur kissed Rhianon briefly,

savagely, on the mouth, refusing to think the thought that it might be the last kiss of all. 'Go inside the gates,' he said.

'No, I am staying here—'

He shook his head. This was one time when he had to make her listen and obey. 'Do as I ask, Rhianon.'

Her eyes searched his, desperately, fearfully, her hand trembling as it rested a moment over his heart. Then, with a nod, she turned and walked to the gates of the mill house.

Peredur watched her go, his heart following her every step. Maelgwn had watched Rhianon walk away too and, in his green eyes, lust and fear and malevolence became one.

'Your wife is even tastier now than when I kissed her at your wedding feast, brother. Truly a delicious morsel, deserving of a *real* man.'

The remark, meant to incite, did exactly that, though not in the way Maelgwn had doubtless intended. The odds made no difference now, impossible or not. He had to beat those odds and stay alive for Rhianon. He *would* beat them because that was what it would take to keep her safe.

Unclasping his cloak, Peredur flung it to the side of the road. 'A kiss that was both uninvited and insulting,' he said, as coolly as the fire in his blood allowed. 'And an impertinence that has been awaiting a redress too long already.'

At the moment, the miller appeared, silently, at his side and Peredur, still with one eye on his brother, turned sharply to meet him, his sword levelled.

'You have arrived in the nick of time, my lord,' Hywel said, grimly but not lifting his sword in return.

'My son and I had begun to fear we'd have to defend your lady by ourselves.'

Peredur stared at him but there was nothing in the man's words, or in his face, to suggest treachery. Had he been wrong about the miller all along? Perhaps…the ice over his heart thawed a little, but even so, the less blood spilled here today the better. It was enough that Hywel wasn't against him, for that evened the ground a little.

'Then you have my gratitude, Hywel, but this is between me and my brother now.'

The miller nodded and moved back. Maelgwn's face went whiter still as the meaning of the words hit home. For a long moment, nobody moved or made a sound. In the silent calm before the storm, Peredur glanced beyond to the men-at-arms behind him, none of whom met his eyes, and just like that, he felt the balance shift.

One against three—as it had unexpectedly turned out—were still poor odds. But one against one were the fairest odds of all.

It was Maelgwn who finally broke the silence. 'Are you challenging me to a fight… *Fleming*?'

There was a sneer on his brother's mouth but behind his words, fear sounded. Even his charm wouldn't save him now and Maelgwn knew it.

Peredur pulled the gauntlet from his right hand—one of the pair Rhianon had given him—and threw it down on the ground.

'Let us have this out between us two alone,' he announced, loud and clear, so that everyone watching would hear. 'Let us finish this once and for all, Maelgwn, man to man, brother to brother. After all, we both know it is long overdue.'

* * *

Inside the mill gates, Rhianon was gathered into Elen Felin Ddŵr's arms as if she was one of her own brood. She let herself be gathered, heedful of only what was happening outside the gates, as Peredur's dreadful challenge filled her ears.

For a moment, Maelgwn didn't move. His eyes slid to one side then the other, his body braced as if unsure whether to stand or run. And then, slowly and with visible reluctance, his drew his weapon. Peredur lifted his sword and squared up, leaving his brother no option now but to face his wrath.

And wrath it was, and more. As the two men engaged, Rhianon's heart shuddered and slowed down, weighted so heavily with the horror that unfolded that it hardly seemed to beat at all.

For this was nothing like that day she'd watched Peredur mock fight with Guto Bren on the training ground. This was brutal, punishing and relentless, without quarter and without pity.

The first flashing arc of steel was blinding in the sunlight, the clash of his blade upon Maelgwn's ringing loud, silencing everything else. There was deadly intent in every movement of foot and hand, his whole being bent on vanquishing his opponent or else dying in the attempt.

Rhianon had never seen that look on Peredur's face, never even imagined he *could* look as he did now, for all his warrior reputation. Even though Maelgwn wore gambeson and mail, and Peredur himself was without armour, it made no difference. He had gone somewhere both inside and outside of himself, oblivious of everything else around him—even her—as he set about the work of killing.

Maelgwn was a skilled enough swordsman but he was no match for his brother. Almost before the contest had begun, he was on the back foot, defending instead of attacking, parrying the blows of Peredur's sword but returning hardly any of his own.

Sweat began to stream down his face, his mouth was agape, his gasping for breath becoming loud and awful to hear. Slowly but surely, he was forced to retreat, stumbling as the force of his brother's attack sent him off balance.

Peredur's blade caught Maelgwn's cheek and a line of red blood opened. He staggered backwards into his mounted men, causing them to scatter to either side of the road.

And each time he fell, each time his sword drooped in his hand, Peredur stood back and waited, his body poised and his countenance without mercy, for him to rise again, which Maelgwn did, slower and more unwillingly each time.

Rhianon's heart began to beat fast again and her stomach churned sickeningly. Tears of pity rose up behind her eyes, for her husband clearly meant this to be a fight to the death.

Finally Maelgwn fell to his knees, exhausted, the slash of Peredur's weapon shearing his in two. The severed half veered across the road and into grass at the verge. This time, he made no attempt to rise. He simply waited, the broken hilt slack between his fingers, the blood from the wound in his cheek trickling into his mouth.

Peredur's sword arced and glinted and Rhianon cried

out. She flung her hands wide in entreaty as its point went to his brother's throat. 'No!'

The blade held without even a quiver. For a long moment, the only sound was Maelgwn's agonising panting breaths. He half lay on the ground at Peredur's feet, his face ashen, his eyes wide and afraid as he faced certain death.

And then, as the echo of her cry faded, the sword point lowered. Peredur stooped and, taking hold of his brother's collar, hauled him to his feet. 'Now, tell me, without guile or lies, what mischief you have caused in Gwynedd.'

He was breathless too but his words were steady, his demand brooking no refusal. Maelgwn's answer came instantly, through trembling lips, low and barely audible.

'N-none. Owain Gwynedd…has no interest…or intent…of attacking Ceredigion. He is preparing his forces…to meet a campaign by the King.'

'So, Owain sent you back from whence you came with your tail between your legs!' Even from where she stood, Rhianon heard the contempt and the relief in her husband's voice. 'A wise prince indeed.'

His next question was as punishing as his sword had been. 'Was it *you* who ordered the murder of the castle garrison?'

Maelgwn nodded, seemingly lacking the strength to speak, or else the will to speak of a deed too treacherous for words.

'*Grist annwyl*!' Peredur's tone rang with disgust. 'Why, in God's name, did *they* have to die?'

'Because the fewer men you had here…the better for my plans.'

'How was it done?' His fingers clenched tighter in Maelgwn's collar. 'And by whom?'

His brother's head jerked towards the men behind him, each of whom shifted uncomfortably in their saddles. 'By night…and with stealth.'

'The garrison allowed you entry into the castle?'

Some of Maelgwn's arrogance returned. 'Why would they refuse entry to a son of Eilyr, the Lord Rhys's loyal man, who requested shelter for the night?'

'And then…?'

'Then, when they'd retired to their beds, we took them, one by one. It was easy, though the man at the gate put up a fight—futile, of course.'

There was a taut silence and Rhianon began to pray that that was it, and that her husband's tortuous questioning was done. Despite everything, even she began to feel compassion for the wretched, broken man that hung from Peredur's fingers like a rat in the jaws of a wolf.

'And the bonfires?' Peredur asked, showing no mercy. 'Was that your doing too?'

Maelgwn's dark head sank low again, his arrogance dimming. 'Signals… I hoped to persuade the Prince of Powys to join me at Pennal…he didn't come.'

'So you went to his court at Tafolwern and got the same response as you did at Pennal?'

'Yes.'

There was a stunned silence and then Peredur dropped his brother to the ground, shaking his head in disbelief. 'You have had a lucky escape this time—which is far more than you deserve. I will leave it to our father and the Lord Rhys now to decide what to do with you.'

Then he squatted down and, taking hold of Maelgwn's chin, forced his face up to his. 'But if you ever touch my wife again, I *will* kill you…*brother*!'

Then, rising swiftly to his feet, he glared at the two men-at-arms. As one, and without a word being uttered, they sheathed their weapons. Their demeanour now was one of fear for their *own* skins, complicit as they were in treachery and in cold-blooded murder.

'Escort my brother back to Llanbadarn,' Peredur said curtly, turning his back on Maelgwn, as if for ever. 'And there you also may throw yourselves on the mercy of the Lord Rhys.'

The soldiers dismounted and aided their leader up onto his horse. Maelgwn's head was bowed, his face hidden, his charming tongue silent now. Then the group moved slowly off, the miller's dog running out and barking at their horses' heels, as if to send them on their way.

Then Peredur marched straight over to Hywel Felin Ddŵr. 'Did you know about this conspiracy? Or the murder of the garrison?'

The miller shook his head. 'No, my lord, I didn't. Although I suspected that Lord Maelgwn had a hand in the dispatching of those men. This last week wasn't the first time he's ridden past my house at night.'

'Yet you kept silent about it?'

Hywel shrugged. 'How was I to know it wasn't a case of brothers in arms? That you were not equally treacherous? All I knew of you was what I'd heard about you.'

The miller's words echoed those she herself had said to Peredur on their wedding night. And, as they hung on the air, Rhianon finally knew them for what they were—words that had no basis in truth or reality, born only of ignorance and fear.

'Then I trust now you know differently?' her husband said next.

The miller nodded and the hint of a smile twisted the scar on his cheek, though not mockingly as it had before. 'I am beginning to know it, my lord.'

Peredur looked down at the broadsword in Hywel's hand, its point resting on the ground. 'That is a fine weapon,' he said, conciliation in his tone, meeting the miller halfway. 'It might prove quite valuable in the service of the Lord Rhys.'

'It might at that, my lord.'

Then, finally, her husband held out his arm, a gesture of friendship, and more. After a slight hesitation, the miller grasped it. 'Then come to the castle tomorrow, Hywel, and we will talk more.'

At a nod and a word from his father, Hywel Fychan ran and, catching Tarth, led the stallion up. 'Your horse, my lord,' the boy said, with a little bow.

Taking the reins, Peredur nodded his thanks, and then sheathed his sword. Another boy—Idwal, was it?—ran out through the gate and, retrieving her husband's cloak from where it still lay in the dirt, held it out.

'Your cloak, my lord.'

Peredur stared down at the boy for a moment. Then he smiled and clapped a hand on the thin shoulder. 'My thanks, *fy ngwas i*.'

And, suddenly, with that smile, that gesture, those words, it was all over. The miller lifted a hand in salute and, with his children at his heels, disappeared into the house, the dog too, its tail wagging as if for a job well done.

Only Elen and Esyllt remained. The former, releasing Rhianon from within her arms at last, dropped a curtsey, as if suddenly remembering the difference in their status. But her eyes, as green and as cunning as her daughter's were, twinkled merrily.

'I'll send some of my oatcakes up with my husband tomorrow, my lady. Your uncle enjoyed them very much.'

Rhianon, still dazed, murmured her thanks and then started as Esyllt gave her arm a confiding little squeeze. 'Do you wish me to return to the castle with you, *meistres*?'

She shook her head. 'No, there is no need today, come tomorrow.'

Her maid skipped into the house behind her mother, where no doubt, much excited talk was about to commence. And then there was only the running of the river and the turning of the waterwheel, with nothing but scuffles on the ground to show that anything at all had happened in the place.

Peredur hadn't looked in her direction once and he didn't now. Instead, he stooped to pick up the gauntlet he'd thrown down, an eternity before, it seemed. He stared at it for a long moment, his mouth a thin line, and then his fingers curled tightly over it.

His head lifted and his eyes met hers. Tucking the gauntlet into his belt, he held out his hand. With the mill folk indoors, only she saw how that hand shook, not just with the aftershock of brutal conflict, but with the culmination of a lifetime of bitter enmity, surely ended here now, once and for all.

And then he said, quietly, 'Come.'

Rhianon longed to fly to him but she walked, slowly and steadily. Halting, she took his hand and a look passed between them, a look that reached right down inside her. Then he pulled her into his arms and held her tightly to him.

His entire body shook, she realised, as she pressed herself close, letting all the violence of what had just happened flow from him to her, embracing his emotions so that they might be hers too, sharing the burden of the pain she knew he must feel, even though what he'd done had been necessary, inevitable.

They stood for a long time without speaking and then, at last, his trembling ceased. And all at once, it was as if time, frozen for an interim, started moving forward again.

'Let us go home,' he said, pressing his lips to her hair.

She nodded. 'Yes, let us go home.'

Peredur lifted her up into the saddle and then mounted behind her, settling her against him. And his arm safely around her waist, as he'd done when they'd ridden from the church of Llanbadarn, they turned homeward.

Rhianon glanced down as they passed by the little clay pot of wimberry she'd dropped. It was smashed to pieces, its sweet red contents mashed into the dirt along with Maelgwn's blood. And as they made their way leisurely along the road to the castle, just as the sun passed its zenith in the sky above, she remembered.

The sun was a glowing ball of fire on the horizon when, that evening, Rhianon sought her husband on the battlements. She hadn't seen him all afternoon since, after a late and hurried dinner, he'd sat with Meirchion to write urgent letters. One to Owain Gwynedd and another to the Prince of Powys, in the name of the Lord Rhys, explaining that Maelgwn's treachery was his alone, and would be condemned and duly punished by his overlord.

Now, going to stand beside him, she looked out as he did towards the northern shore. Neither spoke for a while. The water was dappled gold and the sunset bathed the snow-capped mountains in crimson, making Gwynedd seem not just a different kingdom, but another world entirely.

A world from which no threat would come—not for now, at least.

'Everything is so quiet now the *morloi* have gone,' she said, breaking the silence at last. 'Do they always go like that, suddenly, as one entity?'

'I don't know,' he said, not looking at her. 'I have not been here before at this time to witness it.'

Rhianon drew a breath, drawing the silence into her lungs. 'Their noise stopped my ears, made it difficult to hear my own thoughts at times,' she said, feeling her way into a conversation that had to be had. 'And yet it seems strange without them, lonely somehow.'

Peredur's hand found hers, his fingers locking as if he too was feeling his way, tentatively yet hopefully. 'They will be back again next winter.'

Next winter. It seemed an age away, the long months ahead as endless as *this* winter had seemed to her on the day they'd set out from Llanbadarn. Then, she'd wondered what her life with Peredur would be like, whether she'd discover his heart, or find out that he really didn't possess one.

Rhianon turned and looked at him. The last rays of the sun glanced off his golden hair though his face in profile was sombre, his eyes narrowing against the glare on the water. All at once, a rush of overwhelming love flooded through her, deeper even than the sea that surrounded them.

Yes, he had a heart, she knew that now without a doubt. A heart that was full of courage and compassion and honour—yet could it hold even more?

'How did you find your father?' she asked, since she'd had no opportunity to do so before, and because she didn't know how to begin to broach that other question.

'Impatient to be out of his convalescent bed!' His features softened. 'The physician told me he is improving daily.'

'And how did he take the news about Maelgwn's treachery?'

There was pause. 'With sadness.'

Rhianon paused a moment too, and then she voiced what had been burning on her tongue ever since they'd left the mill. 'Would you have killed Maelgwn today?'

He shook his head, his gaze still on the shore opposite, where tonight no bonfires burned. 'No. Killing in battle is one thing but killing a man in cold blood is another thing entirely.'

'Yet it wouldn't have been in cold blood,' she said. 'It *was* a battle and he'd accepted your challenge. He would have killed *you* without hesitation.'

Peredur turned to meet her gaze then. 'I know,' he said, with chilling simplicity.

How had she ever thought his eyes to be ice-like, as cold as a stormy sky? Now, even though his face was turned away from sunset, they burned brighter than any sun ever could.

'What punishment do you think he will face?' Rhianon asked, still skirting around what she really wanted to ask. The little jar of red wimberry might be crushed into the ground, no longer required, but there was still something else that needed to be resolved, now, tonight.

A grim smile touched his mouth and a muscle moved in his cheek. 'None, since I suspect he will not have returned to Llanbadarn to answer for his treachery, but will have fled, his men too.'

'Fled?' she repeated, the idea of that not occurring to her before, though what else could Maelgwn and his henchmen have done? 'But where to?'

'Ireland, mayhap, or to one of the Marcher lands, perhaps even into England. As far out of the reach of the Lord Rhys as is possible, anyway.'

'Did you know he would run when you let him go, even though he is guilty of treason and of murder?'

He nodded and his shoulders lifted in a heavy sigh. 'For all his faults—and they are many—Maelgwn is still my brother. It is for a higher power to judge him now, not I.'

'But he's not your brother in blood.'

'Does that matter?'

Rhianon shook her head. 'No. My own family are proof that blood ties do not necessary mean there is compassion or kindness...or love.'

She laced her fingers tighter in his, anchoring herself to ask something else that had simmered uncomfortably below her skin for too long. 'And would you have killed Letard, as you said, that night we sat late at table?'

Peredur's face grew sober still. 'Thanks to Anarawd ap Gruffudd, that is something I'll never know.'

Then, turning fully to face her, he took both her hands in his. 'Today could have gone so very differently, Rhianon. You could have been hurt, killed...if I'd been defeated, my brother would have taken you as his.'

'But I wasn't, and he didn't,' she said, although her flesh shuddered at the thought of it. 'Everything ended well.'

He nodded but his eyes clouded as the dusk encroached and enveloped them and a cool breeze lifted from the water below. 'I would have given my life to keep you safe, Rhianon, and I will always.'

'I know,' Rhianon said, her love flowing deeply in the confines of her heart, as surely as that water flowed into the sea. A pair of curlew passed low overhead, their haunting, bubbling call sending a thrill down her spine, as if daring her to speak as loudly as they did.

And, as they disappeared, she finally found the courage to ask. 'But do you…*desire* me, Peredur?'

His eyes flew wide. 'Desire you? *Dduw trugarog*, Rhianon. I *love* you!'

Her heart jerked against her ribs and the breath left her body in a rush. 'You…you love me?'

'Do you doubt it?' he asked, drawing her close into the warmth of him. '*Can* you doubt it after these last two nights we have lain together?'

Rhianon searched his eyes. But they hadn't lain *together*, had they? They'd lain *next* to each other, albeit in each other's arms. He'd given her so much yet he'd left her strangely bereft, lacking something she didn't know how to express.

Yesterday, when she'd almost hurled the jar of wimberry at the wall, it had expressed itself in anger. But it wasn't anger she felt now. That had gone when the little jar had fallen and smashed on the ground. Now she was left only with a keen and inexpressible yearning.

'Yet, these last two nights…despite…' she began and then stopped, turning her head away, as the embarrassment and humiliation came washing back, like the evening tide that had begun to lap at the shore.

His hand lifted, cupped her cheek, and he turned her face back towards him. 'Rhianon…you are the most desirable woman I have ever known. You are the only woman I have ever loved.'

Dipping his head, he kissed her, softly at first and then, with a sharp intake of breath and a jolt of his body, with all the intent she'd witnessed him wield his sword earlier that day.

'I love you too, Peredur,' she breathed, through their kiss. 'I love you so very much.'

The sun sank into the sea, disappearing from sight, leaving only a thin line of gold on the horizon to the west. In its wake, embarrassment and humiliation sank too and vanished, as if they'd never been, leaving only love behind.

Leaning back against the parapet wall, Rhianon brought him with her and wound her arms around his neck. Threading her fingers into the golden hair, she drew his head down so that his kiss went deeper still and his body grew hard against hers.

Surely now there was no doubt, as he said? Surely this *was* desire and love, all come together at last? Never now to be doubted, or vanquished, but destined to grow so strong, so steadfast, that nothing could come between them again.

The voice of the watch announcing the hour for supper broke through the moment. The echoing cry of an owl somewhere overhead answered him through the twilight. The waves lapped closer to the shore, rippling quietly like an echo of her longings.

Peredur's head lifted and he stared down at her, his

eyes gleaming, his chest heaving. Rhianon too was gasping for breath, her breasts aching, her belly warm and heavy.

'We…should go down to supper…' he said, his words trailing into reluctance.

Rhianon shook her head, equally reluctant. 'I'm not hungry.'

She saw the swallow of his throat, the flash of scarlet along his cheekbones, the darkening of his eyes as he nodded, slowly. 'Nor am I, *f'anwylyd.*'

My beloved! A surge of hope filled her as the endearment—the first he'd ever uttered—sounded in her ears. It drowned out owl and curlew, the rattle of water on sand and pebble. It was still echoing, in her heart not just in her ears, as, hand in hand, they descended the steps and made for their bedchamber.

Chapter Sixteen

The sounds of supper hadn't yet died away and the hall below was still lively. The moon was high, sending a shaft of silver in through a gap in the shutter at the window. The sound of men singing, harsh and unmusical, drifted upwards through the boards in the floor.

The quivering of Rhianon's body hadn't died away either, when Peredur stretched out a hand to douse the candle, then drew her towards him and, with a kiss on her mouth, settled her into the curve of his body.

She stared into the darkness, listening to his uneven breathing, feeling the thundering of his heart beneath the palm that she pressed to his chest. This night had been a repeat of the two other nights they'd shared this bed. This night too he'd touched her and kissed her, aroused her and incited her, given her indescribable pleasure.

And yet, he had still not taken his own pleasure, still not taken *her*.

Leaning her forehead into the hollow of his shoulder, Rhianon bit her lip in frustration. How could a man—a husband—restrain himself so? And why? *Why?* What was so wrong with Peredur that he didn't want her? Or rather…what was so wrong with *her*?

She cleared her throat and, frustration turning to foreboding, lifted her head. 'Light the candle again, Peredur.'

He shifted and she sensed his eyes—which she knew hadn't been shut any more than hers had been—look down at her. 'Is something amiss?'

Rhianon nodded. 'Yes.'

There was a pause and then he got out of bed. Taking up the candle, not yet cold in the oil, he passed through the curtain to light it from the fire. A moment later, he returned, the candlelight illuminating the astonishment on his face when he saw her standing there at the side of the bed, naked.

'Rhianon?' He put the candle down on the table and some of the oil spilled and seeped into the wood. 'What is wrong?'

Rhianon steeled her limbs not to tremble, her voice not to shake as she spoke what she must. 'You said, aloft on the battlements, that you desired me.'

Peredur nodded, his gaze bemused as he pulled the curtain across again. 'Yes, I did.'

'And you also said that you…loved me.'

He nodded again, his features softening as he turned back towards her. 'Yes… I do. I love you very much, Rhianon.'

Rhianon drew a deep breath, anguish filling her throat as she witnessed on his face the truth of his words, yet heard below them the ring of evasion.

'Then why will you not bed me?' she asked, her anguish even louder now than the singing below. 'Properly, as a husband should?'

* * *

Peredur stared at Rhianon. The flame from the candle flickered over her lovely form, lighting on the swell of her breasts and belly, the curve of her hips. Her gaze was bright and dark at the same time, the gentian hue like midnight as it held his.

She was so beautiful and so desirable that his body, still strung taut from what had taken place earlier, pulled tighter still. And the perplexity on her face, the hurt in her accusation, tore at his heart until he thought it would burst out through his ribs.

Taking a step towards her, he reached out his hand, touched her cheek where the flush of passion still glowed. But she shook her head, causing his hand to drop away.

'No! I don't want you to touch me.' Her eyes flashed. 'I want you to tell me what is…so *wrong* with me that you will not make me your wife proper?'

Peredur felt the blood leave his face. 'Wrong with you? *Dduw annwyl*, Rhianon, there is *nothing* wrong with you. You are…perfection.'

'Then why don't you *want* me?'

He drew a deep breath and, reaching out, took her hand in his. Sitting down on the bed, he drew her to sit beside him, her nakedness dancing tantalisingly before his eyes and the scent of her stirring his senses.

'*Why*, Peredur?' she asked again. 'If you find me desirable as you claim, if you love me as you say you do, then you *must* tell me!'

Peredur looked down to where her wedding ring glinted on her finger. The token of marriage and the pledge he'd made at the altar a month ago. No, less. It hadn't even been a month yet it felt like a lifetime of sheer purgatory.

And it was *he* himself who had made their marriage a purgatory, he alone. 'Rhianon, I love you more than I thought I could ever love. I've never *known* this sort of love, before you,' he said, meeting her eyes again. 'You must know that?'

Her gaze softened, searched his deeply. 'I think I know it…and I love you too, Peredur, very much. But then, if we both love…what is it that still lies between us?'

Peredur swallowed as the words he'd never expected to hear from her, never looked for, struck his heart like a fatal blow. How *could* she love a man—a half-man—like him? But she did, he saw it in the stark honesty on her face, and that only made the words even more difficult to say.

'It is *because* I love you that I cannot bed you, Rhianon.'

Her hand grew cold in his and she drew in a sharp breath. 'I don't understand.'

'But I told you, the night Edwin came with the news of my father's accident.'

She frowned. 'You spoke of what happened at Pebidiog, when Letard was killed, yes, I remember.'

Peredur nodded. 'I also spoke of…something else.'

'That your grandmother took you in only because Letard paid her to raise you as his son.'

'Do you not recall what I said the night before I rode for Llanbadarn?'

Her frown creased deeper. 'You told me she hated you so much that she urged Anarawd to kill you. But… as wicked and unforgivable as that is…what does it have to do with us, now?'

A surge of desperation rose up into his throat. 'I see that you missed the meaning altogether, Rhianon.'

'What meaning?' Her fingers gripped his. 'For God's sake, Peredur! What meaning?'

'It is simple.' Peredur hesitated. It *should* be simple but suddenly it was not. 'My mother died when I was born...*because* I was born.'

She shook her head 'Yes, I know. You said that to me too.' Instead of abating, the confusion in her eyes increased. 'But...'

Unable to look into those eyes any longer, he leapt to his feet, crossed to the curtain and fisted his fingers in its folds. 'I have known other women die in child-birth, Rhianon,' he said, 'Eilyr's first wife among them.'

Peredur ran the fingers of his other hand through his hair, wiped away the sweat that broke out on his brow. '*Grist annwyl*, even Tarth's dam died birthing him, her blood pouring out of her, all over my hands as I pulled him from her womb, her agony too terrible to bear!' His voice broke. 'Therefore... I must not... I *will* not...'

Rhianon finished his words, quietly but with a dawning comprehension that was dreadful to hear. 'You will not bed me in case I die in childbirth too?'

He nodded, stared at his hand, the knuckles gone white where they clutched the curtain so tightly. Neither he nor Rhianon moved nor seemed even to breathe, only the singing from the hall, the lustful, bawdy soldiers' song filling the awful silence, fittingly ironic.

Then, just when it seemed the tension must snap, she spoke again, low and strangely without inflection. 'You haven't asked me why I was at the mill today... when Maelgwn came.'

Peredur half turned his head, astonishment eclips-

ing everything and nothing making sense any more. He
shivered, not because of the cold, but at the thought of
the danger she'd been in, at what might have happened
had he not defeated Maelgwn.

'Why *were* you there?' he asked, grasping at the
abrupt and perplexing change of topic, relieved at it,
and yet knowing it couldn't be left just like that. There
would be more to ask, more to answer, more to deny.
This was only an interlude, just as the merriment downstairs ceased momentarily, doubtless for a replenish-
ing of cups and moistening of dry and thirsty throats.

'I went to return something to Elen Felin Ddŵr. A
jar of red wimberry.'

Peredur relinquished the curtain and turned around
to fully face her, the explanation so strange that, for a
moment, he doubted he'd heard right. 'A jar of wimberry?'

She nodded, her raven hair catching the candlelight.
'The *red* wimberry. Elen takes it to prevent a babe coming. I intended to take it for the same reason. But then
it became clear to me, the morning you left, that there
would be no need to take it.'

He stared at Rhianon, her words, bluntly said, piercing
him like a knife all the same. Remorse filled his throat
and poured into his mouth until he felt it would choke
him. 'I cannot put you at such risk. If anything happened, Rhianon, if you conceived…and then if you….'

Peredur took a step towards her, and then stopped.
How could he go to her now? Touch her? Kiss her?
Hold her tight and lie in that bed with her after what
he'd just told her?

'I'm sorry,' he said, the futility of the excuse damning his ears and his heart cringing with the shame of it.

'Now it is *you* who have missed the meaning.' A little smile touched her mouth and then was gone as her gaze became grave again. 'I was angry this morning, when I went to take the wimberry back. You weren't here and I felt unwanted, rejected…hurt.'

The revelry started up again downstairs but her words came louder, despite the softness of tone. 'It was too quiet, my head so free of sound that suddenly I was able to think but too clearly, hear my thoughts but too loudly, and yet I couldn't understand what I was *feeling*.'

Peredur shook his head. 'I don't understand either, Rhianon.'

'Then I'll explain it to you.'

She got to her feet and came towards him, her movements graceful and her face radiant, in the candlelight. 'I had planned to take the wimberry because *I* was afraid too, Peredur. I feared that, if I had children, I might not be able to protect them from harm, from brutality, from violence, as my mother failed to protect me and my brothers.'

Peredur's gut twisted. 'Because you feared I might be exactly like your father?'

She nodded. 'When we were first wed, how could I know that you were *not*, since I only knew what I had heard about you? And, if you *had* been so, how could I have borne to see my children suffer? How could I have stood apart, helpless with fear, as my mother did, and then live with my shame?'

Her hand lifted and she pressed her palm to the right side of his chest, the contact—light though it was—striking him deep. 'Then, at the ford, when you showed me where your heart lay… I began to see the truth—to see *you*—and I know full well now the sort of man you are.'

Peredur felt his heart leap beneath her palm. 'Then you know, also, that I never could, never would, hurt you, nor anyone, man, woman or child.'

A shadow flickered in her eyes, a veil of hurt dimming the radiance of her face. 'Yes, I know it…but what does that matter now, if we are to *have* no children?'

Her words seemed to flay the skin from his bones. 'We have one another, Rhianon.'

She shook her head. 'It's not enough.'

'It is for me,' he said, but even as he said it, he knew it wasn't true. And so did Rhianon.

'Is it? I don't believe that.' She traced a fingertip along the scar on his chest. 'I believe that in your heart, in your soul, you want what I want.'

As her palm smoothed down over his stomach, Peredur drew a breath, inhaling the essence of her deep into his lungs. 'Any man would want you, Rhianon,' he said, for that at least was the truth. 'I *want* you…but I've just told you why that is impossible.'

Her fingers were following his ribs now, a light tickle that made his flesh quiver. 'I believe you have the same lusts, the same needs, the same passion as any other man, Peredur.'

Her gaze dropped to his loins, where his manhood visibly betrayed him, despite all his efforts to subdue those needs that she saw all too clearly.

'That you master them where another man would not, that you give pleasure selflessly yet take none for yourself, is rare and commendable,' she said. 'But in the end, it will count for naught, because it can only be destructive. It might even break both our hearts.'

Her eyes lifted to his again, burning with an intensity that was every bit as urgent, every bit as prophetic, as her words. 'You see, I returned the wimberry because I *want* a babe, Peredur. I want *your* babe.'

Her hand on his stomach pressed hard, as if she meant to drive her words deep into his bowels, into his soul. 'Do you not see that, by denying yourself, and me also, you are denying us the family we never had?'

In the light of the candle, burning low now, Rhianon saw the blood drain from Peredur's face. He began to tremble, as if her words, the words she'd had to say, had been hammer blows on his body.

But still he didn't reach for her, didn't respond, even though the need that she'd accused him of denying was evident in every line of his body. Visible, undeniable, yet determined to prove her wrong.

And she knew she had to prove *him* wrong, now, this very night, before his resolve, seemingly stronger even than his needs, defeated her. Her heart racing, she stepped closer, moved her hand lower and curled her fingers over the waistband of his braies.

'And also, do you not know, Peredur, that you are denying us both the chance to love our children as we were never loved when *we* were children?'

Rhianon went up on her toes and kissed his mouth. His lips were cold so she pressed her own hard upon them, willing her warmth, her desire, her love into him. His hands closed about her upper arms and, although his mouth yielded a little, still she felt the restraint, the holding back of the passion she longed to release in him.

Slowly, she uncurled her fingers and, smoothing her hand downwards, she pressed her palm over his manhood, hard and erect below the linen. The convulsive shudder he gave made her totter on her tiptoes and she felt his fingers tighten on her arms.

And then, steady once more but her heart anything but, she whispered softly through her kiss. 'Take your braies off, Peredur…come back to bed and make me your wife.'

His head jerked back and his eyes blazed down into hers. He shook his head savagely, as if an insurmountable struggle was raging inside him. A battle of restraint, a war with himself that he seemed determined to wage—and to win.

Rhianon swallowed as she realised how much she was asking…demanding…of him. And how much she was willing to give him in return. Everything and all that she was.

'I am your wife, Peredur,' she said, curling her hand tighter around him, pressing herself closer, praying that this would be the one battle he would lose. 'I love you, I desire you, and I want you. Can you not love and desire and want me too? Can you not let go of your fear as I have done?'

There was a beat of silence, an instant of utter stillness, and then, with an inarticulate sound, Peredur stopped trembling. Then he was threading his fingers through her hair, kissing her ardently, hungrily, and backing her towards the bed.

As she fell into the furs, Rhianon's fingers worked at the ties of his braies. And when he came down beside her, the linen was finally gone. She clasped him to her and hooked her leg over his hip, ready for him, willing and longing to take him inside herself. His naked manhood was hard and urgent, and digging her fingers into his flanks she opened up her whole self to receive him.

But abruptly, he drew back, his breath hot on her face, his eyes stormier than she'd never seen them before. And, deep inside them, she saw that the battle was still raging.

'Rhianon….'

She placed a palm over his lips. 'Don't speak.'

If he did, she might lose this precarious piece of ground she'd won and be forced to retreat before the strength of his will. She might never again have the advantage over him that she'd gained this night, one that had taken him—and her too—by surprise.

Too quickly for him to react, she pushed him onto his back with a strength that astonished her. Lifting herself up, she straddled his hips, trapping him between her legs but resisting the instinctive and overpowering urge to take him inside her at once. Instead, placing her hands on his shoulders, she stilled for a moment and looked down into his face.

'Stop fighting, Peredur, and, just this once, let yourself be vanquished.'

The light from the candle fell over his chest, turning his skin to bronze, picking out muscle, shadowing the hollows at his throat where a pulse beat erratically.

'I cannot…'

But in the taut and powerful body beneath her, Rhianon felt his response, felt him begin to yield, to accept a defeat that was rather a victory, for him, for her.

'Yes…you can.'

Hardly daring to hope, she leaned forward, letting her hair cascade down upon him, the groan he gave sending a thrill of excitement through her. His hands closed about her waist and his eyes locked intently on hers, dark and fever bright with desire, just as she knew her own eyes to be.

'You can,' Rhianon repeated, softly, persuasively, as she watched his denial finally crumble. 'If you love me, then you can.'

Slowly moving her hips, she sensed her way, feeling him grow harder still beneath her. For a long moment, she did nothing else, just rocked gently, back and forth, leaning on his chest, their gazes holding in utter silence.

Then she touched her lips lightly to his, and breathed softly. 'Do you *truly* love me, Peredur?'

Against her mouth, he breathed back, a rasping sound of need. 'Yes, with all my heart.'

Rhianon's heart heaved in her breast, violently and with a growing certainty. 'And I love you, *fy ngŵr annwyl*, but I need you to *prove* you love me.'

Peredur shuddered, his whole body tensing as Rhianon levered herself up on her hands, lifted her hips, and took him slowly inside her. He gasped, as did she, her eyes never leaving his as she sank low, letting him fill her, welcoming him, closing her warmth around him.

For an instant he lay still, unable to move, the experience overwhelming him with its beauty, its wonder, its exquisite and utter sense of awe and gratitude and… freedom.

Rhianon enveloped him, not just with her body, but with her whole essence, her soul, her love. Peredur gasped again as, with a smile, she began to rock once more, gently, inciting and enticing, asking him to embrace and accept what she was giving him, and to give her what she asked in return.

His eyes filled and for a moment, he struggled to breath, to see, to think. All he could do was feel. And then, with a hoarse cry that tore from somewhere deep inside him, he embraced it, embraced her, finally and wholly.

Rolling them both over so that Rhianon was beneath him, he moved his hands from her waist and cupped her bottom, lifting her to him, so that he filled her deeper still, until he could fill her no more.

And, as he did, his fear left him, and only need and love remained. He buried his face into her neck, the scent of her skin swamping his senses, her hair tickling his face, hiding his tears as he finally surrendered all his control and handed mastery to her.

And she took it, as she took him, wrapping her arms tightly about him, entwining him with her legs, arching up to meet him and encasing him in a prison of utter and indescribable joy.

Peredur closed his eyes, tears seeping through his lashes and falling onto her neck, and fisted his hands in her hair. He murmured her name, in between broken words of love, kissing her throat, her lips, her breasts as he thrust into her, not needing to think.

There was no need for thought any more than there was a need for fear. His instincts guided him, her answering murmurs, her sighs, her movements guiding him too.

Her fingernails scored the flesh of his back, the sweat of his skin trickled into hers, as he moved ever harder, ever faster inside her. Pleasure built and engulfed him, engulfed them both, soaring to unbearable heights of feeling that seemed impossible to bear.

His body began to shudder and he groaned as fire

raged in his blood and consumed him. Rhianon's body quivered too, her moans filling his ears as she clung to him, possessing him as he possessed her.

Their bodies were joined together, not just in one part, but encompassing all parts—every pore of skin, every flow of blood, every gasping breath, deep into the marrow of their bones—never to be separated again.

And as his seed spilled deeply into her womb and his cry of release echoed her own, Peredur knew that, finally, truly and for ever, his heart too joined and beat with hers.

The thin shaft of sunlight through the shutter woke Peredur soon after dawn. A strange sort of silence, of eerie stillness, filled the air and immediately his senses sharpened, his ears pricked, his body tensed.

He listened for a long time and then all at once, with a jolt of dread, he knew what it was. It wasn't the slumberous time before the day began, nor the quiet before a storm, nor even the seasoned instinct that warns a warrior of unseen danger.

It wasn't even the new and wondrous sensation of a satiated body, freed after a lifetime of imprisonment. It was instead a dreadful sense of utter fear.

Peredur looked down at the woman in his arms. Rhianon lay sleeping still, her eyes still shut, her hair cascading down over her shoulders, and her hand, as always, pressed to his right breast.

The heart within him swelled with love, and in its wake fear flooded fast and cold, encasing him in an icy tomb. He shuddered and the languid warmth of his limbs, the drowsy state of his senses, vanished as if they'd never existed.

Rhianon must have felt his movement, for her eyes opened and found his, soft with sleep. *'Bore da.'*

Peredur lifted a hand and touched her cheek. *'Bore da.'*

He'd lost count of how many times they'd joined together during the night. But during one of those times, as he'd shed his tears and his innocence, and spilled his love deep inside her...surely a babe had been made.

She smiled and pressed herself closer. 'The morning has come very soon,' she murmured, her breath tickling his throat.

Peredur felt beads of sweat break out on his brow and trickle down his temple. Yes, the morning had come all too quickly, which wasn't surprising, since they had only lately succumbed to sleep, exhausted with lovemaking, and moments spent in quiet and soul-baring talk.

For a moment, he thought she'd drifted off into sleep again but then he felt her stiffen in his arms. Her eyes flew open and her head lifted sharply. 'Peredur...what's wrong?'

He looked down into her face and a rush of love almost eclipsed the fear. Fear that, an instant later, increased a hundredfold because of that love and dropped into the hollow of his gut.

Shaking his head, he kissed her lips, feeling his own tremble with anguish. 'Nothing is wrong, *f'anwylyd.'*

But she lifted herself up on one elbow, her palm slipping from its place over his heart, leaving his skin colder still. She frowned, her eyes raking his face keenly. 'Yes, there is.'

Peredur started to deny it but then stopped himself. He could try and hide his fear from her, for a year, the year after that—for ever, even but she would seek it out eventually, just as she'd sought his heart out.

Beneath the covers, he placed his palm over her belly, flat and warm, the skin soft, the life that may lie within impossible to discern. Yet it might be there already, it might grow, thrive for a while, bring hope and joy—and then…

He looked into her eyes, a vice closing around his throat. 'Rhianon, what if…?'

But he didn't need to ask it. She knew. Her hand came to cover his and she pressed it firmly to her belly. 'What if we have made a babe this night?'

Peredur nodded. 'It is possible…likely.'

She smiled, her eyes sparkling with joy. 'I know!'

His fear squeezed the breath from his lungs, the thought that those sparkling eyes might one day dim with pain, with sorrow, with unbearable loss. Rhianon saw his fear, he knew, for the joy faded from her face, and concern darkened the gentian eyes.

'Peredur, listen to me.' Her fingers curled over his. 'Yes, you are right in what you said. Some women do die in childbirth. But many do not.'

He stared at her, said nothing, the earnest conviction making him feel even more a coward before her courage, her faith, her love.

'Some men die in battle, many *do* die,' she went on. 'But others do not. They live instead and die old men in their beds.'

Peredur thought of her brother Rhodri, dead before his time, but the thought was fleeting, for she was speaking again, more urgently than ever.

'There will always be death, Peredur, but there will always be life too, long or short, peaceful or violent, we don't know. We must accept that some things are meant and we cannot change them.'

Her hand lifted to his cheek then, soft and tender. 'If it was meant that you mother died birthing you, then that cannot be changed, only accepted. But it wasn't meant that you should live in fear all your days after. That is not meant…it is a choice.'

Her eyes grew sombre still. 'It was cruel and it was wrong of your grandmother to make you believe yourself guilty of your mother's death. It was wicked and unforgivable of her to urge Anarawd to take your life in return. You were innocent, Peredur, you *are* innocent, no matter how she made you believe otherwise all these years.'

Peredur tried to speak then, but she stopped him. 'I have not finished yet,' she said.

After a pause, she went on.

'I understand your fear because I have also felt fear of the unknown, of what *might* happen. And because of my fear, I intended to prevent a babe coming, to avoid the pain *my* mother must have felt, until she stopped feeling at all.'

She shook her head.

'But that would have been wrong too, and wicked, since it would have robbed us of what is meant to be.'

Peredur gazed into her face, radiant once more as a beam of sunlight slanted in through the shutter and fell across the bed. All at once, his vision blurred, and he didn't even try to pretend it had anything to do with the sunlight. Rhianon's eyes had grown moist too, though her smile was wide, and lit his soul brighter than any sun ever could.

'*We* are meant to be, Peredur, and so are our babes. All will be well, I know it will, and so must you.'

Rhianon held her breath, all her words running out now at the look of awe on Peredur's face, the sheen of moisture in the once cold eyes. And then an overwhelming surge of joy, and hope, and love bubbled up inside her.

'I want to be the mother of your children, Peredur. I want to give you heirs of your blood, sons and daughters, as many as the miller has, even more perhaps, if God wills it so.'

She felt his palm grow warm again on her belly, where perhaps the first of those babes already lay.

'And I believe…no, I *know* that is what you want too,' she said. 'And so, since I may be with child already… can you believe that all will be well? Will you *choose* to believe, Peredur?'

Peredur looked at her for a long moment of silence, his face paler then she'd ever seen it, and his gaze— not icy or stormy, as she'd so often witnessed, but so turbulent that even the walls of the castle seemed to shake around her.

Rhianon took a deep breath and, when he still didn't speak, she pressed her lips to his heart, hidden below the scar but beating strongly. 'Has the *bwgan* stolen your tongue, husband?'

His body gave a tremendous shudder and then his hand went under her chin and he brought her face up to his. And even before he spoke, Rhianon saw the belief and the hope and the joy, all merged into one wonderful blaze of love in his eyes.

'No, *fy ngwraig annwyl*, my tongue is intact, as is

the whole of me…now. *You* have made me whole, Rhianon. And one day, I might even be able to become the husband you deserve.'

'You already are, *fy nghariad ŵr.*'

He touched her cheek tenderly. 'And I swear I will give you the family you never had, the love you were never shown, the life you deserve.'

'All the things we *both* deserve, Peredur.'

He smiled and, dipping his head, he took her mouth. Rhianon gave it willingly, as she'd given him everything. Her body responded like a flame to his kiss and, as she pressed herself closer, she felt him grow hard against her.

Bold now, she brushed her fingertips down his body, caressing the smooth bronzed flesh. Then, curling her palm over his manhood, she pushed her hips towards his. And, through the kiss that she never wanted to end, she teased him.

'Your brother, Maelgwn, told many tall tales of you the night of our wedding, Peredur, but he lied in one respect, that is evident.'

His eyes danced merrier than she'd ever seen them, with a joy she'd never thought she would witness in him. 'And what lie was that?'

'When he called you his virgin brother.'

Peredur grinned and gave a rueful shake of his head. 'That was one thing my brother *did* indeed speak true.'

Rhianon felt her mouth drop open, her eyes fly wide. 'But…no…surely not?'

'Surely yes,' he said, his gaze becoming serious again. 'How could it be otherwise, until now…until you.' His hand cupped her breast and made her senses start to quiver with anticipation. 'But he was definitely incorrect in something else that he said.'

'What?' she asked

'When he said my heart had been left in the ruins of the village of Pebidiog,'

He moved over her and she revelled in the weight of his body upon hers, the warmth of his skin, the feel of his flesh. She entwined her limbs with his as he shifted and entered her and her body closed tightly around him, welcoming him, bringing him home once more.

Peredur settled and then stilled, deep inside her, his gaze devouring her as his body was about to do. And in that moment of stillness, when their eyes held and the sun fell across the bed and bathed their forms, and their souls became moulded together once more, he truly showed her his heart.

'My heart wasn't left in Pebidiog at all. It is here, where it belongs—with you, Rhianon.'

Epilogue

Easter 1158

They came out of Capel Edwin, the new church at Ab-ereinion, into bright sunlight. Rhianon, with her babe in her arms, walked with Peredur across the grass to Ffynnon Non. It was a lovely spring afternoon and the holy well was full of water that sparkled like jewels.

Life sparkled too, these warm days, despite the threat of war that was gathering behind the mountains to the east. The King of England had subdued Owain Gwynedd last year—by truce after an ill-fated campaign, not through victory in battle—and soon it might be the turn of the Lord Rhys to bend the knee and kiss the royal hand.

Rhianon touched her lips to her daughter's golden head, refusing to think of a war that might or might not come. Better to live in this moment, in the joy of their child, born from a love that she knew would withstand any war and emerge victorious.

As if her daughter agreed, sleepy blue eyes opened, found hers, and the rosebud mouth twitched. And then, as the soft lashes fluttered closed again, Rhianon looked up at Peredur, her world bursting with love.

'It is fitting that my uncle baptised her Marared today, for your mother,' she said.

He smiled, handsomer than ever, his gaze brighter than the spring day. 'Thank you for our daughter,' he said, taking her hand and kissing her palm. 'Thank you for giving me a family.'

Rhianon smiled too. He hadn't shown it but, since he could no longer hide anything from her, she'd seen how his fear had lingered, grown with every month her belly had grown. And then, with the safe, even easy birth of their daughter three months since, she knew Peredur would never fear again—at least not any more than other men did when their wives approached their birthing time.

'Thank *you* for making me a mother,' she said, lifting her mouth for a kiss, and infusing a twinkle into her eyes. 'Though as I remember, I did have to *insist* on it rather strongly.'

Peredur pressed his lips to hers, his eyes twinkling too. 'And now that your lying-in time is over, will you insist again tonight?'

Rhianon giggled, a blush scorching her cheeks. She might well have been the one to abstain these last months of her lying-in, but it had been *her* turn to give pleasure, in ways that she was sure would shock even the miller's wife!

'I might indeed. After all, did I not tell you I wanted even more children than Elen Felin Ddŵr?'

'So you did.' His face was full of the love that she no longer needed to look for, any more than she did his heart. 'And I will do my utmost to surpass the miller in that respect.'

As if their jesting had reached his ears, Hywel Felin Ddŵr, at the head of his brood, called his farewell, his wife gathering the children who were running at games among the trees. Hywel had become Peredur's staunchest supporter during this last year, her husband's loyal ally now, not his enemy.

Peredur raised a hand in return and then dropped his arm around her shoulder, drawing her close. They stood in silence for a moment, in the sunshine, and looked at the wider family that had come together to make this day even sunnier.

In the shade of the church porch, Tangwystl was talking to Edwin, their heads close together, friends now instead of lovers. Beneath the leafy branches of an oak, Esyllt and Guto Bren stood in silence, hand in hand and very much the lovers.

Beside the boundary wall, where the graves of the murdered men of the garrison were flanked with bright spring flowers, her brother Llywelyn was talking earnestly to Eilyr ap Bleddyn, not about love at all, but doubtless about the King's rumoured campaign in Deheubarth.

Rhianon gave a little shiver as a cloud passed over the sun. Llywelyn was much changed. He was a warrior now, hard and ruthless, not pious and gentle as he'd once been. Even their father stood in awe, and in fear, of him.

Peredur's arm tightened and, as he so often did, he read her mind with accuracy. 'I'm glad to see your mother here today, Rhianon. We have Llywelyn to thank for that, I think.'

Rhianon banished the wisp of worry that had settled

briefly overhead. 'I suppose, like us all, Llywelyn must find his own path,' she said. 'I just pray it will not be too difficult a one.'

Peredur kissed the top of her head. 'In time, perhaps Llywelyn too will be able to unlearn his harsh childhood lessons and choose how his life will be, as *we* chose ours, Rhianon.'

At the moment, the miller's dog sped across the grass in pursuit of a blackbird that was close by, pecking for worms. The bird took to the wing, squawking alarm. The dog leapt high and almost caught it in his jaws but fell instead into the well with a splash.

The water wasn't deep and Peredur fished it out quickly, handing it by the scruff of its neck to one of the children that came running. The girl—Anest, who one day might well take Esyllt's place as lady's maid—clutched the squirming and excited dog tight in her arms.

'Thank you, my lord,' she said shyly.

Peredur touched a hand to her hair. 'You are welcome, but best keep the beast on a leash, *forwyn*, since he is clearly very fierce!'

But there was laughter in her husband's voice as he went on, echoing the question she'd asked, so long ago now it seemed, the day she'd gone against his wishes and visited the mill to ask for Esyllt.

'I've always wondered why he is called Fawrgi,' he said, pulling the dog's ear gently. '*Big Dog* is a strange name indeed for such a small creature.'

The other child—Lleucu, the miller's youngest daughter—piped up. 'He may be small, my lord, but his heart is…' she spread her thin arms wide '…this big.'

Elen Felin Ddŵr called then and the two girls ran off to return with their parents to the mill. Settling

Marared again in the crook of her arm, Rhianon turned and placed her palm on Peredur's chest where his heart beat strong and steady.

'Fawrgi isn't the only creature with a big heart,' she said, the harsh lessons of their childhoods things of the past now. Lessons that *their* children would never be forced to learn. 'I know another who possesses the biggest heart of all.'

As always, his hand came up to rest over hers and he gazed down into her eyes. 'Even if it is in the wrong place?'

Rhianon lifted herself up on her toes and kissed his mouth, her joy and her love far deeper than the water in Non's Well. More vast even than the bottomless ocean that surrounded their home and stretched as far as the eye could see, and where no demons lurked.

'It's not in the wrong place at all,' she said. 'It's exactly where it should be.'

* * * * *

*If you enjoyed this story, be sure to read
Lissa Morgan's other great romances!*

The Welsh Lord's Convenient Bride
An Alliance with His Enemy Princess

Available now!

Historical Note

Twelfth-century Wales, unlike England, was divided into individual kingdoms, each with its own ruler. As the Norman and Angevin kings gradually asserted sovereignty over these fiercely independent territories, and to define their own status, the Welsh rulers began to drop their ancient title of *brenin*—king—and adopt *tywysog*—prince—instead.

Owain ap Cynan of Gwynedd and Rhys ap Gruffudd of Deheubarth were two exceptional and dominant Welsh princes who, by turns, resisted, complied or adapted in order to keep their kingdoms intact and even expand them.

Ceredigion, in which the *cantrefi* of Penweddig and Uwch Aeron lay, was part of the ancient kingdom of Deheubarth, held by the ancestors of the Lord Rhys. It was invaded first by the Normans, and then brought under the rule of Gwynedd. Rhys ap Gruffudd drove Owain Gwynedd out of Ceredigion in 1156 and re-established Deheubarth in its entirety.

Rhys is unique in that he formed a canny relationship with Henry II and served as the King's Justiciar of

South Wales from 1171 to 1189. Unlike any other medieval Welsh prince, he has the singular appellation of Yr Arglwydd Rhys—the Lord Rhys—a title that reflected his unusual and exalted status.

Wales in that period witnessed frequent conflict between individual kingdoms as rulers sought to enlarge their territories. The Welsh nobility was also wracked by extreme family discord and violence. Male relations fought each other bitterly for ascendancy, frequently killing, blinding or castrating their rivals in a dynastic disunity that the Anglo-Normans took full advantage of.

When the Lord Rhys died in 1197, his kingdom of Deheubarth was fragmented for ever as his sons quarrelled over their inheritance.

King Henry I had invited a great number of Fleming warriors to colonise Dyfed in the early 1100s, and Letard was among the most infamous of these invaders. Although very little is known about him, the Welsh village of Pebidiog was renamed Letterston (Letard's Town)—an indication of his reputation and his nickname of 'Little King.' He was killed in battle in 1136 by Anarawd ap Gruffudd, elder brother of the Lord Rhys.

The mound of the motte and bailey castle of Abereinion is still evident at Ynys Hir, and in the care of Cadw. Although overgrown and inaccessible for decades, there is now an exciting project in motion to clear the mound and install an information board retelling the history of this important castle.

Santes Non was indeed the mother of Dewi Sant—St David—and her well is located in the churchyard of St Michael's Church in Eglwysfach. There, legend claims, an earlier church called Edwin's Chapel once stood, built in the seventh century by a king of Northumbria to commemorate a victory in battle.

The red wimberry—also called whortleberry and bilberry—is listed in *Culpepper's Complete Herbal* as having the virtue of 'staying women's courses.' Whether it was effective in preventing conception is uncertain, of course, but the black wimberry still grows in abundance in the uplands of Mid and South Wales.

Grey seals—the *morloi* of the story—don't come ashore at Glan Dyfi to birth and breed, and probably never did. But they do inhabit the waters of Cardigan Bay and the estuary, and can very occasionally be seen basking on the beach where Rhianon walked.

HARLEQUIN
PLUS

Try the best multimedia subscription service for romance readers like you!

Read, Watch and Play.

Experience the easiest way to get the romance content you crave.

Start your **FREE TRIAL** at
<u>www.harlequinplus.com/freetrial</u>.